Free Fall

Books by William Golding

LORD OF THE FLIES

THE INHERITORS

FREE FALL

PINCHER MARTIN

THE SPIRE

THE PYRAMID

THE SCORPION GOD

✲

THE BRASS BUTTERFLY

✲

THE HOT GATES

A Harbinger Book

HARCOURT, BRACE & WORLD, INC.
NEW YORK & BURLINGAME

ISBN 0-15-633468-2

First American edition 1960
First Harbinger Books edition 1962

Library of Congress
Catalog Card Number: 60-5431
Printed in the
United States of America

LMNOP

I have walked by stalls in the market-place where books, dog-eared and faded from their purple, have burst with a white hosanna. I have seen people crowned with a double crown, holding in either hand the crook and flail, the power and the glory. I have understood how the scar becomes a star, I have felt the flake of fire fall, miraculous and pentecostal. My yesterdays walk with me. They keep step, they are grey faces that peer over my shoulder. I live on Paradise Hill, ten minutes from the station, thirty seconds from the shops and the local. Yet I am a burning amateur, torn by the irrational and incoherent, violently searching and self-condemned.

When did I lose my freedom? For once, I was free. I had power to choose. The mechanics of cause and effect is statistical probability yet surely sometimes we operate below or beyond that threshold. Free-will cannot be debated but only experienced, like a colour or the taste of potatoes. I remember one such experience. I was very small and I was sitting on the stone surround of the pool and fountain in the centre of the park. There was bright sunlight, banks of red and blue flowers, green lawn. There was no guilt but only the plash and splatter of the fountain at the centre. I had bathed and drunk and now I was sitting on the warm stone edge placidly considering what I should do next. The gravelled paths of the park radiated from me: and all at once I was overcome by a new knowledge. I could take whichever I would of these paths.

There was nothing to draw me down one more than the other. I danced down one for joy in the taste of potatoes. I was free. I had chosen.

How did I lose my freedom? I must go back and tell the story over. It is a curious story, not so much in the external events which are common enough, but in the way it presents itself to me, the only teller. For time is not to be laid out endlessly like a row of bricks. That straight line from the first hiccup to the last gasp is a dead thing. Time is two modes. The one is an effortless perception native to us as water to the mackerel. The other is a memory, a sense of shuffle fold and coil, of that day nearer than that because more important, of that event mirroring this, or those three set apart, exceptional and out of the straight line altogether. I put the day in the park first in my story, not because I was young, a baby almost; but because freedom has become more and more precious to me as I taste the potato less and less often.

I have hung all systems on the wall like a row of useless hats. They do not fit. They come in from outside, they are suggested patterns, some dull and some of great beauty. But I have lived enough of my life to require a pattern that fits over everything I know; and where shall I find that? Then why do I write this down? Is it a pattern I am looking for? That Marxist hat in the middle of the row, did I ever think it would last me a lifetime? What is wrong with the Christian biretta that I hardly wore at all? Nick's rationalist hat kept the rain out, seemed impregnable plate-armour, dull and decent. It looks small now and rather silly, a bowler like all bowlers, very formal, very complete, very ignorant. There is a school cap, too. I had no more than hung it there, not knowing of the other hats

I should hang by it when I think the thing happened—the decision made freely that cost me my freedom.

Why should I bother about hats? I am an artist. I can wear what hat I like. You know of me, Samuel Mountjoy, I hang in the Tate. You would forgive me any hat. I could be a cannibal. But I want to wear a hat in private. I want to understand. The grey faces peer over my shoulder. Nothing can expunge or exorcise them. My art is not enough for me. To hell with my art. The fit takes me out of a deep well as does the compulsion of sex and other people like my pictures more than I do, think them more important than I do. At heart I am a dull dog. I would sooner be good than clever.

Then why am I writing this down? Why do I not walk round and round the lawn, reorganizing my memories until they make sense, unravelling and knitting up the flexible time stream? I could bring this and that event together, I could make leaps. I should find a system for that round of the lawn and then another one the next day. But thinking round and round the lawn is no longer enough. For one thing it is like the rectangle of canvas, a limited area however ingeniously you paint. The mind cannot hold more than so much; but understanding requires a sweep that takes in the whole of remembered time and then can pause. Perhaps if I write my story as it appears to me, I shall be able to go back and select. Living is like nothing because it is everything—is too subtle and copious for unassisted thought. Painting is like a single attitude, a selected thing.

There is another reason. We are dumb and blind yet we must see and speak. Not the stubbled face of Sammy Mountjoy, the full lips that open to let his hand take out a fag, not the smooth, wet muscles inside round teeth, not the gullet, the lung, the heart—those you could see and touch if you took a knife to him on the table. It is the unnameable, unfathomable and invisible darkness that sits at the centre of him, always awake, always different from what you believe it to be, always thinking and feeling what you can never know it thinks and feels, that hopes hopelessly to understand and to be understood. Our loneliness is the loneliness not of the cell or the castaway; it is the loneliness of that dark thing that sees as at the atom furnace by reflection, feels by remote control and hears only words phoned to it in a foreign tongue. To communicate is our passion and our despair.

With whom then?

You?

My darkness reaches out and fumbles at a typewriter with its tongs. Your darkness reaches out with your tongs and grasps a book. There are twenty modes of change, filter and translation between us. What an extravagant coincidence it would be if the exact quality, the translucent sweetness of her cheek, the very living curve of bone between the eyebrow and hair should survive the passage! How can you share the quality of my terror in the blacked-out cell when I can only remember it and not re-create it for myself? No. Not with you. Or only with you, in part. For you were not there.

And who are you anyway? Are you on the inside, have you a proof-copy? Am I a job to do? Do I exasperate you by translating incoherence into incoherence? Perhaps you found this book on a stall fifty years hence which is an-another now. The star's light reaches us millions of years after the star is gone, or so they say, and perhaps it is true.

What sort of universe is that for our central darkness to keep its balance in?

There is this hope. I may communicate in part; and that surely is better than utter blind and dumb; and I may find something like a hat to wear of my own. Not that I aspire to complete coherence. Our mistake is to confuse our limitations with the bounds of possibility and clap the universe into a rationalist hat or some other. But I may find the indications of a pattern that will include me, even if the outer edges tail off into ignorance. As for communication, to understand all they say is to pardon all. Yet who but the injured can forgive an injury? And how if the lines at that particular exchange are dead?

I have no responsibility for some of the pictures. I can remember myself as I was when I was a child. But even if I had committed murder then, I should no longer feel responsible for it. There is a threshold here, too, beyond which what we did was done by someone else. Yet I was there. Perhaps, to understand, must include pictures from those early days also. Perhaps reading my story through again I shall see the connection between the little boy, clear as spring water, and the man like a stagnant pool. Somehow, the one became the other.

I never knew my father and I think my mother never knew him either. I cannot be sure, of course, but I incline to believe she never knew him—not socially at any rate unless we restrict the word out of all useful meaning. Half my immediate ancestry is so inscrutable that I seldom find it worth bothering about. I exist. These tobacco-stained fingers poised over the typewriter, this weight in the chair assures me that two people met; and one of them was Ma. What would the other think of me, I wonder? What celebration do I commemorate? In 1917 there were victories and defeats, there was a revolution. In face of all that, what is one little bastard more or less? Was he a soldier, that other, blown to pieces later, or does he survive and walk, evolve, forget? He might well be proud of me and my flowering reputation if he knew. I may even have met him, face to inscrutable face. But there would be no recognition. I should know as little of him as the wind knows, turning the leaves of a book on an orchard wall, the ignorant wind that cannot decipher the rows of black rivets any more than we strangers can decipher the faces of strangers.

Yet I was wound up. I tick. I exist. I am poised eighteen inches over the black rivets you are reading, I am in your place, I am shut in a bone box and trying to fasten myself on the white paper. The rivets join us together and yet for all the passion we share nothing but our sense of division. Why think of my dad then? What does he matter?

But Ma was different. She had some secret, known to the cows, perhaps, or the cat on the rug, some quality that rendered her independent of understanding. She was content with contact. It was her life. My success would not impress her. She would be indifferent. In my private album of pictures, she is complete and final as a full stop.

At odd moments when the thought occurred to me I asked her about my dad but my curiosity was not urgent. Perhaps if I had insisted, she might have been precise—but what was the need? The living space round her apron was sufficient. There were boys who knew their fathers just as there were boys who habitually wore boots. There were shining toys, cars, places where people ate with grace;

but these pictures on my wall, this out-thereness amounted to a Martian world. A real father would have been an unthinkable addition. So my inquiries were made in the evening before the "Sun" opened, or much later in the evening when it shut again and Ma was mellow. I might have asked as indifferently for a story and believed it as little.

"What was my dad, Ma?"

Out of our common indifference to mere physical fact, came answers that varied as her current daydream varied. These were influenced by the "Sun" and the flickering stories at the Regal. I knew they were daydreams and accepted them as such because I daydreamed too. Only the coldest attitude to the truth would have condemned them as lies, though once or twice, Ma's rudimentary moral sense made her disclaim them almost immediately. The result was that my father was sometimes a soldier, he was a lovely man, an officer; though I suspect Ma was past the officer and gentleman stage by the time I was conceived. One night when she came back from the Regal and pictures of battleships being bombed off the shores of America, he was in the Royal Air Force. Later still in our joint life—and what was the celebration this time? What prancing horses, plumed helmets and roaring crowds? Later still, he was none other than the Prince of Wales.

This was such tremendous news to me, though of course I did not believe it, that the red glow behind the bars of the grate has remained on my retina like an afterimage. We neither believed it but the glittering myth lay in the middle of the dirty floor, accepted with gratitude as beyond my own timid efforts at invention. Yet almost before she threw the thing there, she was prepared to snatch it back. The story was too enormous, or perhaps the daydream too private to be shared. I saw her eyes shift in the glow, the faint, parchment colour of her lighted face move and alter. She sniffed, scratched her nose, wept an easy gin-tear or two and spoke to the grate where there could well have been more fire.

"You know I'm a sodding liar, dear, don't you?"

Yes. I knew, without condemnation, but I was disappointed all the same. I felt that Christmas had disappeared and there was no more tinsel. I recognized that we should return to Ma's fictitious steady. The Prince of Wales, a soldier, an airman—but whores claim to be the daughters of clergymen; and despite all the glitter of court life, the church won.

"What was my dad, Ma?"

"A parson. I keep telling you."

On the whole, that has been my steady, too. There would be nothing in common between us but our division yet we should at least recognize it: and I should know behind the other face, the drag, the devil, the despair, the wry and desperate perceptions, conforming hourly to a creed until they are warped as Chinese feet. In my bitter moments I have thought of myself as connected thereby to good works. I like to think then that my father was not doing something for which he had either an excuse or moral indifference. My self-esteem would prefer him to have wrestled desperately with the flesh. Soldiers traditionally love them and leave them; but the clergy, either abstemious or celibate, the pastors, ministers, elders and priests—I should be an old anguish once thought forgiven now seen to be scarlet. I should blow up in some manse or parsonage or presbytery or close, I should blow up like a forgotten abscess. They are men as I am, acquainted with sin. There would be some point to me.

Which branch, I wonder? Only a day or two ago I walked down a side street, past the various chapels, the oratory, round the corner by the old church and the vast rectory. Of what denomination shall I declare my fictitious steady to be? The church of England, the curator's church? Would not my father have been a gentleman first and a priest afterwards, an amateur like me? Even the friars walk round with trousers showing under their well-cut habits. They remind me of the druids on Brown Willie, or somewhere, coming in cars and spectacles. Shall I choose a Roman Catholic to my father? There is a professional church even when you hate her guts. Would a bastard tug one of them by the heart as well as the sleeve? As for the ranks of nonconformity so drearily conforming, the half-baked, the splinter parties, the tables, and tabernacles and temples—I'm like Ma; indifferent. He might as soon be an Odd Fellow or an Elk.

"What was my dad, Ma?"

I lie. I deceive myself as well as you. Their world is mine, the world of sin and redemption, of showings and conviction, of love in the mud. You deal daily in the very blood of my life. I am one of you, a haunted man—haunted by what or whom? And this is my cry; that I have walked among you in intellectual freedom and you never tried to seduce me from it, since a century has seduced you to it and you believe in fair play, in not presuming, in being after all not a saint. You have conceded freedom to those who cannot use freedom and left the dust and the dirt clustered over the jewel. I speak your hidden language which is not the language of the other men. I am your brother in both senses and since freedom was my curse I throw the dirt at you as I might pick at a sore which will not break out and kill.

"What was my dad, Ma?"

Let him never know. I am acquainted with the warm throb myself and think little enough of physical paternity compared with the slow growth that comes after. We do not own children. My father was not a man. He was a speck shaped like a tadpole invisible to the naked eye. He had no head and no heart. He was as specialized and soulless as a guided missile.

Ma was never a professional any more than I am. Like mother, like son. We are amateurs at heart. Ma had not the business ability nor the desire to make a career and a success. Neither was she immoral for that implies some sort of standard from which she could decline. Was Ma above morals or below them or outside them? Today she would be classed as subnormal, and given the protection she did not want. In those days, if she had not clad herself in such impervious indifference she would have been called simple. She staked small but vital sums on horses in the "Sun", she drank and went to the pictures. For work, she took whatever was available. She charred for chars, she—we—picked hops, she washed and swept and imperfectly polished in such public buildings as were within easy reach of our alley. She did not have sexual connection for that implies an aseptic intercourse, a loveless, joyless refinement of pleasure with the prospect of conception inhibited by the rubber cup from the bathroom. She did not make love, for I take that to be a passionate attempt to confirm that the wall which parted them is down. She did none of these things. If she had, she would have told me in her slurred, rambling monologues, with their vast pauses, their acceptance that we are inescapably here. No. She was a creature. She shared pleasure round like a wet-nurse's teat, absorbed, gustily laughing and sighing. Her casual intercourse must have been to her what his works are to a real artist—themselves and nothing more. They had no implication. They were meetings in back streets or fields, on boxes, or gateposts and buttresses. They were like most human sex in history, a natural thing without benefit of psychology, romance or religion.

Ma was enormous. She must have been a buxom girl in the bud but appetite and a baby blew her up into an elephantine woman. I deduce that she was attractive once, for her eyes, sunk into a face bloated like a brown bun, were still large and mild. There was a gloss on them that must have lain all over her when she was young. Some women cannot say no; but my ma was more than those simple creatures, else how can she so fill the backward tunnel? These last few months I have been trying to catch her in two handfuls of clay—not, I mean, her appearance; but more accurately, my sense of her hugeness and reality, her matter-of-fact blocking of the view. Beyond her there is nothing, nothing. She is the warm darkness between me and the cold light. She is the end of the tunnel, she.

And now something happens in my head. Let me catch the picture before the perception vanishes. Ma spreads as I remember her, she blots out the room and the house, her wide belly expands, she is seated in her certainty and indifference more firmly than in a throne. She is the unquestionable, the not good, not bad, not kind, not bitter. She looms down the passage I have made in time.

She terrifies but she does not frighten.

She neglects but she does not warp or exploit.

She is violent without malice or cruelty.

She is adult without patronage or condescension.

She is warm without possessiveness.

But, above all, she is there.

So of course I can remember her only in clay, the common earth, the ground, I cannot stick the slick commercial colours on stretched canvas for her or outline her in words that are ten thousand years younger than her darkness and warmth. How can you describe an age, a world, a dimension? As far as communication goes there are only the things that surrounded her to be pieced together and displayed with the gap that was Ma existing mutely in the middle. I fish up memory of a piece of material which is grey with a tinge of yellow. The one corner is frayed—or as I now think, rotted—into a fringe, a damp fringe. The rest is anchored up there somewhere about my ma and I swing along, fingers clutched up and in, stumbling sometimes, sometimes ungently removed without a word said, by a huge hand falling from above. I seem to remember searching for that corner of her apron and the pleasure of finding it again.

We must have been living in Rotten Row then for certain directions were already as settled as the points of the compass. Our bog was across worn bricks and a runnel, through a wooden door to a long wooden seat. There was an upthereness over our room, though surely not a lodger? Perhaps we were ever so slightly more prosperous then, or perhaps gin was cheaper, like cigarettes. We had a chest of drawers for a dresser and the grate was full of little iron cupboards and doors and things that pulled out. Ma never used these but only the little fire in the middle with the hot metal disc that closed the top. We had a rug, too, a chair, a small deal table and a bed. My end of the bed was near the door and when Ma got in the other end, I slid down. All but one of the houses in our row were the same, and the brick alley with a central gutter ran along in front of them. There were children of all sizes in that world, boys who stepped on me or gave me sweets, girls who picked me up when I had crawled too far and took me back. We must have been very dirty. I have a good and trained colour sense and my memory of those human faces is not so much in passages of pink and white as of grey and brown. Ma's face, her neck, her arms—all of Ma that showed was brown and grey. The apron which I visualize so clearly I now see to have been filthily dirty. Myself, I cannot see. There was no mirror within my reach and if Ma ever had one it had vanished by the time I was a conscious boy. What was there in a mirror for Ma to linger over? I remember blown washing on wire lines, soap suds, I remember the erratic patterns that must have been dirt on the wall, but like Ma I am a neutral point of observation, a gap in the middle. I crawled and tumbled in the narrow world of Rotten Row, empty as a soap bubble but with a rainbow of colour and excitement round me. We children were underfed and scantily clothed. I first went to school with my feet bare. We were noisy, screaming, tearful, animal. And yet I remember that time as with the flash and glitter, the warmth of a Christmas party. I have never disliked dirt. To me, the porcelain and chromium, the lotions, the deodorants, the whole complex of cleanness, which is to say, all soap, all hygiene, is inhuman and incomprehensible. Before this free gift of a universe, man is a constant. There is a sense in which when we emerged from our small slum and were washed, the happiness and security of life was washed away also.

I have two sorts of picture in my mind of our slum. The earlier are the interiors because I can remember a time when for me there was no other world at all. The brick path and gutter down the middle ran between the row of houses and the row of yards with each a bog. At one end and to our left was a wooden gate; at the other, a passage out to the unvisited street. At that end, the "Sun" was an old and complicated building and the back door was inside the alley. Here was the focus of adult life; and here the end house in the row extended across the passage and joined the pub overhead so it was in a position of some eminence and advantage. When I was old enough to notice such things I looked up, together with the rest of our alley, to the good lady who lived there. She had two rooms upstairs, she was mortared to the pub, she did for nice people and she had curtains. If I told you more of our geography and put us in the general scheme of things I should be false to my memories; for I first remember the alley as a world, bounded by the wooden gate at one end and the rectangular but forbidden exit to the main road at the other. Rain and sunshine descended on us between the shirts flapping or still. There were poles with cleats on and a variety of simple mechanisms for hoisting away the washing where it would catch the wind. There were cats and what seems to me like crowds of people. I remember Mrs. Donavan next door who was withered and Ma who was not. I remember the loudness of their voices, used straining from the throat with heads thrust forward when the ladies quarrelled. I remember the fag-end of one quarrel, both ladies moving slowly away from each other sideways, neither in this case victorious, each reduced to single syllables full of vague menace, indignation and resentment.

"Well then!"

"Yes!"

"Yes!"

"Ah——!"

This remains with me because of the puzzle that Ma had not won outright. She did, usually. Withered Mrs. Donavan with her three daughters and many troubles was not Ma's weight in any sense. There was one occasion of apocalyptic grandeur when Ma not only won but triumphed. Her voice seemed to bounce off the sky in brazen thunder. The scene is worth reconstructing.

Opposite each house across the brick alley with the gutter down the middle was a square of brick walls with an entry. The walls were about three feet high. In each square on the left-hand side was a standpipe and beyond it, at the back of the square, was a sentry-box closed by a wooden door which had a sort of wooden grating. Open the door by lifting the wooden latch and you faced a wooden box running the whole width between the walls and pierced by a round, worn orifice. There would be a scrap of newspaper lying on the box, or a whole sheet crumpled on the damp floor. Some dark, subterranean stream flowed slowly along below the row of boxes. If you closed the door and dropped the latch by means of a piece of string which dangled inside, you could enjoy your private, even in Rotten Row. If someone from your house entered the brick square—for you saw them through your grating—and lifted a hand to the latch, you did not move, but cried out, inarticulately avoiding names or set words so that the hand dropped again. For we had our standards. We had progressed from Eden—that is, provided the visitor came from your own house. If, on the other hand, they had loitered in the alley and made a mistake you might be as articulate as you pleased, be wildly Rabelaisian, suggest new combinations of our complex living patterns to include the visitor until the doorways were screaming with laughter and all the brats by the gutter screamed, too, and danced.

But there were exceptions. In the twenties progress had caught up with us and added a modern superstition to the rest so that we firmly believed a legend about lavatories. Rotten Row sometimes suffered from more than a cold in the head.

It must have been a day in April. What other month could give me such blue and white, such sun and wind? The clothing on the lines was horizontal and shuddering, the sharp, carved clouds hurried, the sun spattered from the soap suds in the gutter, the worn bricks were bright with a dashing of rain. It was the sort of wind that gives grown-ups headaches and children frantic exultation. It was a day of shouting and wrestling, a day aflame and unbearable without drama and adventure. Something must happen.

I was playing with a matchbox in the gutter. I was so small that to squat was natural but the wind even in the alley would sometimes give me a sidelong push and I was as much in the soapy water as out. A grating was blocked so that the water spread across the bricks and made a convenient ocean. Yet my great, my apocalyptic memory is not of stretched-out time, but an instant. Mrs. Donavan's Maggie who smelt so sweet and showed round, silk knees was recoiled from the entrance to our brick square. She had retreated so fast and so far that one high heel was in my ocean. She was caught in act to turn away, her arms were raised to ward off. I cannot remember her face—for it is mesmerized in the other direction. Poor Mrs. Donavan, the dear withered creature, peeps out of her own bog with the air of someone unfairly caught, someone who could explain everything, given time—but knows, in that tremendous instant, that time is not to be given her. And from our bog, our own, private bog, with its warm, personal seat, comes my ma.

She has burst out for the door has banged against the wall and the latch hangs broken. My ma faces Maggie, one foot in front of the other for she has come out of the narrow box sideways. Her knees are bent, she is crouched in a position of dreadful menace. Her skirts are huddled up round her waist and she holds her vast grey bloomers in two purple hands just above her knees. I see her voice, a jagged shape of scarlet and bronze, shatter into the air till it hangs there under the sky, a deed of conquest and terror.

"You bloody whore! Keep your clap for your own bastards!"

I have no memory of majesty to match that one from Rotten Row. Even when the Twins Fred and Joe, who dealt so deviously in scrap at the other end of the alley near the wooden gate, were fetched away by two giraffe-like policemen the drama dwindled down into defeat. We watched one of the coppers walking, rolling up the alley and we muttered, I not knowing why. We watched Fred and Joe dash out of their house and bundle themselves through the wooden gate; but of course the second copper was standing on the other side. They ran right into him, small men, easily grabbed in either hand. They were brought down the alley handcuffed between two dark blue pillars surmounted by silver spikes, the van was waiting for them. We shouted and muttered and made the dull tearing sound that was Rotten Row's equivalent of booing. Fred and Joe were pale but perky. The coppers came, took, went, unstoppable as birth and death, the three cases in which Rotten Row accepted unconditional defeat. Whether the extra mouth was coming, or the policeman's van, or the long hearse that would draw up at the end of the passage, made no difference. A hand of some sort was thrust through the Row to take what it would and no one could stop it.

We were a world inside a world and I was a man before I achieved the intellectual revolution of thinking of us as a slum. Though we were only forty yards long and the fields lapped against us we were a slum. Most people think of slums as miles of muck in the East End of London or the jerry-built lean-to's of the Black Country. But we lived right in the heart of the Garden of England and the hop gardens glowed round us. Though on the one side were brick villas, schools, warehouses, shops, churches, on the other were the spiced valleys through which I followed my ma and reached for the sticky buds. Yet that takes me out of our home and I want to stay in it for a while. I will put back the picture postcards of dancing, flame-lit men, and creep back under the lid. True there were bonfires, rivers of beer, singing, gipsies and a pub set secretly among trees, wearing its thatch like a straw hat pulled down over the eyes; but our slum was the point of return. We had a pub, too. We were a huddle. Now I am out in the cold world away from my crying shame in the face of heaven I am surprised to find what number of people will go to any length just to get themselves into a huddle. Perhaps then I was not deceived and we had something. We were a human proposition, a way of life, an entity.

We centred on the pub. There was a constant coming and going through the blistered brown door with its two panes of opaque glass. The brass knob of the door was worn uneven and gleamed with use. I suppose there were licensing laws and forbidden hours but I never noticed them. I saw the door from ground level and it is huge in my memory. Inside was a brick floor, some settles and two stools by a counter in the corner. This was the snug; a warm, noisy, mysterious, adult place. Later I went there if I wanted my ma urgently; and no one ever told me that my presence was illegal. I went there first, because of our lodger.

Our lodger had our upstairs, use of the stove, our tap and our bog. I suppose he was the tragedy about which so many sociologists and economists wrote so many books in the nineteenth and twentieth centuries. I can re-create him in my mind easily enough. To begin with, even from my ground level, he was small. I think he must have been, so to speak, the fag-end of a craftsman, for he was neat, and in a sense, distinguished. A plumber? A carpenter? But he was very old—always had been, for who could think of him as anything else? He was a tiny skeleton, held together by skin and a shiny blue suit. He wore a brown muffler tucked down inside the serge of his suit and I cannot remember his boots—perhaps because I was always looking up at him. He had interesting hands, complicated with knots and veins and brown patches. He always wore a trilby, whether he was sitting by the window in our upstairs, or shuffling down the alley or going into the bog, or sitting by the counter in the "Sun". One remarkable thing about him was his moustache, which faced downwards and seemed of the texture and whiteness of swan's feathers. It covered his mouth and was very beautiful. But even more remarkable, was his breathing, quick as a bird's and noisy, in out, in out, in out, all the time, tick tick tick, brittle as a clock with the same sense of urgency and no time to waste, no time for anything else. Over the moustache, under hanging brows on each side of his sharp nose, his eyes looked out, preoccupied and frightened. To me, he always seemed to be looking at something that was not there, something of profound interest and anxiety. Tick tick tick all the time all the time. Nobody cared. I didn't, Ma didn't; and he was our lodger, hanging on to the fag-end of his life. When I was going to sleep in the night or when I woke in the morning I could hear him up there, through the single deal boards, tick tick tick. If you asked him a question he answered like a man who has just run a four-minute mile with fuff and puff and inspiration of grasped breath, with panic need to stay alive like a man coming up for the third time in out in out in out. I asked him as he sat staring through the stove. I wanted to know. He fuffed the panel answer back at me—just got the words out and then caught up with the air again like a man who snatches a cup from his ankles an inch above shattering.

"Wart——" fuff gasp tick tick "in me——" tick tick tick—"chest". Fuff fuff and another desperate, lunging inspiration towards the end.

I never saw him eat; though I suppose he must have

eaten. But how? There was no time. What number of days must run before the body uses all the fat and flesh, all the stored fuel? How long then can the spirit hold itself up by its own bootstraps, focused as it seemed to be, in the eyes? Tick tick tick and though he went into the "Sun" with the others he could never drink much if anything and that was why the downward tufts that covered his mouth were like white swan's feathers. As I remember him and his breathing it occurs to me that what he had was lung cancer; and I notice with a certain wry amusement my instant effort to fit that uninformed guess into a pattern. But then I remember that all patterns have broken one after another, that life is random and evil unpunished. Why should I link that man, that child with this present head and heart and hands? I can call to mind a technical crime of this period, for I stole tuppence from the old man once—bought liquorice for which I still have a passion—and got clean away with it. But those were days of terrible and irresponsible innocence. I should be literary if I shaped my story to show how those two pennies have lain on the dead eyes of my spiritual sight for I am clear of them. Then why do I write? Do I still expect a pattern? What am I looking for?

Our bed downstairs was within an arm's reach of the chest of drawers and our alarm clock stood near the edge. It was an early make, round, on three short legs, and it held up a bell like an umbrella. It would shatter Ma into wakefulness when she had to go out charring in the early dark and my sleeping ears would note the noise and dream on. Sometimes if the night had been long and thick, Ma would take no notice or groan and bury herself. Then the clock woke me. All night it had ticked on, repressed, its madness held and bound in; but now the strain burst. The umbrella became a head, the clock beat its head in frenzy, trembling and jerking over the chest of drawers on three legs until it reached a point where the chest would begin to drum in sympathy, sheer madness and hysteria. Then I would wake Ma and feel very business-like and virtuous till she rose in the dark like a whale. But during the night if I woke myself or could not get to sleep the clock was always present and varied as I felt. Sometimes and most often it was friendly and placid; but if I had my seldom night terrors, then the clock had them, too. Time was inexorable then, hurrying on, driving irresistibly towards the point of madness and explosion.

Once, near midnight, I woke with a jolt because the clock had stopped so that I was menaced and defenceless. I was frightened and I had to find Ma. There was the same compulsion on me as there is now before this paper, a compulsion irrational and deep. I fell out of bed, went scrambling and crying through the door and into the alley, along and across the gutter to the back door of the pub. There was no light from the panes of glass. The pub was blind. I scrabbled and reached up for the brass handle and swung there.

"Ma! Ma!"

The brass turned under my hand and pulled me into the back snug, still half-swinging. I squatted on the floor and there were shadowy people looking down at me, shadows that moved a little in the dull light from the fire. Ma was sitting on most of a settle facing the door and she held a little glass buried in her hand. The place was larger than daylight. Now I know they were only a few neighbours drinking after hours—but then they presented the whole mystery of adult life in one shadowy picture.

"The clock's stopped, Ma."

I could not convey the impossibility of returning by myself to the dark silence; I was wholly dependent on their understanding and goodwill. They loomed and muttered. So the party broke up without much kindness but some noise so that for two or three minutes the alley rang with comfortable voices. Ma shoo'd me across the gutter and switched on our naked bulb. She took the alarm clock in one hand—it was hidden almost as the glass had been hidden—and held it to the side of her head. She set it down again with a bang and turned to me with a punitive hand lifted.

And stopped.

She looked slowly up at the ceiling where our lodger lay a few feet over my head and listened; listened in such silence that now I found that I had made a quite incomprehensible mistake, for I could hear clearly how the alarm clock was still hurrying on towards the hysterical explosion, hurrying on, brittle, trivially insistent, tick tick tick.

Did our lodger subscribe to some burial insurance? I remember the stately car that came for him so that his body was much more important to the Row dead than alive. Rotten Row believed in death as a ritual and spectacle, as a time to mourn and rejoice. Why then did I never see his body? Did the Row cheat me or is there some mystery here? Normally, the dead held higher court than the newly born. They were washed, straightened out, tidied; and received homage as if they were Pharaoh bandaged and with a belly full of spices. I cannot think of death in Rotten Row without the word "royal" coming to mind. To the backward sight which hangs events in their symbolic colours, Rotten Row is draped for death in hatchments of black and violet and purple, is big with the enjoyment of booze and sorrow.

Why then did I not see his or any other body? Had those shadowy adults from the snug, some lore or theory of my nightmare knowledge? Did I know too much? I had a special reason for feeling cheated. I was told that under his trilby there was a thatch of that same swan's feather whiteness; and in my mind it became a precious thing, exquisite as the cap that fits the head of the Swan Maiden herself. Evie told me about the swan's feathers under the hat. She saw him in his box. She had touched him, too—been made to touch him by her mother. That way, went our belief, the child will never fear a dead body. So Evie touched him, reaching out her right forefinger to his sharp nose. She showed me the finger, I looked, I saw, I was awed and admired Evie. But I never saw or touched him. Death rolled by me in the high black car behind panes of chased and frosted glass. Then, as always, I stood, only partly comprehending, on the pavement. But Evie was always at the heart of things. She was a year or two older and she bossed me. How could I be jealous of Evie who knew so much? Even though he had been our own private lodger with use of our bog, not Evie's mum's, I could not grudge her the sharp nose of death. She was majestic. It was her right. But I could feel insufficient and I did. For me there was no thatch of white but only the frosted glass rolling away down the street. I made fantasies of myself daring the most awful and gruesome loneliness to know the very feel of death. But it was too late. I can see that time in my mind's eye if I stoop to knee height. A doorstep is the size of an altar, I can lean on the sloping sign beneath the plate-glass of a shop window, to cross the gutter is a wild leap. Then the transparency which is myself floats through life like a bubble, empty of guilt, empty of anything but immediate and conscienceless emotions, generous, greedy, cruel, innocent. My twin towers were Ma and Evie. And the shape of life loomed that I was insufficient for our lodger's thatch, for that swan-white seal of ultimate knowing.

I wonder if he had a thatch at all? As I ponder the empty bubble from knee-height, I see for the first time that I only had Evie's word for it. But Evie was a liar. Or no. She was a fantasist. She was taller than I was, brown and thin, with a bob of lank brown hair. She wore brown stockings with wrinkles concertina'd under each knee. She had a variety of immense and brilliant hair-ribbons; and I adored these and desired them with hopeless cupidity. For what was the good of a hair-ribbon without the hair to tie it in? And what was the good of that symbol without the majesty and central authority of Ma and Evie? When she bent sideways to talk out of the world of what people ought really to be, her hair fell and leaned out and the pink bow flopped sideways, august and unattainable.

Yet I was in her hands and content to be so. For now I was to go to the infant school and she was to convoy me. In the morning I would be out first by the gutter waiting for her to come out of her door. She would appear and the world would fill with sunlight. She would call and I would rush into her collection. She cleaned me up at the tap, took me by the hand, talking all the time and led me out past the "Sun", past the window of the lady with the leathery-green plant and into the street. The school was three hundred yards away or a little more, along, across round a corner, across the main road and along a pavement. We stopped to examine everything and Evie was much more interesting than school in her explanations. Most of all I remember the antique shop. What must have been the firm's name was displayed in huge gold letters on a sloping sill just below the window and my nose. I can only remember one golden W. Perhaps I had reached that letter in the alphabet.

There were some ornate candlesticks in that shop. They stood on a gold-gilded table and each one held up a dunce's cap as our alarm clock held up the umbrella. Evie explained that you had only to turn the dunce's cap over, pour in the melted wax and it would burn for ever. Evie had seen them doing so in her cousin's house in America—not a house exactly, a palace, rather. She elaborated the house all the way down the road and when I was set before a piece of paper with crayons at my side, I drew her house—her cousin's house, a huge downstairs and a huge upstairs; and the dunce's caps burning with flames of gold.

There was a little spoon among some litter, a spoon which was much longer than a spoon should be. Evie explained that they'd given a man poison with this by mistake, thinking it was medicine. He had bitten the spoon with his teeth and started to jerk about on the bed. Then they realized of course that they had given him poison instead of friar's balsam but it was too late. They had pulled and pulled but the spoon wouldn't come out. Three of them had held him down and three had pulled as hard as they could but the spoon only stretched and stretched—then Evie was running away down the pavement, knees hitting each other, heels kicking out; she was twitching and giggling and horrified, and I was running after her, crying Evie! Evie!

There was a suit of armour in the dim back of the shop. Evie said her uncle was inside the suit. Now this was demonstrably ridiculous. You could see through the suit where the pieces did not quite join. Yet I never questioned that he was there for my faith was perfect. I simply felt that he was an unusual creature with all those holes in him; and this may have been because he was a duke. Evie explained that he was waiting there until he could rescue her. She had been stolen by the people she lived with—she was really a princess and one day he would come out and take her away in his car. She described the car, with frosted and chased glass, and I recognized it. The people would cheer, said Evie; but I knew I should stand on the pavement and the hair-ribbon would vanish as the white cap of swan's feathers had vanished.

Evie must have watched my lifted and trusting eyes for a flicker of doubt; because soon her stories took wings to themselves. I know now that I was privileged to see a soul spread out before me; was introduced to one of our open secrets. But my innocent credulity was a condition of the sights so that I learned nothing. She was, she confided to me, she was sometimes a boy. She told me that, but first she swore me to a secrecy which I violate now for the first time. The change, she said, was sudden, painful, and complete. She never knew when, but then pop! out it came and she had to stand up in the bog—*had* to, she explained, she couldn't do anything else. She had to pee the way I did. What was more, when she changed she could pee higher up the wall than any of the boys in our

Row, see? I saw and was appalled. To think of Evie, putting off the majesty and beauty of her skirt and pulling on common trousers—to see her cut short the lank hair, abandon hair-ribbons! Passionately I implored her not to be a boy. But what could she do, she said? Hesitantly I grasped at the only comfort. Might I perhaps change into a girl, wear skirts and a hair-ribbon? No, she said. It only happened to her. So there I was, on the pavement again.

I adored Evie. I was grief-stricken and terrified. She nursed this terror as a tribute to the reality of the situation. Next time it happened, she said, she would show me. But that would mean that she would vanish out of my life; for I understood that no boy could possibly take me by the hand and lead me to school. How should I pass the long spoon and her uncle in safety without her? I begged her not to change—knowing all the while that we were powerless in the face of this awful thing yet preserving the faith that Evie of all people could control our world even if no one else could. I watched her closely for symptoms. In the playground, if she vanished into the girl's lavatory, I stood in anguish, wondering if she had gone to look. I hung about, I pestered her; and at last I bored her. Somehow, in some way that is not clear to me, she detached herself. So there I was, going to school unattended, crossing the road to keep away from the long spoon and her uncle, going in the gate to a different world.

This was my first break with Rotten Row, for Evie's stories had linked it to school and I was unaware of any transition. But now Rotten Row fell into a geographical context and was no longer the whole world. Yet when I see in popular magazines some excavated plan of dwellings and read the dry précis of conjectured life, I wonder how Rotten Row will fare under the spade, two thousand years after the V2 hit it. The foundations would tell a story of planned building and regimentation. They would be a bigger, if duller liar than Evie. For Rotten Row was roaring and warm, simple and complex, individual and strangely happy and a world unto itself. It gave me two relationships which were good and for which I am still grateful: one, for my mother, blocking out the backward darkness: two, for Evie, for the excitement of knowing her and for my trust in her. My mother was as near a whore as makes no matter and Evie was a congenital liar. Yet if they would only exist there was nothing more I wanted. I remember the quality of this relationship so vividly that I am almost tempted into an aphorism: love selflessly and you cannot come to harm. But then I remember some things that came after.

So I moved out of Evie's shadow and became the inhabitant of two linked worlds. I liked them both. The infants' school was a place of play and discovery in which the mistresses leaned down like trees. There were new things to do, a tall jangly box out of which one of the trees beat entrancing music. At the end of prayers while we were still standing in rows, the music changed and became marching music. If I heard a brass band in the street today, I should break step, refusing the shame of so simple a reaction; but in those days I stamped and stuck my chest out. I could keep step.

Minnie could never keep step and no one expected her to. She was lumpy. Her arms and legs were stuck on the corners of her square body and she had a large, rather old face which she carried slightly tilted to one side. She walked with an ungainly movement of the arms and legs.

She shared a table desk with me so that I noticed her more than the others. If Minnie wanted to pick up a crayon she would make perhaps three sideways movements at it with one hand while the other was held up in the air and jerked in sympathy. If she reached the crayon she made hard, crushing movements with her fingers until somehow they fastened round it. Sometimes the sharpened end of the crayon would be uppermost; and then Minnie would make scratches on the paper for a moment or two with the blunt end. Usually, a tree would lean down at this point and reverse the crayon; but then one day the crayons appeared on her side of the desk sharpened at both ends, so life was easier. I neither liked nor disliked Minnie. She was an appearance, to be accepted like everything else. Even her voice, with its few, blunted words, was just the way Minnie spoke and nothing more. Life was permanent and inevitable in this shape. The pictures on the wall of animals and people in strange clothes, the clay, the beads, the books, the jar on the window-sill with its branch of sticky chestnut buds—these and Johnny Spragg and Philip Arnold and Minnie and Mavis, these were an unchanging entity.

There came a time when we sensed that the trees were tossed by a high wind. There was to be an inspection and the trees whispered the news down to us. A taller tree was coming to find out if we were happy and good and learning things. There was much turning out of cupboards and pinning up of especially good drawings. Mine were prominent which is perhaps one reason why I remember the occasion so vividly.

One morning there was a strange lady at prayers and by then we had been wrought to a state of some tension. We had our prayers and a rather tremulous hymn and waited for the marching music which would take us back to our room. But things were altered. While we stood in our rows the strange lady came along and bent down and asked each of us our names in turn. She was a nice lady and she made jokes so that the trees laughed. She was coming to Minnie. I could see that Minnie was very red.

She bent down to Minnie and asked her name.

No answer.

One of the trees bent down to help.

"My name is M——?"

The nice lady guessed. She was helping, too.

"Meggie? Marjorie? Millicent?"

We began to giggle at the idea of Minnie being called anything but Minnie.

"May? Mary?"

"Margaret? Mabel?"

Minnie pissed on the floor and the nice lady's shoes. She howled and pissed so that the nice lady jumped out of the way and the pool spread. The jangly box struck up, we turned right, marked time, then filed away to our room. But Minnie did not come with us. Neither did the trees for a time. We were impressed and delighted. We had our first scandal. Minnie had revealed herself. All the differences we had accepted as the natural order, drew together and we knew that she was not one of us. We were exalted to an eminence. She was an animal down there, and we were all up here. Later that morning Minnie was taken home by one of the trees for we watched them pass through the gate, hand in hand. We never saw her again.

2

The general has left his house along the road. The gate house is still there, projecting across the wide pavement from the high wall that surrounded his acres of shrub and garden. The house has been taken over by the health service and I cannot claim much social prestige from living almost next door. The slums are not what they were; or perhaps there are no slums. Rotten Row is a dusty plan outlined among rubble. The people who lived there and in similar huddles live now in an ordered housing estate that crawls up the hill on the other side of the valley. They have money, cars, telly. They still sometimes sleep four in a room but there are clean sheets on the bed. Here and there where the old, filthy cottages are left, either in the town or in the country, beams are blue or red. The sweet-shop with its two windows of bottle-glass, is yellow, picked out in duck's egg blue. There are the usual offices indoors now, and the dreamy couple who live there throw pottery in the shed. The town does not stand on its head for the head is gone. We are an amoeba, perhaps waiting to evolve—and then, perhaps not. Even the airfield that lay on the other hill is silent now. The three inches of soil are ploughed up and planted with wheat that sometimes grows as much as a foot high, reaching for the government grant. In winter you can see the soil smeared away from the chalk by the rain like the skin from a white skull. Is my sickness mine, or do we all suffer?

Once the airfield was a Mecca for children. I and Johnny

Spragg used to climb the escarpment towards the edge, our feet bent sideways by the slope as we tacked up to get our breath again. There was a grassy ditch at the top, one of those sprawling relics that are smoothed into the downs at every few miles from coast to coast. The wire ran along the farther lip and we could lie side by side, among the scabious, the yellow cowslips and purple thistles; we could watch all the tiny crawling and flying things in the tall grass and wait for the planes to buzz out over us. Johnny was a great sage in this. He had that capacity which many small boys have—but not I—of absorbing highly technical knowledge through the pores of his skin. He had no access to the appropriate publications but he knew every plane that came within sight. He knew how to fly almost, I think, before he could read properly. He understood how the planes sat in the air, had an instinctive, a loving grasp of the balanced, invisible forces that kept them where they were. He was dark, chunky, active and cheerful. He was absorbed. If the planes were high up, not just circling and landing, he liked us to lie on our backs to watch them. I think that gave him some sort of sense of being up there with them. I guess now, with my adult sympathy, that he felt he was turning his back on the immobile earth and sharing the lucid chasms, free heights of light and air.

"That's the old DH. They went all the way to—somewhere—in one like that."

"He's going into a cloud."

"No. Too low. There's that Moth again."

Johnny was an expert. He knew things that still astonish me. We were watching a little plane once that was hanging half a mile over the town in the valley when Johnny shouted.

"Look, he's going to spin!"

I made jeering noises but Johnny hit out sideways with his fist.

"Watch!"

The plane flicked over, nose down and spun, flick, flick, flick. It stopped turning, the nose came up, it flew sedately over us, the sequences of engine noises following each manœuvre a second or two later.

"That's an Avro Avian. They can't spin more than three times."

"Why?"

"Couldn't come out."

But for most of the time we watched the planes taking off and landing. If we followed the ditch and turned the corner at the shoulder of the hill we could see them from the side for the prevailing wind blew to the hill across the town. They were an enchantment to Johnny and the figures that climbed out of them, gods. I caught a little of his enthusiasm and became fairly knowledgeable. I knew that a plane should touch down with both wheels and the skid at the same time. This was fun, because very often the gods would err and the plane land twice in fifty yards. These occasions filled me with excitement but they hurt Johnny. He felt, I think, that each time a plane was strained, or a strut in the landing gear buckled, his chances of learning to fly when he was old enough were lessened. So part of our duty was to identify the planes and note when they were out of the hangars, serviced again, and flying. As far as I can remember, there was always at least one of the half a dozen off the air, being mended. I was not very interested but watched obediently; for in some ways I gave Johnny the devotion that I had once given Evie. He was very complete. If there was no flying we would be off along the downs, in the rain and wind, Johnny most of the time with his arms held out as wings.

One day it hardly seemed worth climbing the hill for we could only just see the top. But Johnny said to go and we went. That must have been in some Easter holiday. The early afternoon had not been so bad—windy but clear enough—but now the rain and mist were sweeping right through the valley. The wind pushed us up the hill and the rain searched us out. If we turned for a moment our cheeks bulged where the wind got in them. The windsock at the top was roaring and shorter than usual for the end was being frayed and torn away. They ought to have taken it down, we agreed, but there the windsock was, stays singing, the mast whipping in the rain. Johnny climbed through the wire.

I hung back.

"We better not."

"Come on."

We could not see more than fifty yards of the airfield at a time. I followed Johnny, running over the shuddering grass; for I knew what he wanted. We had argued about the marks that a plane would make on landing and we wanted to see—or at least Johnny did. We kept our eyes open because this was sacred and forbidden ground and children were not encouraged. We were well out from the wire, getting towards the patch where planes landed, when Johnny stopped.

"Down!"

There was a man, just visible in the rain ahead of us. But he was not looking our way. He had a square can at his feet, a stick in his hand and he had something huddled under his raincoat.

"We better go back, Johnny."

"I want to see."

The man shouted something and a voice answered out of the mist upwind of him. The airfield was crowded.

"Let's go home, Johnny."

"We'll get round the other side of him."

We retreated carefully into the rain and mist and ran downwind. But there was another man waiting by another can. We lay close, wet through, while Johnny bit his fingers.

"There's a whole row of 'em."

"Are they after us?"

"No."

We got round the last man and were between the line and the hangar. I was tired of this game, hungry, wet and rather frightened. But Johnny wanted to wait.

"They can't see us if we keep away from them."

A bell clanged and rang by the hangar, a bell familiar to me and yet not to me in these surroundings.

"What's that?"

Johnny smeared his nose with the back of his hand.

"Nambulance."

The wind was not so strong but the air was darker now. The low clouds were bringing down the evening.

Johnny tensed.

"Listen!"

The man just visible by his can had heard something too, for we could see him waving. The DH appeared over us, hanging in the air, misted to a ghost, her antique profile slipping away into invisibility. We heard the engine of the ambulance start up by the hangar and someone shouted. The man was jabbing fiercely at his can. A light flickered upwind of him in the mist and a stream of black smoke swept past him. He had a bundle of cloth on a stick and suddenly it was ablaze. Downwind we could just see another fire. There was a line of them. The DH droned past again.

The mist was driving thick now so that the man and his flare were nothing but a vague patch of light. The DH droned round, now coming near, now receding. Suddenly she was near us in the mist, a dark patch crawling over us and on over the hangar. Her engine snarled, rose to a roar. There was a great sound of rending and tearing wood, then a dull boom like the report of a big gun. The line of flares broke formation and began to hurry past us in the mist.

Johnny whispered to me as if we might have been overheard, whispered with cupped hands.

"We better get out by the hangar and into the lane."

We ran away in the lee of the hangar, silent and awed. Smoke was drifting past the dark end and there was a smell in the wet air. A big fire was glowing and pulsing on the windward side of the hangar. As we rounded the end and made a bolt for the road a man appeared from nowhere. He was tall and hatless and smeared with black. He shouted:

"You kids shove off! If I catch you here again I'll put the police on you."

So then, for a time, Johnny avoided the airfield.

The other hill where I live now had the general's house on it. He was one of the Planks, he shot big game and his wife opened bazaars. His family owned the brewery by the canal and you could not tell where the gasworks began and the brewery ended. But this was an entrancing piece of canal, dirty and coloured and enlivened by the pipes of hot water that discharged there continually. Sometimes barges lay up under the greasy wall and once we even got aboard one and hid under the tarpaulin. But we were chased out of there, too, and that was the first time we ever climbed the streets to the other hill. We ran all the way because the bargee was a giant and disliked children. We were excited by the exploit and trapped into another one by our exhilaration. We reached the wall of the general's garden in the late evening. As soon as we got our breath back Johnny danced on the pavement. No one could catch us. We were too quick for them. Not even the general could catch us.

"You wouldn't go in!"

Johnny would.

Now this was not so daring a vaunt as it appeared. Nobody could get into the general's garden because there was a very high wall all round; and this combined with his reputation for shooting lions had started the rumour that wild animals roamed those secluded acres—a rumour which we believed, in order to make life a little more exciting.

Johnny would. What was more—secure in the knowledge of the unclimbable wall—he would look for a way in. So off we padded along the road, excited by our daring, to look for a hole which was not there. We went along by the gatehouse to the corner, passed down the south-east side and round to the back. Everywhere the brick wall was impenetrable and the trees looked over. But then we stopped, without saying anything. There was really nothing to say. Thirty yards of the wall was down, fallen inward among the trees, the gap darkling and shaped like a lower lip. Someone knew about the gap. There was a gesture of chicken wire along the lower edge, but nothing that could keep determined climbers out.

Now it was my turn to be excited.

"You said you would, Johnny——"

"And you're coming, too."

"I didn't say I would!"

We could hardly see each other under the trees. I followed him and near the wall, shrubs and creepers grew thick and apparently unvisited.

I smelt lion. I said so to Johnny so that we held our breath and listened to our hearts beating until we heard something else. The something was far worse than a lion. When we looked back we could see him in the gap, his dome-shaped helmet, the top half of his dark uniform as he bent to examine the disarranged netting. Without a word spoken we made our choice. Noiselessly as rabbits in a hedge we stole forward away from the policeman and towards the lions.

That was a jungle and the land inside the walls was a whole country. We came to a part where there were furrows and small glass boxes in rows on the ground and there we saw another man, working in the door of a shed; so we nipped away again into shrubs.

A dog barked.

We peered at each other in the dull light. This was far more than an adventure.

Johnny muttered:

"How we going to get out, Sam?"

In a moment or two we were recriminating and crying

together. Coppers, men, dogs—we were surrounded.

There was a wide lawn in front of us with the back of the house running along the other side. Some of the windows were lighted. There was a terrace below the windows because as we watched we saw a dark figure pace along by them in ritual solemnity, and carrying a tray. Somehow this dignity was even more terrifying than the thought of lions.

"How we going to get out? I want to go home!"

"Keep quiet, Sam, and follow me."

We crept away round the edge of the lawn. The tall windows let long swathes of light lie across the grass and each time we came to one of these we had to duck into the bushes again. Our nerve began to come back. Neither the lions nor the policeman had spotted us. We found a dark corner by a white statue and lay still.

Slowly the noises of people died down and our tremors died away with them so that the lions were forgotten. The high parapet of the house began to shine, a full moon lugged herself over the top and immediately the gardens were translated. There was a silver wink from a pool nearer the house, cypresses, tall and hugely still, turned one frosted side to her light. I looked at Johnny and his face was visible and bland. Nothing could hurt us or would hurt us. We stood up and began to wander without saying anything. Sometimes we were waist-deep in darkness and then again drowned and then out in full light. Statues meditated against black deepnesses of evergreen and corners of the garden were swept by dashes of flowering trees that at that month were flowering nowhere else. There was a walk with stone railings on our right and a succession of stone jars with stone flowers draped round them. This was better than the park because forbidden and dangerous; better than the park because of the moon and the silence; better because of the magic house, the lighted windows and the figure pacing by them. This was a sort of home.

There was a burst of laughter from the house and the dog howled. I spoke again mechanically.

"I want to go home."

What was the secret of the strange peace and security we felt? Now if I invent I can see us from outside, starry-eyed ragamuffins, I with nothing but shirt and trousers, Johnny with not much more, wandering together through the gardens of the great house. But I never saw us from outside. To me, then, we remain these two points of perception, wandering in paradise. I can only guess our innocence, not experience it. If I feel a kindly goodwill towards the ragamuffins, it is towards two unknown people. We went slowly towards the trees where the wall had broken down. I think we had a kind of faith that the policeman would be gone and that nothing would embarrass us. Once, we came to a white path and found too late that it was new, unset concrete where we slid; but we broke nothing else in the whole garden—we took nothing, almost we touched nothing. We were eyes.

Before we buried ourselves in undergrowth again, I turned to look back. I can remember this. We were in the upper part of the garden, looking back and down. The moon was flowering. She had a kind of sanctuary of light round her, sapphire. All the garden was black and white. There was one tree between me and the lawns, the stillest tree that ever grew, a tree that grew when no one was looking. The trunk was huge and each branch splayed up to a given level; and there, the black leaves floated out like a level of oil on water. Level after horizontal level these leaves cut across the splaying branches and there was a crumpled, silver-paper depth, an ivory quiet beyond them. Later, I should have called the tree a cedar and passed on, but then, it was an apocalypse.

"Sammy! He's gone."

Johnny had undone the chicken wire and poked out his heroic head. The road was deserted. We became small savages again. We nipped through and dropped down on the pavement. We left the wall to be rebuilt and the tree to grow, unseen of us, in the garden.

I see now what I am looking for and why these pictures are not altogether random. I describe them because they seem to be important. They contributed very little to the straight line of my story. If we had been caught—as later I was indeed caught—and taken by the ear to the general, he might have set in motion some act that changed my whole life or Johnny's. But they are not important in that way. They are important simply because they emerge. I am the sum of them. I carry round with me this load of memories. Man is not an instantaneous creature, nothing but a physical body and the reaction of the moment. He is an incredible bundle of miscellaneous memories and feelings, of fossils and coral growths. I am not a man who was a boy looking at a tree. I am a man who remembers being a boy looking at a tree. It is the difference between time, the endless row of dead bricks, and time, the retake and coil. And there is something even more simple. I can love the child in the garden, on the airfield, in Rotten Row, the tough little boy at school because he is not I. He is another person. If he had murdered, I should feel no guilt, not even responsibility. But then what am I looking for? I am looking for the beginning of responsibility, the beginning of darkness, the point where I began.

Philip Arnold was the other side of our masculine triangle. How shall I describe Philip? We had moved on from the infants' school. We were boys in a boys' school, elementary school, windy and asphalt. I was tough, sturdy, hard, full of zest. There is a gap between the pictures of Sammy Mountjoy with Evie and Sam Mountjoy with Johnny and Philip. One was a baby and the other a boy; but the steps have vanished. They are two different people. Philip was from outside, from the villas. He was pale, physically an extreme coward and he seemed to us to have a mind like a damp box of matches. Yet neither the general nor the god on the airfield, nor Johnny Spragg, nor Evie nor even Ma, altered my life as Philip altered it.

We thought him wet and violence petrified him. That made him a natural target for if you wanted something to hurt, Philip was always to hand. This was sufficient for the odd kick, or scragging; but anything more elaborate required careful preparation and Philip found a simple way of avoiding this. To begin with, he could run very fast; and when he was frightened he could run faster than anyone else. Sometimes, of course, we cornered him; and he evolved a technique for dealing with this, too. He would cower without fighting back. Perhaps it was an instinct rather than an invention, but a very effective one. If you find no resistance you do not become suddenly one with your victim; but after a time you become bored. Philip crouched like a rabbit under a hawk. He looked like a rabbit. Then, as he said nothing, but jerked about under the blows that fell on him, the savour went out of the game. The scurrying victim had become a sack, dull and uninteresting. Without knowing that he was a political philosopher, Philip achieved the end to be desired. He turned the other cheek and we wandered away to find a sport with more savour.

I am anxious that you should not make too simple, too sympathetic a figure out of Philip. Perhaps he sounds like the hero of one of those books which kept turning up in the twenties. Those heroes were bad at games, unhappy and misunderstood at school—tragic, in fact, until they reached eighteen or nineteen and published a stunning book of poems or took to interior decoration. Not so. We were the bullies but Philip was not a simple hero. He loved fighting when anyone else was being hurt. If Johnny and I were fighting, Philip would come running and dance about, flapping his hands. When there was a heaving pile in the playground, our pale, timid Philip would be moving round the outside, giggling and kicking the tenderest piece he could reach. He liked to inflict pain and a catastrophe was his orgasm. There was a dangerous corner leading to the high street; and in a freeze-up, Philip would spend all his spare time on the pavement there, hoping to see a crash. When you see two or three young men on a street corner, or at a country cross-road, at least one of them is waiting for just this. We are a sporting nation.

Philip was—is—not a type. He is a most curious and complicated person. We said he was wet and we held him in contempt; but he was far more dangerous than any of us. I was a prince and Johnny was a prince. We had rival gangs and the issue of battle always hung in doubt between us. I think with rueful amusement of those two barbaric chieftains, so innocent and simple, who dismissed Philip as a wet. Philip is a living example of natural selection. He was as fitted to survive in this modern world as a tapeworm in an intestine. I was a prince and so was Johnny. Philip debated with himself and chose me. I thought he had become my henchman but really he was my Machiavelli. With infinite care and a hysterical providence for his own safety, Philip became my shadow. Living near the toughest of the lot he was protected. Since he was so close, I could not run after him and my hunting reflexes were not triggered off. Timorous, cruel, needing company yet fearing it, weak of flesh yet fleet of fear, clever, complex, never a child—he was my burden, my ape, my flatterer. He was, perhaps, to me, something of what I had been to Evie. He listened and pretended to believe. I was not quite the fantasist that Evie was; my stories were excess of life, not compensation. Secret societies, exploration, detectives, Sexton Blake—"with a roar the huge car leapt forward"—he pretended to believe them all and wove himself nearer and round me. The fists and the glory were mine; but I was his fool, his clay. He might be bad at fighting but he knew something that none of the rest of us knew. He knew about people.

There was the business of the fagcards. We all collected them as a matter of course. I had no dad to pass them on to me and Ma smoked some awful cheap brand that relied on the poverty of its clients rather than advertisement. No one who could have afforded anything better would have been content to smoke them. This is the only feeling of inferiority I can trace right back to the Row but it was strictly limited; not that I had no dad, but just that I had no fagcards. I should have felt the same if my parents had been married non-smokers. I had to rely on pestering men in the streets.

"Got a fagcard, mister?"

I liked fagcards; and for some reason or other my favourites were a series of the kings of Egypt. The austere and proud faces were what I felt people should be. Or do I elaborate out of my adult hind-sight? The most I can be certain of is that I liked the kings of Egypt, they satisfied me. Anything more is surely an adult interpretation. But those fagcards were very precious to me. I begged for them, bargained for them, fought for them—thus combining business with pleasure. But soon no one with any sense would fight me for fagcards because I always won.

Philip commiserated, rubbed in my poverty; pointed out the agony of my choice—never to have any more kings of Egypt or else exchange those I had for others and thus lose the first ones for good. I toughed Philip up mechanically for insolence but knew he was right. The kings of Egypt were out of my reach.

Now Philip took the second step. Some of the smaller boys had fagcards which were wasted on them. What a shame it was to see them crumpling kings of Egypt they were unable to appreciate!

I remember Philip pausing and my sudden sense of privacy and furtive quiet. I cut right through his other steps.

"How we going to get 'em?"

Philip went with me. Immediately I had jumped to the crux, he adapted himself to my position without further comment. He was elastic in such matters. All we—he said we, I remember that clearly—all we had to do was to waylay them in some quiet spot. We should then remove the more precious cards which were of no use to them. We needed a quiet place. The lavatory before school or after school—not in break time, he explained. Then the place would be crowded. He himself would stand in the middle of the playground and give me warning if the master or mistress on duty came too near. As for the treasure, for now the cards had become treasure, and we, pirates, the treasure should be divided. I could keep all the kings of Egypt and he would take the rest.

This scheme brought me one king of Egypt and Philip about twenty assorted cards. It did not operate long and was never really satisfactory. I waited in the smelly shed, idly looking at the graffiti of our more literate members, graffiti rendered more conspicuous by their careful deletion. I would wait in the creosoted quiet as the cisterns filled automatically and discharged—filled and discharged all day and night, whether they had customers or not. If a small victim appeared, I did not mind twisting his arm, but I disliked taking his fagcards. And Philip had miscalculated, though I am sure he profited by the lesson. The situation was never as simple as we had envisaged. Some of the older boys got to know and wanted to share the loot, which gave me more but unprofitable fights and some of them actually objected to the whole business. Then the supply of small boys dried up and only a day or two went by before I found myself being interviewed by the head teacher. A small boy had been found being excused behind a brick buttress by the boiler-shed. Another had wetted himself handsomely in class, burst into tears and sobbed that he was frightened to be excused because of the big boy. The ordinary course of their instruction was immediately interrupted. Soon there was a file of little boys outside the head teacher's room all waiting to give evidence. The fingers pointed straight at Sammy Mountjoy.

This was a humane and enlightened school. Why punish a boy if you can make him conscious of his guilt? The head teacher explained carefully the cruelty and dishonesty of my actions. He did not ask me whether I had done it or no, for he would not give me a chance to lie. He traced the connection between my passion for the kings of Egypt and the size of the temptation that had overcome me. He knew nothing about Philip and found out nothing.

"It's really because you like pictures, eh, Sammy? Only you mustn't get them that way. Draw them. You'd better give back as many as you can. And—here. You can have these."

He gave me three kings of Egypt. I believe he had gone to great trouble over those fagcards. He was a kindly, careful and conscientious man who never came within a mile of understanding his children. He let the cane stay in the corner and my guilt stay on my back.

Is this the point I am looking for?

No.

Not here.

But that was not the profoundest thing that Philip achieved for me. His next was a masterpiece of passion. It was, I suppose, a clumsier exhibition, a botched job from his prentice hand. It reveals Philip to me as a person in three D, as more than a cutout. Like the appearing ice, a point above water, it gives evidence of great depths in Philip. He has always had much in common with an iceberg. He is still pale, still involved and subtle, still dangerous to shipping. He avoided me for a time after the fag-card case. As for me, I fought more than ever; and I do not think it an adult wisdom to say that now I fought with a more furious desire to compel and hurt. At this time I had my greatest hour with Johnny. Out of an obscure and ungovernable rage against something indefinable, I went for the only thing I knew would not flinch at a battering—Johnny's face. But when I hit his nose he tripped and cut his head open on the corner of the school building. So then his ma came and saw the head teacher—Johnny was most anxious that I should understand he had asked her not to—and I was in trouble again. I can still sense my feelings of defiance and isolation; a man against society. For the first, but not the last time I was avoided. The head teacher thought a period in Coventry would show me the value of social contact and persuade me to stop using people as a punchball.

During this period Philip slid alongside again. He assured me of his friendship and we quickly became intimate because he was the only friend I had. Johnny always had a great respect for authority. If the head teacher said no talk, then Johnny was mum. Johnny was adventurous but dared an authority he respected. Philip had no respect for authority, but caution rather. So he quickly slid alongside again. Perhaps among the teachers he may even have built up a little credit as a faithful friend. Who knows? Certainly I was grateful.

As I piece together and judge our relationship during those few weeks I am overcome with astonishment. Can it be possible? Was he so clever so early? Was he even then so cowardly, so dangerous, so elaborate?

When he had got me fast to him Philip led the conversation round to religion. This was unbroken ground for me. If I were baptized now the baptism would have to be conditional. I slipped through the net. But Philip was C. of E.; and what was unusual in those days, his parents were strict and devout. I explored the fringes of this incredible situation by report, understanding very little. We had prayers and a hymn at school, but all I remember of them is the march which got us back to our rooms and the occasion when Minnie showed us the difference between a human being and an animal. We were visited once or twice by a parson but nothing happened. True; I liked what we heard of the Bible. I accepted everything within the limits of a lesson. I should have fallen into the hands of any denomination that made the gesture like a plum.

But Philip, even at that raw age, had begun to watch his parents objectively and had come to certain conclusions. He could not quite take the plunge but he hesitated on the verge of thinking the whole thing daft. Yet not quite. The trouble was the curate. Philip had to go to some class or other—were they confirmation classes or was he not far too young? The rector had nothing to do with this class. He was a strange, lonely old man. He was rumoured to be writing a book and he lived in the vast rectory with a housekeeper almost as old as he.

How had religion touched us so far? I was neutral and Philip tormented. Perhaps Johnny Spragg had the best of it with his unthinking acceptance and untroubled mind. He knew where he was with Miss Massey who ensured that we knew what we ought to know. And you knew where you were with her—scared out of your wits and struck by lightning if your attention wandered. She was fair but fierce. She was a thin, grey-haired woman, in complete control of everything. We were having a lesson with her one day on a fine afternoon with piles of white clouds and blue sky outside the window. We were watching Miss Massey because no one dared to do anything else—all of us except Johnny. His ruling passion had caught up with him. The Moth had appeared among the clouds, climbing, looping, spinning and threading the high valleys over Kent. Johnny was up there, too. He was flying. I knew what was going to happen and I made cautious attempts to warn him; but the whistle of the wind in the wires and the smooth roar of the engine drowned out my whisper. We knew that Miss Massey had noticed because of an additional awe in the atmosphere. She went on speaking as if nothing out of the way was happening. Johnny spun.

She finished her story.

"Now do you remember why I told you those three little stories? What do they show us, children? Could you tell us, Philip Arnold?"

"Yes, miss."

"Jenny?"

"Yes, miss."

"Sammy Mountjoy? Susan? Margaret? Ronald Wakes?"

"Miss. Miss. Miss. Miss."

But Johnny was diving for a loop. He was sitting, building up under his seat the power that would swing him into his sky. He was helmeted, assured, delicate at the rudder-bar and joystick in the fish-'n-chip smell of the engine oil and great wind. He pulled the joystick back slowly, a huge hand thrust him up and he rolled off the top of the loop while the irrelevant dark earth reeled sideways as easy as a shadow.

"Johnny Spragg!"

Johnny made a crash landing.

"Come here."

He clattered out of his desk for the pay off. Flying was always expensive—three pounds dual and thirty shillings solo, for an hour of it.

"Why did I tell you those three stories?"

Johnny's hands were behind his back, his chin on his chest.

"Look at me when I speak to you."

The chin lifted, ever so slightly.

"Why did I tell you those three stories?"

We could just hear his muttered answer. The Moth had flown away.

"Idunnomiss."

Miss Massey hit him on both sides of the head, precisely with either hand, a word and a blow.

"God——"

Smack!

"—is——"

Smack!

"—love!"

Smack! Smack! Smack!

You knew where you were with Miss Massey.

So religion, if disorganized, had entered our several lives. I think Johnny and I accepted it as an inevitable part of an enigmatic situation which was quite beyond our control. But we had not met Philip's curate.

He was pale, intense, sincere and holy. The rector had withdrawn from a multitude of fears and disappointments into secluded eccentricity; and more and more of the church work fell into the hands of Father Anselm. He enthralled and frightened his little pitchers. He adjusted his discourse to their level. He got Philip. He slipped past his guard and menaced his knowledge of people, his selfishness. He took them to the high altar and made them kneel. He was not emotional, no Welsh hwyll for him. He made everything concrete. He showed them the cup. He talked about the *Queen Mary* or some other great work then a-building. He talked about wealth. He held out the silver cup. Have you a sixpence, children, a silver sixpence?

He bowed the cup towards them. Look, children; that is what they think, the kings of Egypt. The cup is lined with pure gold.

Philip was torn down to the soles of his feet. So there was something in it after all. They treated the reality of this subject with the same practical reverence as they treated anything else. They gave it gold. In his clever, tortuous mind, religion swam up out of deceit and gooseberry bush into awful power. The curate would not let him be. Having knocked him down with the cup he finished him off with the altar.

You cannot see it, dear children; but the Power that made the universe and holds you up, lives there. Mercifully you cannot see it as Moses could not see though he asked to. If the veils were lifted from your eyes you would be blasted and destroyed. Let us pray, meekly kneeling on our knees.

You may go now, dear children. Take with you the thought of that Power, uplifting, comforting, loving and punishing, a care for you that will not falter, an eye that never sleeps.

Philip walked away on riven feet. He could not tell me what the matter was but I know now. If what they said was true, and not just another bit of parental guff then what future was there for Philip? What of the schemes, the diplomacy? What of the careful manipulations of other people? Suppose there was indeed another scale of values in which the means were not wholly justified by the results? Philip could not express this. But he could convey his urgent, his desperate desire to know. Gold has never been a metal to me but a symbol. I picked it delightedly out of school, myrrh and fine gold, a golden calf—what a pity they had to grind it to powder!—golden fleece, Goldilocks, Goldilocks let down, golden apple O golden apple, they irradiated my mind's eye and I saw nothing in Philip's cup but another bit of myths and legend. But I was isolated now and in Coventry. It was for this reason that Philip had slid alongside again. With that dreadful perspicacity of his he had assessed my loneliness and resentment, my braggadocio. He knew, even then, the right man and the right moment for a job.

Because how could you test the truth of what Father Anselm said? The only way, surely, was the method used with an unlighted house. I was to ring the bell and run away. Philip would be stationed where he could watch and judge by the ensuing reaction whether anyone was at home or not. I was to be manœuvred into that position, using as a lever my isolation and the excesses of my character. He got me grateful first. Here we were, walking together by the canal. He had talked to me in break when the master on duty was not looking. He was my only true friend. Not that I cared about them of course, did I? No. I cared for nobody like the Miller and I would break the head teacher's window as like as not, just to show.

"Bet you wouldn't."

"Would."

"Wouldn't."

I'd break a policeman's window, see?

Philip introduced the subject of the church. It was autumn and growing dusky. It was the right hour for a desperate deed.

No, not the window, said Philip; but he bet and he bet. So we moved by dare and vaunt and dare and vaunt until I was where he wanted me. Before the light had drained down and the dusk turned to darkness—I might lick every boy in the school but not this, I wouldn't, I wouldn't dare—honest, Sammy, you better not! and giggling, appalled and flapping his hands at awed promise of an accident——

"I would, then, see? I'd piss on it."

Giggle flap tremor, heart-thud.

And so by dare upon dare in the autumn streets I found myself at last engaged to defile the high altar. O streets, cold with copper smoke and brazen noise, with brown profile of warehouse and gasworks glory be for you under the eternal sky. Glory be for the biggest warehouse of all, huddled away from the shining canal among trees and bones.

Philip led the way with his dance and flap and I followed in the net. I was not cold particularly but my teeth had a tendency to shake in my mouth if I did not clench them. I had to cry to Philip to wait a bit under the bridge over the canal and I made concentric, spreading circles in the water and a speck of foam. He ran ahead and came back like a puppy, for all the world as if I were the master.

As we went, I found that something seemed to be wrong with my guts and I had to stop again in a dark alley. But Philip danced round me, his white knees gleaming in the dusk. I wouldn't, he bet.

We came to the stone wall, the lych-gate, the glooming yews. I stopped again and used the wall that the dogs used and then Philip clicked the latch and we were through. He went on tiptoe and I followed with strange shapes of darkness expanding before my eyes. The stones were tall about us and when Philip lifted a longer latch in the yawning porch it sounded like a castle gate. I crouched in after him, hand out to feel him in this thicker darkness but still we were not inside. There was another door, soft-covered; and when Philip pushed, it spoke to us.

Wuff.

I followed still, Philip let me through. I did not know the drill and the released door spoke again behind us.

Wubb wuff!

There were miles of church—first a sense of a world of hollowed stone, all shadow, all guessed-at glossy rectangles dim as an after-image, sudden, startling figures near at hand. I was nothing but singing teeth and jumping skin and hair that crawled without orders. Philip was as bad. His need must have been deep indeed. I could see nothing of him but hands and face and knees. His face was close to mine. We had a fierce and insane argument under the shadow of the inner door with Prayer Books piled on a table at shoulder height.

"It's too dark, I tell you! I can't see!"

"You're a coward then, you can just talk that's all——"

"It's too dark!"

We even struggled there, unhandily, I made impotent

by his unpredictable female strength. And then it was not too dark. The distances were visible. I cannoned into something wooden with green lights revolving round me; then saw a path stretching and guessed rather than knew that this was the way on. Blasts of hot air blew up my legs from metal grilles in the ground. At the end of the path a clutch of dully shining rectangles went careering away up into the sky and below them there was a great shape. There was a light by the altar jazzing as if a maniac were holding it. Silence began to sound, to fill with a high, nightmare note. There were steps to mount and then a blankness of cloth with a line of white at the top. I ran back to Philip, pattering through the blasts of hot air from the grilles in the floor. We argued and tussled again. The awe of the place was on me; even on my speech.

"But I been three times, Phil—don't you see? I can't pee any more!"

Philip raged at me out of the darkness, raged weakly, vilely, cleverly—my brother.

"All right then. I can't pee. But I can spit."

I went back through the hot air and a brass eagle ignored me. Though evening had come on there was more light rather than less—enough to show high fences of carved oak on either hand, a carpet, a pattern of black and grey in the stone floor. I stood as near as I dared to the bottom step; but now my mouth was dry, too. I was involutely thankful for that dry mouth. I snatched wildly and legalistically at the hope of another misfire.

Leaning forward, the green lights swimming round me, I made my motions loud so that Philip should hear them.

"Ptah! Ptah! Ptah!"

The universe exploded from the right-hand side. My

right ear roared. There were rockets, cascades of light, catherine-wheels; and I was fumbling round on stone. A bright light shone down on me from a single eye.

"You little devil!"

I tried mechanically to get my body on its feet but they slithered under me and I fell down again before the angry eye. Through the singing and roaring I heard only one natural noise.

Wubb. Wuff.

I was being hauled across the stone floor and the eye was dancing a beam of light over carved wood, books and glittering cloth. The verger held me all the way and as soon as he had me in the vestry he switched on a light. It was a fair cop. But I could manage neither the insolence nor the stoicism of Black Hand when unmasked by Sexton Blake and Tinker. The floor and the ceiling could not decide between them on up and down. The verger had me cornered literally in an angle and when he let me go I slid all the way down the wall and was a boneless heap. Life had suddenly rearranged itself. On one side of my head life was bigger and more portentous than on the other. The sky, with stars of infinite velocity and remote noise that patterned their travel had opened into me on the right. Infinity, darkness and space had invaded my island. What remained of normal inspected a light, a wooden box, white cloaks hanging up and a brass cross—looked through an arch, and saw that it was lighted now. This world of terror and lightning was only a church being prepared for an evening service. I did not look at the verger, cannot remember at that time what sort of face he had, saw only black trousers and shiny shoes—for at any moment I might have dropped off the floor and broken my bones on the ceiling by the single electric light. A lady appeared in the arch, a grey lady carrying a sheaf of flowers and the verger talked a lot, calling her madam. They talked about me and by that time I was sitting on a low stool, inspecting the lady in one direction and the universe in the other through the hole that had been blown in the side of my head. The verger said I was another of them. What was he going to do? He had to have help, that was what it had come to and the church must be kept locked. The grey lady looked down at me across whole continents and oceans and told him that the rector must decide. So the verger opened another door and led me through into darkness on gravel. He was talking down to me, I deserved the birch and if he had his way I should get it—boys! They were young devils and getting worse every day, like the world and where it would end he didn't know and no one else seemed to, either. The gravel felt as if it had been ploughed and my feet were unclever. I said nothing but tried to get along without tumbling over. Then I found the verger was holding my hand instead of my ear and soon after that he was bending sideways with his hand under my elbow and the other somewhere round my waist. He talked all the time. We came to another door and another grey lady who opened it but carried no flowers and the verger was still talking. We went up some stairs and crossed a landing to a big door. This was a bog because I could hear someone straining inside.

"Ooh! Aah-ooh!"

The verger tapped on the door and inside someone scrambled to his feet.

"Come in then, come in! What is it?"

We went through into a dark room over limitless carpet. There was a parson standing in the middle. He was so tall that he seemed to me to ascend into the shadows that surrounded and roofed everything. I looked at what I could with a strange lack of fear or interest. The nearest thing to me was a section of the parson's trousers. They were sharply creased except at the knees just below my face where the cloth was rounded and shone like black glass. Once more two people argued above me and my attention, in terms which meant nothing to me and which I have forgotten. I was more concerned with and puzzled by my tendency to lurch sideways; and I thought I would like to kneel down, not because of the parson but because if I rolled into a ball there might be no need to wonder so absurdly about which way was up. All I knew was that the parson was refusing to do something and that the verger was pleading with him.

Then the parson spoke loudly and as I now think, with a kind of despair.

"Very well, Jenner. Very well. If I must be invaded—"

I was alone with him. He moved away, sat down in a mother-shaped chair by the dead fire.

"Come here."

I moved my feet carefully over the carpet and stood by the arm of the chair. He bent his head, beyond the length of black thigh, looked searchingly into my face, examined me carefully from head to foot. He came back at last to my face.

He spoke slowly, absently.

"You'd be a pretty child if you kept yourself clean."

He gripped the arms of the chair deep and a goose walked over his grave. I saw that he was straining away from me and I looked down in sudden shame for the girl's word "pretty" and for my so obviously distasteful dirt. We fell into a long silence while I saw that his narrow shoes were turned in towards each other. And on the right-hand side the universe was still roaring and full of stars.

"Who told you to do it?"

That was Philip, of course.

"A little boy like you couldn't have an idea like that without someone suggesting it."

Poor man. I glanced up and then down again, I inspected the enormous explanation, saw it was beyond me and gave up.

"Now tell me the name of the man who told you to do it and I'll let you go."

But there was no man. There was only Philip Arnold and Sammy Mountjoy.

"Why did you do it then?"

Because. Because.

"But you *must* know!"

Of course I knew. I had a picture in my mind of the whole transaction that had led me into this position—I saw it in elaborate detail. I did it because that other parson who talked to Philip had made it seem possible that the church contained more excitement and adventure than the pictures; because I was an outcast and needed something to hurt and break just to show them; because a boy who has hit Johnny Spragg so hard that his mum complained to the head teacher has a position to keep up; because, finally, among the singing stars, I'd been, three times and couldn't pee any more. I knew so many things. I knew I should be interrogated with terrible, adult patience. I knew I should never grow up to be as tall and majestic, knew that he had never been a child, knew we were different creations each in our appointed and changeless place. I knew that the questions would be right and pointless and unanswerable because asked out of the wrong world. They would be righteous and kingly and impossible from behind the high wall. Intuitively I knew this, that the questions would be like trying to lift water in a sieve or catch a shadow by the hand: and this intuition is one of the utter sorrows of childhood.

"Now then. Who told you to do it?"

For of course, when the glamour is gone, the phantom enemies, the pirates and highwaymen, robbers, cowboys, good men and bad, we are faced by the brute thing; the adult voice and four real walls. That is where the policemen and probation officers, teachers and parents achieve the breakdown of our integrated simplicity. The hero is overthrown, remains whimpering and defenceless, a nothing.

How long should I have lasted? Should I have lived up to Tinker? He was frequently threatened with some elaborate form of extinction if he refused to tell. But I was saved at that time from any suspicion of my own inadequacy; for suddenly I wanted to go home and lie down; and then even going home seemed an impossible exertion. The universe bored into my head, the milky way swam past, the green lights of the singing stars expanded and were everything that was.

My memories of that time are confused as mountainous country in misty weather. Did I walk home? How could I? But if I was carried, what arms held me? I must have reached Rotten Row somehow. I went to school next day as usual, I remember that clearly. Perhaps I was not quite as usual. I seem to remember feeling as if I had been drizzled on for a long time and had reached the crisis of whimpering; but there was no rain. There was warmth instead on my right side and a deep throbbing in my right ear. How many days? How many hours? Then, at the end, I was sitting in a classroom and it must have been late afternoon because both the naked lights on their long flexes were switched on. I was tired of the throbbing, tired of school, tired of everything, wanted to lie down. I looked at the paper in front of me and I could not think what I had to write. I heard whispering and knew without understanding, that I was the centre of excitement and awe. A boy in front of me and to the left had his coat pulled and looked round. There was more whispering so that the master moved at his desk. Then Johnny Spragg who was sitting to the right of me got out of his seat and put up his hand.

"Please, sir! Sammy's crying."

Ma and Mrs. Donavan knew about earache. There were rituals to be performed. For a while I was an object of interest to all the women in the row. They would gather and nod and look down at me. It comes to me now with faint surprise that we never used our upstairs after the lodger died in it. Perhaps Ma was hoping for another lodger; or perhaps her neglect of the bare room was a symptom of her decline. We had lived and slept downstairs, just as if he were still ticking and fuffing above the whitewashed boards; so I had my earache near the stove which was as comfortable a place as any. Ma kept up a good fire in the centre hole. The lady with the green leathery plant brought in a bucket of coal and some advice. They gave me bitter white pills to swallow, aspirin perhaps; but the universe kept boring in, bringing the earache with it. Things became more than lifesize. I kept trying to get away from the pain but it went with me. Ma and Mrs. Donavan took council with the plant lady and they decided to iron me. Mrs. Donavan brought an iron —perhaps Ma always borrowed?—and it was black, with a piece of brown cloth round the handle. It was really iron too, deeply pitted with rust, and only shiny on the bottom part. The plant lady put a piece of cloth over the side of my head while Ma set the iron on the fire. When she took it off she spat on the shiny side and I saw the little balls of spit dance, dwindle and vanish. She sat by me and ironed the side of my head through the cloth and the plant lady held my hand. Then while I was still accepting the warmth with good faith and hoping the pain would go away, the door opened and the tall parson bowed himself through. Ma took away the cloth and the iron and got up. The pain was worse if anything so that I began to turn on this side and then on that and then lie on my face; and every time I happened to see the tall parson he was still standing in the door with his mouth open. Perhaps they moved and spoke, but I have no memory of it. To my hindsight they seem motionless as a ring of stones. Just then the pain began to knock on the door where I was, my own private, inviolable centre so that I made noises and flung myself about. The parson disappeared and at some remove, over gulfs of fire and oceans of blackness under wild green stars there was a big man in the room who was fighting me, binding me, getting my arms in a hold, fastening me down with terrible strength and saying the same thing over and over again.

"Just the tiniest little prick."

Behind my right ear there is a new moon of scar and a pucker. They are so old that they feel natural and right. I got them that same day, or at least, before the next morning. There was no penicillin, no wonder-drug to control and reduce infection in those days. If the doctor had any doubt at all he operated for mastoid straight away. I came round in a new place, a new world. I was lying over a bowl, too sick and faint to notice anything else but the bowl, whiteness and a brown, polished floor. The pain was reduced to the same dull throbbing that had made me cry at school; but now even crying was too much effort. I lay, drugged and miserable with a turban of gauze and cotton-wool and bandages round my head. Ma appeared at some time or other in that period. I saw her then for the first and last time, not as the broad figure blotting out the darkness but as a person. There is a wan sanity about the drugged eye sometimes that the healthy one does not have. In my misery I saw her as a stranger might see her, a massive, sagging creature, mottled and dirty. Her hair was in wisps over her brown forehead, her face was a square-ish, drawn-down mass with a minute fag sticking in one corner of her mouth. I see now the sausage hands, brown, with discolorations of red and blue, clutching the string-bag into her lap. She sat as she always sat, in majestic indifference; but the gas was escaping from the balloon. She had little enough to bring me, for what has a woman to spare who even borrows an iron? Yet she had taken thought and found what she could. There was a pedestal by the head of the bed and she had placed there a handful of rather dirty fagcards—my cherished kings of Egypt.

3

And still I ask myself: "Well. There?" and myself answers: "No. Not there." He is no more a part of me than any other child. I simply have better access to him. I cannot remember what he looked like. I doubt if I ever knew. He is still this bubble floating, filled with happiness or pain which I can no longer feel. In my mind those feelings are represented by colours; they are as exterior to what I feel, as the child itself. His insufficiency and guilt were not mine. I have my own which sprang out of my life somewhere like weeds. I cannot find the root. However I try I can bring up nothing which is part of me.

The ward was a fine place to be when my head stopped hurting. I got complications, had ups and downs. I was a lifetime in that ward, so that I can switch my mind from the world of Rotten Row to the world of the ward as from planet to planet. I have a sense of timelessness in both places. I cannot remember the doctors or nurses or even the other children at all clearly. Survival in this mode must surely be random or why can I not remember who had the beds to right and left? But there was a little girl who had the bed opposite me. She was tiny and black with tight curls and a round, shining, laughing face. Nobody understood the language she spoke. Now I remember that she had a cot instead of a bed like the older children, because when she stood up at the foot she could hold the top rail and swing up and down. She talked all the time. She laughed and sang, she talked to anyone within reach in her babbling, meaningless talk, talked to doctors, nurses, visitors, matron, children, happily and irrepressibly. She was entirely without fear or sorrow and everybody who saw her loved her. I deduce from the line of bricks that she came, had her graph of sickness, recovered and went. But to me, if I think of the ward, she is always there, a small figure in a white nightdress with two jet black hands and a black, flashing face, swinging and laughing.

I remember the matron, too, because I had a little more to do with her than most of the patients. She was tall and thin. She must have been handsome, in a severe sort of way. Her uniform was dark blue with wings on her head of blinding white. She had stiff, glossy cuffs, small at the wrist but expanding a little up the forearm. When she came into the ward the world stopped turning. We gave the nurses a terrible time; but not matron. She was surrounded by awe. Perhaps the deference of the nurses had something to do with that but as far as I was concerned awe came from her as naturally as comfort from a mother.

She did a job for me.

One of the nurses told me that Ma had been taken poorly which was why she did not come to see me. I accepted this without thought for I was entirely taken up in the endless world of the ward. Somehow my pedestal was as full as the others and the visitors did not seem to belong too particularly to other children. I shared the visitors and everything. Things were so different, so ample, so ordered. One day matron came and sat on my bed instead of standing by it or in front of it. She told me that Ma had died—gone to heaven and was very happy. And then she produced the thing I had been wanting without ever believing it could belong to me; a stamp album and some envelopes of assorted stamps. There were transparent windows in each envelope so that you could see the coloured squares inside. There was a packet of transparent hinges, one side dull, the other shiny with gum. She made me open one of the packets and showed me how to put the hinges on and search through the album for the right country. She must have stayed there a long time because I remember putting in a lot of stamps with great concentration. I am unable to report on sorrow. I cannot even see a colour. All I remember is one vast, vertical sniff because it spilt the bitter liquid in a little glass that matron was holding and she had to send a nurse for another one. So at last I dozed off over my album and when I woke up the ward was the same as it had always been only with another fact added to life—and it seems to me now—already accepted out of a limitless well of acceptance.

I was not entirely without visitors either. The tall parson came to see me and stood, looking down at me helplessly. He brought me a cake from his housekeeper and wandered off, gazing at the ceiling and finding the way out of the door with his shambling feet. The verger came to see me too. He sat anxiously by the bed and tried to talk; but it was so long since he had done anything to children but chase them out of the church if they were noisy that he didn't know how. He was a crumpled little man in daylight, wearing the black clothes of his profession and carrying a black bowler hat. This worried him in the ward and he would put it on the bed and then take it off and try the pedestal and then take the hat back again as if certain that sooner or later he would find the exact spot that was right and proper for a black bowler hat in a hospital. He was used to ritual, perhaps, to an exact science of symbols. He had a high, bald forehead, no eyebrows, and a moustache very like our lodger's in everything but colour. You could see the last wisps of his hair smeared black across the top of his baldness. I was shy of him because he was shy of me and worried. He talked to me as if I were another grown-up so his complicated story eluded me. I could not make out what he meant and only picked up odd bits here and there; and most of these were misunderstandings. There had been trouble with a society, he said, and I inferred a secret society at once. They had had people standing up in the back of the church and shouting during the service. That was bad enough; but the society had gone even further. People—he wouldn't like to name them either, seeing he had no proof and couldn't swear to a single one in a court of law—people had sneaked in during the dark evenings and spoiled ornaments, torn down curtains all because they thought the church was too high. I remembered the sheaf of rectangles soaring dizzily above the altar and thought I understood. The verger said the rector had always been high but in the last few years he had seemed to be getting higher and higher. Then when Father Anselm came, the curate he was, of course, he was just as high as the rector was or even a bit higher—in fact, said the verger, he wouldn't be a bit surprised if one of these days——

But there he broke off, leaving me to wonder mildly how high you could get and what happened when you reached the top. If the curate was as high as the rector then he, too, had his head in shadows when he stood in the middle of the carpet. I ceased to listen when the verger went on. His talk of aumbries, chasubles, images, apparels and thurifers went right over my head. My mind's eye was occupied with a dim church full of elongated clergymen.

Then I realized that he was talking of the time he had heard Philip and me in the church. He never turned the lights on until the last possible minute; if Lady Crosby was waiting for confession, he never turned the lights on until she left. Father Anselm had told him not to. But most evenings he wouldn't anyway. It was the only way he could hope to catch the people from the society. When he heard us he made sure. He got his torch and crept out from the vestry and along the choir stalls. He saw it was only a kid and it made him angry.

I was interested. He was kind to tell me exactly how he had done it, creeping along the choir stalls and then tiptoeing out. He had done a nice bit of work and he had caught me nicely.

He took his bowler hat off the bed and put it on the pedestal. He began to talk urgently. Of course the ear must have been giving trouble but he hadn't known, you see, and they'd had such a time with the society . . .

He paused. He was red. Sallow red. He held out his right hand.

"If I'd known what was going to happen I'd sooner have cut that hand off. I'm sorry, lad, sorrier than I can say."

Something to forgive is a purer joy than geometry. I've found that out since, as a bit of the natural history of living. It is a positive act of healing, a burst of light. It is real and precise as aesthetic enjoyment, not weak or soft but crystalline and strong. It is the sign and seal of adult stature, like that man who reached out both arms and gathered the spears into his own body. But innocence does not recognize an injury and that is why the terrible sayings are true. An injury to the innocent cannot be forgiven because the innocent cannot forgive what they do not understand as an injury. This, too, I understand as a bit of natural history. I guess the nature of our universe is such that the strong and crystalline adult action heals a wound and takes away a scar not out of today but out of the future. The wound that might have gone on bleeding and suppurating becomes healthy flesh; the act is as if it had never been. But how can the innocent understand that?

What was the verger talking to me about then? Was he sorry about the whole story, starting when I and Philip had concocted our plan? But he did not know that story or so I hoped. Was he sorry that little boys are devils, that their brash and violent world would knock down the high walls of authority if it could? As I saw the truth the adult world had hit me good and proper for a deed that I knew consciously was daring and wrong. Hazily and in pictures more than in thought I saw my punishment to have been nicely graded. I had spat though rather drily and inadequately on the high altar. But I had meant to pee on it. My mind flinched away from the possibilities of what might have happened if I had not been three times before we reached the church. Men were hanged but boys got nothing worse than the birch. I saw with a sane and appreciative eye the exact parallel between the deed and the result. Why should I think of forgiveness? There was nothing to forgive.

The verger's hand was still held out. I examined it and him and waited.

At last he sighed, took his bowler off the pedestal and stood up. He cleared his throat.

"Well——"

He turned his hat round and round in his hands, sucked his moustache, blinked. Then he was away, walking quickly and silently on his professional creepers down the centre of the ward and through the double door.

Wubb. Wuff.

When did I discover that the tall parson was now my guardian? I cannot dissect his motives because I never understood him. Was it perhaps the opening of the Bible that decided my fate? Was he touched by me more than I can think? Had the verger any hand in it? Was I an expiation, not of the one blow, but of numberless fossilized uneases and inadequacies, old sins and omissions that had hardened into impenetrable black stone? Or was I only a forbidden fruit, made accessible but still not eaten? Whatever it was, the result did not seem to do him much good, bring him much peace. Other people understood him no more than I did. They always laughed at him behind his back—might have laughed in his face if he had had less care to be solitary and hidden. Even his name was ridiculous. He was Father Watts-Watt. His choirboys used to think it very funny to ask each other: "Do you know what's what?" I wish now I could look back down his story as I can look down my own. He could never have been tough as I was tough. Things must have gone right through him.

So he came fairly often and hung about, trying to talk, trying to find out about me. He would stand, knit his jutting grey eyebrows and swoop a look up under them at the ceiling. All his movements were like that, writhings as though the only source of movement was a sudden pain. There was so much of him, such lengths that you could see the motion travel outwards, bend his body sideways, stretch an arm out and end in the involuntary gesture of a clenched fist. Did I like school? Yes, I liked school. Good—bend, stretch, clench. It was like a nonsense story; talking with him was like a nightmare ride on a giraffe. Yes, bashfully, I liked drawing. Yes, I could swim a bit. Yes, I should like to go to the grammar school, ultimately, whenever that was. Yes, yes, yes, agreement but still no communication. Did I go to church? No, I didn't—at least—Wouldn't I like to go? Yes, I would like to go.

Well—balancing movement, bend stretch clench—good-bye, my dear child, for the time being.

And so the world of the ward must have come to an end.

I have searched like all men for a coherent picture of life and the world, but I cannot write the last word on that ward without giving it my adult testimony. The walls were held up by sheer, careful human compassion. I was on the receiving end and I know. When I make my black pictures, when I inspect chaos, I must remember that such places are as real as Belsen. They, too, exist, they are part of this enigma, this living. They are brick walls like any others, people like any others. But remembered, they shine.

That, then, is all the infant Samuel I can remember. He trailed no clouds of glory. He was spirit and beauty-proof. He was hard as nails and gave better than he got. Yet I should deceive myself if I refused to recognize something special about the period up to mastoid, up to the end of the ward-world. Let me think in pictures again. If I imagine heaven metaphorically dazzled into colours, the pure white light spread out in a cascade richer than a peacock's tail then I see that one of the colours lay over me. I was innocent of guilt, unconscious of innocence; happy, therefore, and unconscious of happiness. Perhaps the full sheaf of colours is never to be experienced by the human being since if he experiences these colours they must lie in the past or on someone else. Perhaps consciousness and the guilt which is unhappiness go together; and heaven is truly the Buddhist Nirvana.

That must be the end of a section. There is no root of infection to be discovered in those pictures. The smell of today, the grey faces that look over my shoulder have nothing to do with the infant Samuel. I acquit him. He is some other person in some other country to whom I have this objective and ghostly access. Why does his violence and wickedness stop there, islanded in pictures? Why should his lies and sensualities, his cruelty and selfishness have been forgiven him? For forgiven him they are. The scar is gone. The smell either inevitable or chosen came later. I am not he. I am a man who goes at will to that show of shadows, sits in judgment as over a strange being. I look for the point where this monstrous world of my present consciousness began and I acquit him in the ward.

Here?

Not here.

And even by the time I was on the bike by the traffic light, I was no longer free. There was a bridge over a skein of railway lines among the smoky huddles of South London and the traffic lights were a new thing there. They sorted the traffic which went north and south beside the lines from the dribble that tried to pick a way round London, east and west. They were so new a thing in those days that an art student like myself could not see them without thinking of ink and wash—ink line for the sudden punch-ball shape, wash for the smokes and glows and the spilt suds of autumn in the sky.

No. I was not entirely free. Almost but not quite. For this part of London was touched by Beatrice. She saw this grime-smothered and embossed bridge, the way buses heaved over its arch must be familiar. One of these streets must be hers, a room in one of these drab houses. I knew the name of the street, Squadron Street; knew, too, that sight of the name, on a metal plaque, or sign-posted might squeeze my heart small again, take away the strength of my knees, shorten my breath. I sat my bike on the downward slope of the bridge, waiting for a green light and the roll down round to the left; and already I had left my freedom behind me. I had allowed myself the unquiet pleasure of picturing her, taken the decisive step of moving toward. I sat, waiting, watching the red light.

There was a large chapel that rose among the houses perhaps a quarter of a mile off in the smoke and the feelings I had thought seared out of me, stirred as if seeds had burst their cases. Make an end and these feelings die at last. But I had not made an end. Sitting there, I could feel all the beginnings of my wide and wild jealousy; jealousy that she was a girl, the most obscure jealousy of all—that she could take lovers and bear children, was smooth, gentle and sweet, that the hair flowered on her head, that she wore silk and scent and powder; jealousy that her French was so good because she had that fortnight in Paris with the others and I was forbidden to go—jealousy of the chapel-deep inexplicable fury with her respectable devotion and that guessed-at sense of communion: jealousy, final and complete of the people who might penetrate her goodwill, her mind, the secret treasures of her body, getting where I if I turned back could never hope to be—I began to scan the men on the pavement, these anonymities who were privileged to live in this land touched by the feet of Beatrice. Any one of them might be he, could be he, might be her landlady's husband or son; landlady's son!

Still the traffic lights said stop. I became aware that the roads were filled with a jam of traffic—so the lights could break down then. We were held up. There was still time to turn round and go away again. A few days and the feelings would sear themselves out. But even as that possibility presented itself I knew that I should not go back; felt myself get off the bike, lift it on the pavement and wheel it under the red light.

Courage. Your clothes are clean if cheap; your hair is cut and combed; your mug if ugly is carefully shaved and slightly scented with a manly scent as in the advertisements. You have even cleaned your shoes.

"I didn't ask to fall in love!"

I found I was fifty yards on, still pushing my bike along the pavement though here the road was free. I was under a huge hoarding which was flourishing beans and red cheeks ten feet in the air. My heart was beating quickly and loud, not because I had seen her or even thought of her, but because in the walk along the pavement I had understood at last the truth of my position. I was lost. I was caught. I could not push my bike back again over the bridge; there was nothing physical to stop me and only the off-chance of seeing Beatrice to push me on. I had cried out aloud, cried out of all the feelings that were bursting their seed-cases. I was trapped again. I had trapped myself.

For to go back is—what? Not only all that has gone before, but also this added: that I had seen her pavements and people, invented an addition in the landlady's son, was far worse off than when I started. Going back would end somewhere—in Australia perhaps, or South Africa—but somewhere it would end in one way only. Somewhere a man would accost me casually.

"Did you ever know a girl called Beatrice Ifor?"

Myself, with reeling heart and straight, painful face:

"A bit. At school——"

"She's——"

She's what? Become a Member of Parliament. Been canonized by the Catholic Church. Is on the hanging committee.

"She's married a chap——"

A chap. She could marry the Prince of Wales. Be queen. Oh God, myself on the pavement. Queen Beatrice, her secret plumbed and known, but not by me——

I was addressing the beans.

"Does everyone fall in love like this? Is so much of their love a desperation? Then love is nothing but madness."

And I do not want to hate her. Part of me could kneel down, could say as of Ma and Evie, that if she would only be meward and if she would be by me and for me and for nothing else, I wanted to do nothing but adore her.

Pull yourself together. You know what you want. You decided. Now move towards that consummation step by step.

They were coming out of the training college already, I could see them, fair heads and mousy ones, giggling and laughing in flocks, tinkling their good-byes and waving, so girlish and free, the thin ones, tall ones, dumpy ones, humpy ones, inky ones, slinky ones, gamesy ones and stern ones with glasses on. I was in the gutter, sitting my bike, willing them to die, be raped, bombed or otherwise obliterated because this demanded split-second timing. And, of course, she might not come out at all—might be —what the hell did you do in a girls' training college at half-past four on an autumn afternoon? The crowd was thinning out. If she saw me first so obviously sitting my saddle in the gutter and waiting, the game would be up. Had to be accident, I had to be riding when she saw me; so I pushed off and balanced along with circus slowness, half-hoping now that the crisis was at hand that she would not come out and my misbehaving heart would be able to settle again, wobble wobble heart and bike and she appeared with two others, turned and walked away without seeing me. But I had rehearsed this too often in my bed for my heart and swelling hands to let me down. The whole thing was mechanical, fruit of terrible concentrated thought and repetition. I rode casually, one hand in my pocket and the other on my hip, look no hands, swaying thisway and that. She was past and behind me. Startled I looked back,grabbed the handle-bars, braked and skidded to a stop by the pavement, looked back brazenly as she approached, grinned brazenly in immense surprise——

"Why, if it isn't Beatrice Ifor!"

So they stopped all three while my rehearsed prattle left her no chance of moving off without being rude; and those other two, those blessed damozels, they were in the freemasonry of this sort of meeting and moved on almost immediately, waving back and giggling.

"—was just cycling past—never dreamed—so this is the training college, is it? I come along this road a lot or shall do in the future. Yes a course. I prefer cycling between the other place and the other place—no buses for me. Can't stand 'em. Course in lithography. Were you going back to your digs? No. I'll walk. Can I carry? Are you enjoying it here? Is the work hard? You seem to be thriving on—yes. Look. I was going to have a cup of tea before I ride the rest—how—oh, but you must! One doesn't meet—and after all these months, too! Lyons. Yes. I can leave the bike——"

There was a small round table of imitation marble on three iron legs. She was sitting on the other side. I had her now for whole minutes, islanded out of all the complexities of living. By sheer hard work and calculation I had brought this about. There was much to be achieved in those minutes, things noted down and decided, steps to be taken; she was to be brought—oh, irony! a little nearer to a complete loss of freedom. I heard my voice babbling on, saying its lines, making the suggestions that were too general to be refused, the delicately adjusted assumptions that were to build up into an obligation; I heard my voice consolidating this renewed acquaintance and edging diplomatically a trifle further; but I watched her unpaintable, indescribable face and I wanted to say—you are the most mysterious and beautiful thing in the universe, I want you and your altar and your friends and your thoughts and your world. I am so jealousy-maddened I could kill the air for touching you. Help me. I have gone mad. Have mercy. I want to be you.

The clever, unscrupulous, ridiculous voice murmured on.

When she got up to go, I went with her, talking all the time, talking an attentive, amusing—oh, the calculated stories! pleasant young man into the picture; erasing the other Sammy, so incalculable, insolent and namelessly vicious. When she stopped dismissively on the pavement I accepted this as if the sky was not reeling round me. I allowed her to go, attached to me by a line no thicker than a hair, but at least, if one could not say that she had swallowed the fly, it was still there, dancing over the water; and she, she was still there—she had not flicked her tail and vanished under weed or rock. I watched her go and turned to my bike with something accomplished—a meeting with Beatrice in the privacy of a crowd, a contact re-established. I rode home, my heart molten with delight, goodness and gratitude. For it was good. She was nineteen and I was nineteen; we were male and female, we would marry though she did not know that yet—must not know that yet, lest she vanish under weed or rock. Moreover there was peace. For she would be working at her books tonight. Nothing could touch her. Until the next afternoon—for who knew what she would do that evening? Dance? Cinema? With whom? Nevertheless the jealousy was to-morrow's jealousy and for twenty-four hours she was safe. I surrounded her with gratitude and love that came out strongly as a sense of blessing, unsexual and generous. Those who have nothing are made wild with delight by very little. Once again as at school I yearned not to exploit but protect.

So my tiny thread was attached to her and I did not see that with every additional thread I myself was bound with another cable. Of course I went back next day, against my better judgment but with a desperate impulse to move on, to hurry things up; and she was not there, did not come. Then I spent an evening of misery and hung about the next day all the afternoon.

"Hullo, Beatrice! It looks as if we are going to meet quite often!"

But she had to hurry, she said, was going out that evening. I left her on the pavement with Lyons like an unvisited heaven and agonized as she vanished into the infinite possibilities of going out. Now I had ample time to consider the problems of attachment. I began to appreciate dimly that a thread must be tied at both ends before it can restrain anything.

Facetious.

"Hullo, Beatrice! Here we are again!"

When we were sitting at the marble-topped table my plans began to come apart.

"Did you enjoy yourself last night?"

"Yes, thank you."

Then, out of the unendurable compulsion to know; with heart beat and damp hand with plea and anger——

"What were you doing?"

She was wearing, I remember, a suit, grey, some sort of smoothed flannel with a vertical stripe, alternately green and white. She had a blouse on beneath it with some throat and chest showing. Two fine gold chains fell down the glossy skin and vanished into the treasury. What was there at the end, between the Hesperides? A cross? A locket with a curl of hair? An aquamarine to shake and glimmer there, a perfection secret and unattainable?

"What were you doing?"

The contrast between the formal suit, the masculinity of the lapels, the neatness of the waist—and the soft body that sat in it—don't you know what you do to me? But there were changes, too, a faint hint of pink now over each cheekbone and under the long lashes a level look. Suddenly the air between us was filled with comprehension—understanding on the small-change level. This was not worded, did not need to be. She knew and I knew; but still I could not keep the fatal word back. It vibrated in my head, was unstoppable as a sneeze, came out with fury and contempt and pain.

"Dancing?"

The hints of pink were definite now. The round chin lifted. The thread stretched and broke.

"Well, really——"

She lifted off the chair, took her books.

"I'm late. I must go."

"Beatrice!"

I had to run after her as she walked along the pavement. I hung by her, walking sideways.

"I'm sorry. Only I—*hate* dancing—hate it! And the thought of you——"

We were stopped and half turned to each other.

"*Were* you dancing?"

There were three steps up to the front door, curved iron railings descending them on either side. Neither of us had the right vocabulary. She wanted to tell me, that assuming what she sensed was correct then I still had no right to insist on knowing. I wanted to cry—look how I burn! There are flames shooting out of my head and my loins and my heart! She wanted to say: however I may have half unconsciously appraised you as a mate—and of course you seemed impossible, only slightly amended by your recent behaviour—however much I have exercised my normal function of female living and allowed you to approach thus far; nevertheless, the rules of the game should have been observed; whereas you have broken them and affronted my dignity.

So we stood, she on the lower step, I, hand on the rails, red tie blown by my own violence over my right shoulder.

"Beatrice! Were you——?"

She had such clear eyes, such untroubled eyes, grey, honest because the price of dishonesty had never been offered to her. I looked into them, sensed their merciless and remote purity. She was contained in herself. Nothing had ever come to trouble her pool. If I held out my hand, desperate and pleading, inarticulate and hot out of raw youth and all the tides that bundled me along, what could she do but examine it and me and wait and wonder what I wanted?

"Were you?"

Indignation and hauteur; but both scaled down because the thread had been after all so hair-thin and to make much of the offence would imply that I had threatened her freedom.

"Maybe."

And so she took herself away wonderfully into the house.

How big is a feeling? Where is the dial that registers in degrees? I found my way back across South London, trying to come up out of my mind. I said that there was no need to exaggerate; you are not an adult, I said—there will be far worse things than this. There will be times when you will say—did I ever think I was in love? All that long ago? He was in love. Romeo was. Lear died of a broken heart. But where is the means of comparison? Where in the long scale did Sammy come? For now there were rough ropes on my wrists and ankles and round my neck. They led through the streets, they lay at her feet and she could pick them up or not as she chose. It was torture to me as I rode away with the miles of rope trailing, that she did not choose. She was perhaps tied herself in another direction? But I did not believe it. At my fever heat, processes went on more than apace. I was a local and specialized psychologist. I had seen her eyes, knew them and her untroubled. What fool was it insisted that he should know where she had been when at the same time he knew how thin that thread was in the beginning? There had been no risk. Her quality was untouched and the only risk was that somewhere and somehow she might meet the inscrutable chance and be set on fire. I walked in my room, beating my hands together.

The party was a relief. Robert Alsopp was in the chair and the air was thick with smoke and importance. The others were standing or sitting or lying, full of excitement and contempt. Everything was bloody, comrades. But passion, we know where we are going if no one else does. Sammy, you're next. Now keep quiet, comrades, for Comrade Mountjoy.

Comrade Mountjoy made a very small report. In fact he had not worked out any report from the Y.C.L. at all. He vamped. But the smoke and the technicalities the urgency and passion were a place hollowed out. So when I came to my lame conclusion I was disciplined and directed to undertake some self-examination. I began it there and it is still going on; but I remember my first decision; namely, to write to Beatrice that very night and be honest. I remember my second decision, too, and that was that I would never bring Beatrice into this home from home because she would have first to go to bed with Comrade Alsopp. He had a wife who didn't understand him just as though he were a bourgeois school teacher instead of a progressive one; but what with the war only a week or two off, the decay and break-up, the excitement, nobody noticed that this was not Marxism but the oldest routine in the world. Nevertheless, it provided our more personable females with a kind of graduation and, as it were, softened them up.

Comrade Wimbury was speaking. He was very tall and vague, and he was another teacher. I remember how we were ruled by Alsopp and Wimbury because they were, if I could only have seen it at the time, an act of low comedy. Alsopp had an immense bald head, a ruined face with a wet lecherous mouth scrawled across it. He was broad and most impressive at the table; but then you found he was not sitting down but standing up. He had the stumpiest legs of any man I have ever seen. He did not sit on a chair. He leaned his seat against it. Wimbury, on the other hand, had a tiny body so that when he sat by Alsopp his narrow chin and rabbit face only just appeared over the table. But if he stood up, this doll's body was elevated on two stilt-like legs that pushed him right up towards the ceiling. That evening, he was giving us our political lecture and he was proving with a wealth of reference and initials that there would be no war. It was all a capitalist plot to do something, I forget what. We listened and nodded wisely. We were on the inside. We knew that in a few years the world would be communist: and of course we were right. I tried to sink myself in listening; but the ropes were still there.

That night I wrote Beatrice a letter. The Christmas card had taught me that words are our only communication, so it was a long letter. I wish I could read it now. I begged her to read the letter carefully—not knowing how common this opening was in such a letter—not knowing that there were thousands of young men in London that night writing just such letters to just such altars. I explained about school, about the rumoured aphrodisiac. I went back to the first day when I had sat by Philip and tried to draw her. I explained what I had seen or thought I had seen. I told her that I was a helpless victim, that pride had prevented me from making this clear to her, but she was the sun and moon for me, that without her I should die, that I did not expect much—only that she should agree to some special relationship between us that would give me more standing than these acquaintances so casually blessed. For she might come to care for me, I said, in my bourgeois pamphlet, she might even—for I have loved you from the first day and I always shall.

Two o'clock in the morning and autumn mist, London

fog about. I sneaked out of the house for the family I lived with were supposed to report my movements to the authorities. I rode off, through the night, not daring to lose a post. First one policeman stopped me and took my name and address and then two stopped me. The third time I was tired enough to be honest and I told the statue in the blue coat that I was in love so he waved me on and wished me luck. At last I came to her door, pushed the package through and heard it fall. I was saying to myself as I nodded on the bike: at least I have been honest, been honest, I don't know what to do.

How do they react in themselves, these soft, cloven creatures? Where is the dial that marks their degrees of feeling? I had had my sex already. The party had seen to that, Sheila, dark and dirty. We had given each other a little furtive pleasure like handing round a bag of toffees. It was also our absurd declaration of independence, a declaration made by behaving as much like Alsopp as possible. It was freedom. But these other contained, untouched girls—how do they feel and think? Or are they like Sammy in Rotten Row, a clear bubble blown about, vulnerable but unwounded? Surely she must have known! But how did the situation present itself? Granted the whole physical process appears horrible and unmentionable—for so it did, I know that—what then does love appear to be? Is it an abstract thing with as little humanity as the dancing advertisements of Piccadilly? Or does love immediately imply a white wedding, a house? She had dressed and undressed herself, tended her delicate body year in year out. Did she never think with faster pulse and breath—he is in love, he wants to do—that—to me? Perhaps now with the spread of enlightenment virginity has lost sacred caste and girls go eager to swim. It was, after all, a social habit. She was lower middle class where the instinct or habit was to keep what you had intact. It was a class in those days of great power and stability, ignoble and ungenerous. I cannot tell what flutter if any I made in her dovecote, could not, cannot, knew and know nothing about her. But she read the letter.

This time I did not pretend to be riding by. I sat my saddle, one hand on the handle-bars one foot on the pavement. I watched them tumble out of the double doors and she came with them. The blessed damozels had been tipped off because they marched away without a giggle. I looked her in the eye and burned with the shame of my confession.

"You read my letter?"

They were not terms on which she blushed. Without a word we went to Lyons and sat in silence.

"Well?"

She did pinken a bit then, she spoke softly and gently as to an invalid.

"I don't know what to say, Sammy."

"I meant every word of it. You've"—spread hands—"got me. I'm defeated."

"How?"

"It's a kind of competition."

But I saw that her eyes were still empty of understanding.

"Forget it, Beatrice. If you can't understand—look. Have goodwill. You see? Give me a chance to—*am* I so awful? I know I'm nothing to look at, but I do"—deep breath—"I do—you know how I feel."

Silence.

"Well?"

"Your course. It won't last for ever. Then you won't come this way."

"My course? What? Oh—that! I mean I thought if you and I—we could go walking in the country and then you could—I'm quite harmless really."

"Your course!"

"So you guessed, did you? I'm cutting the Art School at this moment. There are some things that are more important."

"Sammy!"

Now the untroubled pools began to fill. There was wonder and awe and a trace of speculation. Did she think to herself; it is true, he is in love, he has done a real thing for me? I am that, after all, which can be loved. I am not entirely empty. I have a stature like the others. I am human?

"You'll come? Say you'll come, Beatrice!"

She was commendably virtuous on every level. She would come; but I must promise—not in exchange, for that would be bargaining—must promise I would not cut the art school any more. I think she began to see herself as a centre of power, as an influence for good; but her interest in my future gave me such delight that I did not analyse it.

Not on Sunday. On Saturday. She couldn't come on Sunday, she said, with a kind of mild surprise that anyone should expect her to. And so I met my first, indeed, my only rival. That surprised me then and surprises me now; first, that I should rage so at this invisible rival, second, that I had none physical. She was so sweet, so unique, so beautiful—or did I invent her beauty? Had all young men been as I, the ways where she went would have been crowded. Did no other man have as I this unquenchable desire to know, to be someone else, to understand; was mine the only mixture near her of worship and jealousy and musky tumescence? Were there others, is it the common experience to be granted a favour, and at once to be a tumult of delight and gratitude for the granting and wild rage because the favour had to be asked for?

We walked on the downs in grey weather and I shook out my talent before her. I impressed myself. When I described the inner compulsion that drove me to paint I felt full of my own genius. But to Beatrice, of course, I was describing a disease which stood between me and a respectable, prosperous life. Or so I think; for all these are guesses. Part of the reality of my life is that I do not understand it. Moreover she did not make things easy for she hardly spoke at all. All I know is that I must have succeeded in giving her a picture of a stormy interior, an object of some awe and pity. Yet the truth was on a smaller scale altogether, the wound less tragic and paradoxically less easily healed.

"Well? What do you think?"

Silence; averted profile. We were coming down from the ridge, about to plunge into wet woods. We stopped where they began and I took her hand. The rags of my self-respect fell from me. Nothing venture, nothing win.

"Aren't you sorry for me?"

She let her hand lie in mine. It was the first time in my life I had touched her. I heard the little word float away, carried by the wind.

"Maybe."

Her head turned, her face was only a few inches from

mine. I leaned forward and gently and chastely kissed her on the lips.

We must have gone on and I must have talked yet the words are gone. All I remember is my astonishment.

Not quite all. For I remember the substance of my discovery. I was, by that mutely invited salute admitted to the status of boy friend. The perquisites of this position were two. First, I had a claim on her time and she would not go out with any other male. Second, I was entitled to a similar strictly chaste salute on rare occasions and also on saying good night. I am nearly sure that at that moment Beatrice meant her gesture as prophylactic. Boy friends were nice boys and therefore—so her reasoning may have gone—if Sammy is a boy friend it will make him nice. It will make him normal. Dear Beatrice!

I kept my communism to myself. It would not have suited my rival. He was apparently as jealous as I, holding that they that touch pitch shall be defiled. But to tell the truth, if it had not been for Nick and his socialism I should never have bothered with politics at all. I shouted and nodded with the rest; but went along with them because at least they were going somewhere. If it had not been for Miss Pringle's nephew who now was high up in the blackshirts I might as well have been a blackshirt myself. But there was something special about that time. Though Wimbury convinced himself and us that there would be no war, our bones knew better. The world around us was sliding on and down through an arch into a stormy welter where morals and families and private obligations had no place. There was a Norse sense of no future in the air. Perhaps that was why we could sleep around with such a deep irresponsibility; only the sleeping had to be among the people who felt the same headlong rush. Beatrice was outside it. Workers of the world—unite!

We had a worker. The rest of our branch were teachers and a parson or two, some librarians, a chemist, assorted students like myself and our jewel—Dai Reece. Dai worked in the gas works, trimming coal or something. I believe that Dai had social aspirations and looked on our branch as gentry. He never came within a mile of showing any of the textbook reactions. Our army, in fact, was all generals. Dai did what he was told for a time obediently and did not even guess what it was all about. Then he rebelled and got disciplined. Wimbury and Alsopp and the rest were all closed communists. The only people who could do anything publicly for the party were students like myself and of course our worker, Dai. He got so much that he broke out into a tirade at a branch meeting. "You sit on your fat ass in your 'ouse all the week, Comrade and I 'ave to go out in the cold to sell the bloody *Worker* every night, man!"

So he got disciplined and I got disciplined because it was the night I had let Philip into the branch meeting without authority. I wanted to keep him with me because we could have talked about Beatrice and Johnny. Otherwise be would have gone back and vanished into central London. What astonished me most was the anxiety in Philip's pale face. Almost, one could have fancied him in love; and it was symptomatic of my state that I should begin to wonder whether he, too, had been throwing away his career to move closer to Beatrice. But Philip watched faces and went close to Dai. When the meeting broke up he insisted that we should all three go off for a drink. He cross-examined Dai who treated him with great respect. I began to answer for Dai who was being appallingly bourgeois and not acting like the white hope of the future at all. I became warm and moved on Philip with conviction and heart-throb. But he was elusive and worried. He treated Dai, too, with an authority I could not yet recognize. At last he dismissed him.

"One more half, Dai, and then you must go home. I have some things to discuss with Mr. Mountjoy."

When we were alone, he bought me a drink but would have no more himself.

"Well, Sammy. So you know where you're going."

Helter-skelter, rush down to the dark arch.

"Does anyone?"

"That chap—Wimbury. Does he? How old is he?"

"I don't know."

"Teacher?"

"Of course."

"What's he up to?"

I drank up and ordered another.

"He's working for the revolution."

Philip was following the movements of my drinking with careful eyes.

"Where does he go from here?"

I must have thought for a long time because Philip went on speaking.

"I mean—he's an ordinary teacher? An assistant?"

"That's right."

"Being a communist won't make him a head teacher."

"You are the most bloody awful ungenerous——"

"Listen, Sammy. What does he get out of it? What can he become?"

"Well!"

But what could Comrade Wimbury become?

"Don't you understand, Philip? We aren't in this for ourselves. We've——"

"Seen the light."

"If you like."

"So have the blackshirts. Now look—don't start a fight."

"Fascist bastards!"

"I'm trying to find things out. I've been to their meetings too. Now don't make a fuss, Sammy. I'm—as you would say—uncommitted."

"You're too damned middle-class that's your trouble."

Drink warmed me, gave me virtue and self-righteousness. I began a rambling and laboured exposition. Philip watched me, always watched me. Finally he straightened his tie and smoothed down his hair.

"Sammy. When the war comes——"

"What war?"

"Next week's war."

"There won't be a war."

"Why not?"

"You heard Wimbury."

Philip began to laugh. I had never seen him so genuinely merry. At last he wiped his eyes and looked at me solemnly again.

"Do something for me, Sammy."

"Paint your portrait?"

"Keep me informed. No. Not just about politics. I can read the *Worker* as well as you. Just let me know what it's like in the branch. The feeling. That other chap with the bald head——"

"Alsopp?"

"What does he get out of it?"

I knew what Alsopp got out of it, but I was not going to say. After all, love was free and private life irrelevant—all except your own.

"How should I know? He's an older man than I am."

"You don't know much, do you, Sammy?"

"Have 'nother drink."

"And you respect your elders."

"Hell with my elders."

Beer in those days was cold and flabby for two half-pints and then took off, had golden wings with the third. I peered for Philip.

"What you up to, Philip? You come here—blackshirts and communists——"

Philip was looking back through my haze with an air of clinical detachment. He was tapping his long teeth with one white finger.

"Know Diogenes?"

"Never heard of 'im."

"Went round with a lamp. Wanted to find an honest man."

"You being bloody rude? I'm honest. So's comrades. Bloody blackshirts."

Philip was forward and peering into my face.

"Dai wants booze more than anything. What do you want more than anything, Sammy?"

I mumbled.

Philip was very near and very loud.

"Beetroots? You want beetroots?"

"What do you want then?"

The reeling eye is sometimes as percipient as the drugged one. Essentials only. Philip was isolated in bright light. Feeling my own uncertainties, my lopsided and illogical life, now lugged into a semblance of upright by bass, I could see why he was not drinking. For Philip, pale, freckled Philip who was skimped in every line of his body by a cosmic meanness was keeping himself intact. What I have I hold. Therefore the bony hands and the cut-price face, the brow pushed in on either side as though supplies had run out, were defended against giving, were incapable by nature of natural generosity, were tight and aware.

Let me describe him as I saw him at that instant. His clothes were better than mine, cleaner and neater. His shirt was white, his tie subdued and central. He sat, not hunched, but precisely, on a vertical spine. His hands were in his lap, his knees together. His hair was of a curious indefinable texture—growing all ways, but so weak that it still lay close to his skull like a used doormat. It was so indeterminate that the large, light freckles blurred the hair line on his sloping forehead. His eyes were pale blue and seemed curiously raw in that electric light for he had neither eyebrows nor eyelashes. No, madam, I'm sorry, we don't supply them at that price. This is a utility model. His nose was generous enough but melted, and the sphincter muscles round his mouth, only just sufficient to get it shut. And the man inside, the boy inside? I had schemed with him for fagcards, wrestled with him in the dark church—I had been cheated by him and beaten by him—I had accepted his friendship at a time when friendship was very dear to me.

The man inside?

It could smile. Was doing so now, with a localized convulsion of the sphincter.

"What do *you* want, Philip?"

"I told you."

He got up and began to put on his raincoat. I was about to suggest he should escort me home for I began to feel uncertain of getting there; but while the suggestion was rising to my lips he cut it off.

"Don't bother to come with me to the station. I shall have to hurry. Here's an envelope with my address on it. Remember. Just every now and then—let me know how things go on in the branch. What people are feeling."

"What the hell are you trying to do?"

Philip pulled the door open.

"Do? I'm—I'm inspecting the political racket."

"An honest man. And you haven't found one."

"No. Of course not."

"What if you find one?"

Philip paused with the door open. There was darkness and a glint of rain. He looked back at me out of his raw eyes from a long, long way away.

"I shall be disappointed."

I kept my drinking from Beatrice because she thought of pubs as only one degree less damned than the Church of England. In her little village, three miles beyond Rotten Row, all the boozers were Church of England and all the boys in broad cloth, chapel. Church of England was top and bottom; chapel was middle, was the class grimly keeping its feet out of the mud. I kept an awful lot of things from Beatrice. I see myself haunted and hurrying, dishevelled, my shoes uncleaned, grey shirt unbuttoned, blue jacket bulging on either side with oddments till the pockets looked like panniers. I had a lot of hair and I shaved when

I was going to see Beatrice. I was thankful for the party's red tie; it settled one item of wardrobe for me. As for my hands, the cigarette stain was creeping towards my wrists. I had neither Johnny's sunny simplicity, nor Philip's sense of direction; and yet I was for something. I was intended. When I did as I was told; when I drew and painted in obedience I was praised judiciously. I would make a good teacher, perhaps, a man who knew all the ropes and understood why each thing must be done. Set a problem, and I could produce the straight, the safe academic answer. Yet sometimes I would feel myself connected to the well inside me and then I broke loose. There would come into my whole body a feeling of passionate certainty. Not that—but this! Then I would stand the world of appearances on its head, would reach in and down, would destroy savagely and re-create—not for painting or precisely for Art with a capital A, but for this very concrete creation itself. If, like Philip and Diogenes I had been looking for an honest man in my own particular racket I should have found him then and he would have been myself. Art is partly communication but only partly. The rest is discovery. I have always been the creature of discovery.

I do not say this to excuse myself—or do I? You cannot have two moral standards one for artists and one for the rest. That is a mistaken view on both sides. Whoever judges me must judge me as if I had been a grocer addicted to chapel. If I have painted some good pictures—brought people slap up against another view of the world—on the other hand I have sold them no sugar nor left the early milk on their doorsteps. I say it rather, perhaps to explain what sort of young man I was—explain it to myself. I can think of no other audience. I am here as well as on canvas, a creature of discovery rather than communication. And all the time, oscillating between resentment and gratitude I was straining towards Beatrice as I have seen a moored boat tugged by the tide. You cannot blame the boat if it breaks loose at last and goes where the water carries it. This young man, sucking first pleasure then drug then nothing out of fags until they became as he smoked them no more than a gesture—drinking first for the phosphorescence and reality it brought to a wall or a lintel, then drinking to escape from a world of nonsense into one of apocalyptic meaning—throwing himself into the party because there people knew where the world was going—this young man, wild and ignorant, asking for help and refusing it, proud, loving, passionate and obsessed: how can I blame him for his actions since clearly at that time he was beyond the taste or the hope of freedom?

But Beatrice hoped to do me good. We walked again. We wrote each other little letters. I became familiar with her vocabulary, found out less and less about her. She stood by a tree and I put my arm round her and vibrated, but she never noticed. I was determined to be good, to move on the highest level, to settle once and for all the hauntings. I bent and put my cheek against hers. I was looking where she looked.

"Beatrice."

"Mm?"

"What is it like to be you?"

A sensible question; and asked out of my admiration for Evie and Ma, out of my adolescent fantasies, out of my painful obsession with discovery and identification. An impossible question.

"Just ordinary."

What is it like to hold the centre of someone's universe, to be soft and fair and sweet, to be neat and clean by nature, to be desired to distraction, to live under this hair, behind these huge, unutterable eyes, to feel the lift of these guarded twins, the valley, the plunge down to the tiny waist, to be vulnerable and invulnerable? What is it like in the bath and the lavatory and walking the pavement with shorter steps and high heels; what is it like to know your body breathes this faint perfume which makes my heart burst and my senses swim?

"No. Tell me."

And can you feel them all the way out to the rounded points? Do you know and feel how hollow your belly is? What is it like to be frightened of mice? What is it like to be wary and serene, protected and peaceful? How does a man seem to you? Is he clothed, always, jacketed and trousered, is he castrated like the plaster casts in the art room?

Beatrice made a slight movement as though she would move away from the tree. We were both leaning against it, she against me, too; and my arm was round her waist. I would not let her go.

Above all else, even beyond the musky treasures of your white body, this body so close to me and unattainable, above all else: what is your mystery? This is not a question I can ask you because I can hardly frame it to myself. But as freedom of the will is to be experienced like the taste of potatoes, as I once saw in and round your face what I cannot draw and hardly remember—as I am unable to make a picture of you that remotely resembles the breathing Beatrice; for mercy's sake admit me to the secret. I have capitulated to you. I go with the tide. Even if you do not know what you are at least admit me.

"Where do you live, Beatrice?"

She stirred again suddenly.

"Don't move. No, silly girl, not your address. Inside. The side of my head is against the side of yours. Do you live in there? We can't be an inch apart. I live near the back of my head, right inside—nearer the back than the front. Are you like that? Do you live—just in here? If I put my fingers there on the nape of your neck and move them up am I close? Closer?"

She pulled away.

"You're—don't, Sammy!"

How far do you extend? Are you the black, central patch which cannot examine itself? Or do you live in another mode, not thought, stretching out in serenity and certainty?

But the musk won.

"Sammy!"

"I said I loved you. Oh God, don't you know what that means? I want you, I want all of you, not just cold kisses and walks—I want to be with you and in you and on you and round you—I want fusion and identity—I want to understand and be understood—oh God, Beatrice, Beatrice, I love you—I want to be you!"

It was the moment when she might have got away, got far enough away to write me a letter and avoid me. It was, in fact, her last chance; but she did not know that. And perhaps even to her contained skin there was some warmth and excitement of the body in my stronger arms.

"Say you love me or I shall go mad!"

"Sammy—be sensible. Someone might——"

"To hell with someone. Turn your face round."

"I thought——"

"Thought we were friends? Well, we aren't, are we?"

"I thought——"

"You are wrong. We aren't friends, can't ever be friends. Don't you feel it? We are more—must be more. Kiss me."

"I don't want to. Look, Sammy—please! Let me think."

"Don't think. Feel. Can't you?"

"I don't know."

"Marry me."

"We couldn't. We're both at college—we haven't any money."

"But say you will. Some time. When we can. Will you?'

"There's someone coming."

"If you don't marry me I shall——"

"They'll see us."

"I shall kill you."

The man and woman came up the track, hand in hand, some of their problems settled. They looked everywhere but at us. They passed out of sight.

"Well?"

And rain was beginning to flick and trickle among the naked branches. Killing is one thing, rain another. We moved on, I hanging a little behind her shoulder.

"Well?"

Her face was pink and wet and shiny. Tiny pearls and diamonds hung clustering in her hair.

"We'd better hurry, Sammy. If we miss that bus there won't be another for ages."

I seized her wrist and swung her round on the path.

"I meant it."

They were still clear eyes, still untroubled. But they were brighter, brighter with mutiny or triumph.

"You said you cared for me."

"Oh, my God!"

I looked at her slight body, sensed the thin bone of the skull, the round and defenceless neck.

"We couldn't get married for ages."

"Beatrice!"

She moved a little closer and looked at me squarely with bright, pleased eyes. She put herself in the position for a permitted kiss.

"You will? Say you will!"

She smiled and uttered the nearest she ever knew to saying yes.

"Maybe."

5

For maybe was sign of all our times. We were certain of nothing. I should have said "Maybe" not Beatrice. The louder I cried out in the wake of the party the more an inner voice told me not to be silly, that no one could be certain of anything. Life waded knee-deep in shadows, floundered, was relative. So I could take "maybe" from Beatrice for "yes".

A young man certain of nothing but salt sex; certain that if there was a positive value in living it was this undeniable pleasure. Be frightened of the pleasure, condemn it, exalt it—but no one could deny that the pleasure was there. As for Art—did they not say—and youth with the resources of all human knowledge at its disposal lacks nothing but time to know everything—did they not say in the thick and unread textbooks that the root of art was sex? And was this not certain to be so since so many clever people said so and what was more to the point, behaved so? Therefore the tickling pleasure, the little death shared or self-inflicted was neither irrelevant nor sinful but the altar of whatever shoddy temple was left to us. But there remained deep as an assessment of experience itself the knowledge that if this was everything it was a poor return for birth, for the shames and frustrations of growing up. Nevertheless I had now brought Beatrice into the sexual orbit. Even she must know that marriage and the sexual act are not unconnected. My thighs weakened, my lungs tripped over a hot breath at the thought of it.

"Sammy! No!"

For, of course, there was only one answer to that "maybe" and I tried for a clinch—she unco-operating. Then I was trembling, I remember distinctly, as if love and sex and passion were a disease. I was trembling regularly from head to foot as if my button had been pressed. There in the winter sunlight, among the raindrops and rusted foliage I stood and trembled regularly as if I should never stop and a sadness reached out of me that did not know what it wanted; for it is a part of my nature that I should need to worship, and this was not in the textbooks, not in the behaviour of those I had chosen and so without knowing I had thrown it away. This sadness had no point therefore, and came out at the eyes of that ridiculous, unmanly, trembling creature so that Beatrice was frightened by it. What accepted suitor in a book ever started to tremble and weep? Her better nature or her commonsense would have taken back that binding maybe there and then if I had not turned away and made a dramatic effort to master my emotion. That was a cliché of behaviour and therefore not frightening. The trembling passed and suddenly I was overwhelmed by realization that here was the beginning of the end of that long path. One day, yes, one real day and not in fantasy I should achieve her sweet body. She would be safely mine beyond doubt or jealousy.

I turned again and began to chatter out of my unbearable excitement. So I led her away down the path, chattering and laughing, she silent and astonished. I see now how extraordinary these reactions must have seemed to her; but at the time I felt them as natural to me. It was an instability that I feel now should have ended in madness and perhaps at the time she felt that too. But for me, old scars were vanishing. The pursuer's hate was swallowed up in gratitude. The burns seared into me by overheated emotion were swealed away, I was unfolding, luxuriating in peace of deep heart over which delight danced, wildly invisible.

I don't think for a moment that she loved me then. If it comes to that I have asked myself how many people know at all the complete preoccupation and dependence? She was much more taken up with custom and precedent. She was now engaged and perhaps I was necessary as a shadowy adjunct in the life of the training college; an adjunct which she could accept more easily as she felt how she did me good. If marriage entered her head at all it was far off after college, was so to speak at the end of the film, was a golden glow near enough the end. But I had definite thoughts and purpose.

I am amazed now at my shyness and ignorance. After all the imagined passion of bed, at first I hardly dared kiss her and made the most tentative advances. Of course she warded them off and they served to bring up the central affair and impossibility of years of waiting.

"Girls don't feel like that."

"I'm not a girl!"

Indeed I was not. I have never felt more severely heterosexual. But she was a girl, her emotions and physical reactions enclosed as a nun. She herself was hidden. All the time I knocked and then hammered at the door she remained shut up within. We continued to see each other, to kiss, to plan marriage in several years' time. I got her a ring and she felt achieved and adult. I could place one hand gently on her left breast provided my hand remained outside her clothes. Beyond that point she became very positive. I have never been able to follow the precise train of thought that guided her reactions. Perhaps there was no thought at all and merely reactions. It is better to marry than burn. How I agreed with Saint Paul! But we could not marry. So I kissed the cold edge of her lips, laid one hand on her hidden pap and blazed like a haystack.

I got myself a bed-sitting-room, moving out of the care which a landlady was supposed to give me. If it had not been for Beatrice that room would have been very bleak; but I designed it as a place to seduce her in.

I had no precedents outside the cinema and these I was not in a position to imitate. I could not surround Beatrice with luxury, had no gipsy violinist to shudder his way into her ear. That room with its couch bed, narrow for two unless they were glued together or superimposed, with its brown dado and pink lamp shade gave me no help. The Van Gogh sunflowers of course were prominent—was there a single bed-sitter in London without them? But there was nothing to draw Beatrice there except our poverty. It was cheaper to sit on the couch than drink coffee in a little shop; it was cheaper, even, than walking in the country, because you had to break out of the smoke by train or bus. So when I finally got her there, though I knew why, she herself may very well have believed it was from laudable motives of economy.

She came; and there were huge, desert areas of silence. For this was so unlike my fevered fantasies that she had no immediate attraction for me. She maddened me by being there; yet I could not cross the gulf of her silence. She would sit on the couch, her elbows on her knees and her chin between her two palms and look placidly at nothing.

Sometimes I would squat in front of her and intercept her gaze.

"What are you thinking of?"

She would smile slightly and shake her head. If I stayed there, she would sit up and look past me again. It seemed like boredom; but it was a strange and untouched content with the process of living. She was at peace. The chapel with its assurances was behind her and for the rest she enjoyed sitting in her pretty body. Nobody told her this was a sin, this calm and selfish enjoyment of her own delicate warmth and smoothness; they told her it was virtue rather and respectability. I see now that her nun-like innocence was an obedient avoidance of the deep and muddy pool where others lived. Where I lived. I gesticulated to her from the pool and she was sorry for me. But all that was taken care of, was it not? For she was to marry me; and that was what nice boys wanted, the dual vanish into a golden haze, all folly smoothed away.

"What are you thinking of?"

"This and that."

"About us?"

"Maybe."

Outside the window the long winter road would darken. A sky-sign would become visible, a square of red words with a yellow line chasing round them; a whole mile of street lights would start and quiver into dull yellow as though they suddenly awoke. There would not be many minutes left.

"What are you thinking about?"

The time would come, she would stand up, allow me my careful embrace and then balance away, feminine and untouched.

I wonder what she was thinking of? She baffles me still, she is opaque. Even though she enjoyed being herself innocently as a young cat before the fire, yet surely there must have been some way to her for someone—for some girl, perhaps, if not for me? Would she have seemed accessible to her own children? Would a lifetime with her bring up a transparency first and then reveal in it the complex outlines of the soul in itself?

Yet she was accustomed to my room—to our room as I began to call it. I worked hard at lines of approach, subtle or logical. I did violence to our physical shyness, hid my face in her hair and begged her—unconscious perhaps of the humour of the narrow couch—begged her to sleep with me. She would not, of course; and I played another card. She must marry me immediately. Let it be secret——

Beatrice would not. What was she up to? What did she want? Was she doing nothing but giving me stability? Did she ever intend to marry me?

"Marry me. Now!"

"But we can't!"

"Why not?"

We had no money. She was not supposed to marry, had signed some sort of agreement. It wouldn't be honest——

The poor girl had delivered herself into my hand.

"Then come to bed with me——"

"No."

"Yes. Why not?"

"It wouldn't be——"

"It wouldn't be what? I'm supposed to suffer because you—I've got to wait—you know what a man is—all because you signed some damned agreement to turn you into a sour school marm——"

"Please, Sammy——"

"I love you."

"Let me go."

"Don't you understand? I love you. You love me. You ought to be coming gladly to me, we to each other, all your beauty given, shared—why do you keep me out? Don't you love me? I thought you loved me!"

"So I do."

"Say it then."

"I love you."

But still she would not. We would be sitting and wrestling ridiculously on the edge of the narrow bed; there was nothing but foolishness. After a time even desire would tire of this and we would sit, side by side, I suddenly conversational about an exhibition or the picture I happened to be painting. Sometimes I would take up the conversation if such a monologue was conversation—where I had dropped it a quarter of an hour before.

Beatrice belonged to my only rival. Her body, therefore, was not hers to give. This she thought, this she acted upon. And we could not get married yet. So she came, time after time to my room and sat with me on the edge of the bed. Why did she do it? Was there the taste of salt curiosity in her mouth, was she going as near the edge of excitement as she dared? Or what?

"I shall go mad."

She had a most wonderfully mobile body that seemed to yield wherever you touched it; but when I threw off that obscene remark her body stiffened between my arms.

"You mustn't ever say such a thing, Sammy."

"I shall go mad, I tell you!"

"Don't say it!"

Madness was not quite so fashionable in those days. People did not so cheerfully claim to be unbalanced or schizo. I may claim to have been before my time in this as in many other things. So where today a girl would be sympathetic, in those days Beatrice was frightened. She gave me the lever I wanted.

"I think I *am* mad, a bit——"

Once a human being has lost freedom there is no end to the coils of cruelty. I must I must I must. They said the damned in hell were forced to torture the innocent live people with disease. But I know now that life is perhaps more terrible than that innocent medieval misconception. We are forced here and now to torture each other. We can watch ourselves becoming automata; feel only terror as our alienated arms lift the instruments of their passion towards those we love. Those who lose freedom can watch themselves forced helplessly to do this in daylight until who is torturing who is? The obsession drove me at her.

But, of course, once she had got over her fear and we were bound so closely together by lovemaking, there would be no end to the brightness of the sunlight future.

My madness was Wagnerian. It drove me forth on dark nights forsooth striding round the downs. I should have worn a cloak.

I sent a message in by the porter. Mr. Mountjoy wishes to speak to Miss Ifor.

"Sammy!"

It was a quarter to eight in the morning.

"I had to come and look at you. To make sure you were real."

"But how did you get here at this time?"

"I wanted to see you."

"But how——"

"I wanted—oh that? I've been walking all night, keeping ahead of it."

"But——"

"You are my sanity, Beatrice. I had to come and see you. Now everything is all right."

"You'll be late, Sammy, you must go. Are you all right?"

Compunction in compulsion, almost weeping. What is madness after all? Can a man who pretends to be mad claim to be sane?

Compulsion, weeping.

"I have to do it. I don't know why. I have to."

"Oh look, Sammy—here I'm not supposed to—I'll see you to the bus stop. Come on. You know the number? You're to go straight to bed."

"You won't leave me?"

"Look—dear!"

"As soon as you can then—the very first moment——"

"I promise."

The bus top was among branches part of the way. I was shaking and shuddering by myself with no need to act. I was muttering like a drunk man.

"I don't understand. I don't know anything. I'm on rails. I have to. Have to. There is too much life. I could kick myself or kill myself. Is my living to be nothing but moving like an insect? Scuttering, crawling? I could go away. Could I? Could I go away? Across the sea where the painted walls wait for me, I might. I am tied by this must."

The muscles of the chest get tautened, the sinews stand out in the wrists, the heart beats faster till the air is eaten up with red shapes expanding; and then you understand that you ought to breathe again; for even if compulsion is a pitiless thing a man does not have to let it take charge of his physical reflexes, no, he can suffer emotionally without starving himself of air—there, I thought, I have breathed the load off my back.

She came to me malleable, and at the same time authoritative, for she was very firm about eating regularly and so on. She was very sweet. She only put up a token fight. She was my sanity. I would take any consequences that ensued would I not, who was so breathlessly assuring her that there would be no consequences. And then Beatrice of four years' fever lay back obediently, closed her eyes and placed one clenched fist bravely on her forehead as though she were about to be injected for T.A.B.

And what of Sammy?

There could be no consequences because there was no cause.

What precisely was he after? Why should it be that at this most triumphant or at least enjoyable moment of his career, the sight of the victim displayed humble, acquiescent and frightened should not only be less stimulating than the least of his sexual inventions but should even be damping and impossible? No, said his body, no not this at all. That was not the thing I meant, thing I wanted. How far was I right to think myself obsessed with sex when that potency which is assumed in all literature was not mine to use at the drop of a knicker? It seemed then that some co-operation was essential. If she were to make of herself a victim I could not be her executioner. If she were to be frightened, then I was ashamed in my very flesh that she should be frightened of me. This did not seem to me to tally with the accepted version of a man who was either wholly incapable or heroically ready, aye ready. There were gradations. But neither I nor Beatrice were prepared to admit them. On the other hand my feelings about her were without doubt obsessive if not pathological. Should they not then make my achievement of her easy? But she, out of my suggested madness and her own religious taboos was incapable of thinking about this moment, this pre-marital deed, without a sense that was at once one of sin, one of fear, one of love and consequently one of drama. Unconsciously we were both setting ourselves to music. The gesture with which she opened her knees was, so to speak, operatic, heroic, dramatic and daunting. I could not accompany her. My instrument was flat.

But of course there were other occasions. I was not wise enough to know that a sexual sharing was no way of bringing us together. So instead of abandoning the game then and there—and of course my own opinion of my masculinity was at stake—I persevered. We began to accept that she should submit to caresses and as all old wives know these things come right in the end. I had my warm, inscrutable Beatrice, triumphed in a sort of sorrow and pity; and Beatrice cried and did not want to go away but, of course, she had to, that was the penalty of jumping the gun. She took her secret back to the training college and endured the faces that might guess, then came back, went to chapel, did there whatever she did, came to what arrangement—and went to bed with me again. I was full of love and gratitude and delight, but I never seemed to get near Beatrice, never shared anything with her. She remained the victim on the rack, even a rack of some enjoyment. But there was nothing in this that we could share; for poor Beatrice was impotent. She never really knew what we were doing, never knew what it was about.

"Don't you feel anything?"

"I don't know. Maybe."

Her silences were if anything longer. She wasn't the boss any more. Instead of my searching her face for a clue, wondering what was inside, I found myself being watched. After our one-sided lovemaking, I would wander up and down the room, thinking to myself that if this was all, there was nothing that would give us a unity and substantial identity. She would lie still on the narrow bed and her eyes would follow me, back and forward as long as I liked to walk. She was not unhappy. If, in the time that followed, I think of and visualize Beatrice below me, it is not entirely a sexual image. She was adjusting herself to a conceived place in life. She was beginning to look up, to belong, to depend, to cling, to be an inferior in fact, however the marriage service may gloss it. Instinctively she was becoming what she believed to be a wedded wife. Her contribution, after the heroic sacrifice, was negative. Death of a maidenhead pays for all.

I loved her and was grateful. When you are young, you cannot believe that a human relationship is as pointless as it seems. You always think that tomorrow there will come the revelation. But in fact we had had our revelation of each other. There was nothing else to know.

Sometimes when I was alone I would think of the future. What sort of life would it be? I should paint, of course, and Beatrice would always be around, making tea. She would have children, probably, be a very good mother. I began to think desperately, not of abandoning her but of some way to force myself towards that wonderful person who must be hidden somewhere in her body. Such grace of body could surely not be its own temple, must enshrine something——

"I'm going to paint you, paint your body. Naked. Like this, all slack and given up."

"No. You mustn't."

"I shall. Lie there. Let me pull the curtain back——"

"No! Sammy!"

"They can't see in across the road. Now lie still."

"Please!"

"Look, Beatrice—didn't you admit that the Rokeby Venus is beautiful?"

She turned her face away. She was being injected for T.A.B. again.

"I shan't paint your face at all. I just want your body. No. Don't rearrange it. Just lie still."

Beatrice lay still and I began to draw.

When the drawing was finished I made love to her again. Or rather, I repeated what my pencil had done, finished what my pencil had begun. The lovemaking accepted that she was unable to take part. The lovemaking was becoming an exploitation. I see now that she could not enjoy or welcome our commerce because she was brought up not to. All the little books and the occasional talks, all the surface stuff were powerless against the dead weight of her half-baked sectarianism. All her upbringing ensured that she should be impotent.

It is difficult for a man to know anything about a woman. But how, when he is passionate can he reach her through her obedient stillness? Does she feel nothing but a kind of innocent lubricity? Can she share nothing?

"What are you thinking of——?"

Her body was a perpetual delight. Moving or still she was finished in colour and texture. And yet she was not there.

"What are you thinking about——?"

Nevertheless from the moment that she let me take her virginity the change began between us. Her clear absence of being leaned in towards me, lay against me, clung. As though from conception she had waited for this, now she bowed against me. She watched me with doggie eyes, she put the lead in my hand.

"What shall we talk about?"

I became angry. I tried to force some response. But we could not even row and fight face to face. Always there was to be a difference of levels. As soon as she detected the touch of hardness in my voice she would grab me and hold me tight, she would hide her face against me.

I would try to explain.

"I'm trying to find out about you. After all if we're going to spend our lives together—where are you? What are you? What is it like to be you?"

Her arms would shake—those arms that bent in at the elbows, were so delicate they seemed for receiving only—her breasts and her face would push against me, be hidden.

Impatient and angry. Continue the catechism.

"Aren't you human, then? Aren't you a person at all?"

And with shudders of her wrists and shaking of the long, fair hair she would whisper against me:

"Maybe."

It comes into my memory now that at this time we never met face to face. Either she is a white body, the head hidden in her hair; or she holds me round the waist and looks up at me with big, faithful eyes, her chin against my stomach. She liked to look up. She had found her tower and was clinging to it. She had become my ivy.

There were days of content—there must have been. I must remember that "last time" was never love but only "infatuation". Therefore we went on for nearly two years until the ripples and then waves of war washed round us. We corresponded when we could not meet. I was full of wit and protestations; she full of simplicity and small change. She would buy a dress. Did I think green suited her? The lecturer in hygiene was very nice. She hoped we should be able to afford a little house some time. When we were married she would have to think of making her own clothes. On some of her letters, in the top left-hand corner, was a little cross-sign that for another few weeks we were safe from having children, though by then the risk was small enough. Her work was going badly and she was getting into hot water over it, but she didn't seem to care any more, except about hygiene! The lecturer in hygiene was very nice. Insensibly I drifted rather than went deliberately into the last cruel effort to reach her.

I must be careful. How much was conscious cruelty on my part? How much was her fault? She had never in her life made one movement towards me until I roared over her like a torrent. She was utterly passive in life. Then was that long history of my agony over her, my hell—real as anything in life could be real—was that self-created? Was it my doing? Did I put the remembered light in her face? Did I? I saw her on the platform in the art room with the bridge behind her, and she did not see me. Yet the descent we were now to embark upon and at my hands was one I was powerless to control or stop. What had been love on my part, passionate and reverent, what was to be a triumphant sharing, a fusion, the penetration of a secret, raising of my life to the enigmatic and holy level of hers became a desperately shoddy and cruel attempt to force a response from her somehow. Step by step we descended the path of sexual exploitation until the projected sharing had become an infliction.

Yet even here, in the sewers of my memory, nothing is sure. How did that good girl that uninscribed tablet receive these violations? What did she think of them if she thought of them at all? They made her as far as I could see, more devoted, more dog-like, more secure. They are memories of my own failure, my own degradation, not hers. Those fantasies of adolescence now brought to half realization on my side were sad, dreary and angry. They reinforced the reality of physical life and they destroyed the possibility of anything else; and they made physical life not only three times real but contemptible. And under everything else, deep, was an anguish of helplessness and loss.

These advances in lubricity then, bound her arms more closely round my waist. I could not paint her face; but her body I painted. I painted her as a body and they are good and terrible paintings, dreadful in their story of fury and submission. They made me my first real money—except for the mayor's portrait, of course—and one of them is hung publicly so that I can go back and see that time, my room—our room—and try to understand, without apology or pity. There hangs the finished perfection of her sweet, cleft flesh. The light from the window strikes gold from her hair and scatters it over her breasts, her belly and her thighs. It was after the last and particularly degrading step of her exploitation; and in my self-contempt I added the electric light-shades of Guernica to catch the terror, but there was no terror to catch. There ought to have been but there was not. The electric light that ought to sear like a public prostitution seems an irrelevance. There is gold, rather, scattered from the window. There was dog faith and big eyes and submission. I look at the picture and I remember what the hidden face looked like; how after my act and my self-contempt she lay, looking out of the window as though she had been blessed.

6

Those were the great days of the Communist Party in England. There was a certain generosity in being a communist; a sense of martyrdom and a sense of purpose. I began to hide from Beatrice in the uproar of streets and halls. There was a meeting at the Town Hall in which a local councillor was going to give his reasons for joining the party. The decision has come down from above. He was a business man, so by remaining "closed" he could never hope to be in a better position, that is, one of governmental trust. There was no reason why his faith should not be capitalized there and then. That was in autumn, a chill autumn of blackout and phoney war. "Why I am joining the Communist Party" said the bills and hoardings, and the hall was crowded. He never got a chance to speak really; there were storms of cheering and counter-cheering, chairs overturned, local swirls in the thick blue cigarette smoke, cheers, shouts, boos. Someone went down at the back of the hall and there was a scuffle while paper arched up and glass smashed. I was looking at the councillor and his silent film mouthing so I saw when a bottle hit him over the right eye and he went down behind the green baize table. So I made to help him as someone turned out the lights and a police whistle blew. We huddled his limp body off the platform, through a side door and into his car, I and his daughter, while the police stood guard because after all he was a councillor. There was still much noise and darkness, and out of that uproar

I can remember the first words her unseen mouth said to me.

"Did you see the bastard who threw that bloody bottle?"

I had never met Taffy before, but as my eyes got used to the blackout I could hardly believe what I saw. She was dark and vivid. She had the kind of face that always looks made-up, even in the bath—such black eyebrows, such a big, red mouth. She was the prettiest girl I ever saw, neat in profile, with soft cheeks and two dimples that were in stunning contrast with her tenor voice and scarifying language. She was dabbing her father's head with a scrap of a handkerchief and muttering over and over again:

"I could kill that bloody sod!"

We took him to hospital and waited. Then there came a moment when we both looked at each other, were face to face; and a dozen things were obvious at once to both of us. We took him home and I waited again, below in the hall while he was put to bed—waited though not a word had been said. She came down the stairs and stood and there was nothing to do but look, nothing needing to be said. She took a scarf—her father's, I think—and we went out together. We went to a blacked-out pub and sat hand in hand, both stunned by this overwhelming sense of recognition. We kissed then and there in public without shame or bravado because although people stood within a yard of us, we were alone. We were both deeply committed elsewhere and we both recognized without a moment's doubt that we should never let each other go. I cannot remember how much we said of this or how much we felt. That very night she came to my spartan room and we made love, wildly and mutually. After all, we were communists and our private life was our own concern. The world was exploding. None of us would live long. Then she went home and left me to think of her next coming; and to think of Beatrice. What was I to do about her? What could I do? Give Taffy up? Presumably that would be the standard reply of the moralist. But was I now to live the rest of my life with Beatrice, knowing all the time that I was in love with Taffy?

In the end I did nothing. I merely ensured that they should not meet. But poor Beatrice bored me. The old magic, the familiar nerve was deadened or burned out. I no longer desired to understand her, no longer believed that she had some secret. I was sorry for her and exasperated by her. I tried to hide this; hoping that time would produce some solution but I was just not callous enough to get away with it. Beatrice noticed. She knew that I was colder and more distant. Her grip on me tightened, her face, her breasts bored in at my stomach. Perhaps if I had had the courage then to look her down in the eye I should have seen all the terror and fear that did not get into my pictures of her; but I never met her eye for I was ashamed to. Beatrice clung to me in tears and fear saying nothing.

She was the image of a betrayed woman, of outraged and helpless innocence. At this distance in time I find myself cynical enough or detached enough to question the tilt of her chin. Was she being operatic again? I cannot think that she had the emotional resources. She was sincere. She was helpless and terrified. The grip of her arms had a pitiful strength as though she could hold physically what was escaping her emotionally. Now I became acquainted with tears, now if I had been brutal enough I might have cried quits for the distraught bed of my school days; now I saw the very water of sorrow hanging honey-thick in eyelashes or dashed down a cheek like an exclamation mark at the beginning of a Spanish sentence. In between her visits to my room and when the requirements of her course made it impossible for her to see me, she took a leaf out of my old book. She began to write me letters. They were elaborate in their queries. What was the matter? What had she done? What could she do? Didn't I love her any more?

One day I was walking in a country lane and came out on the high road. I could see then what was making the noise. A car had caught a cat and taken away about five of its nine lives, and the poor, horrible thing was dragging away and screaming and demanding to be killed; and I ran away, my fingers in my ears until I had put the writhing thing out of mind and could play supposing again, or when the ship comes home. For, after all, in this bounded universe, I said, where nothing is certain but my own existence, what has to be cared for is the quiet and the pleasure of this sultan. Therefore the exposed nerve of the monocular homunculus the rack is all, is the point of my hunting Beatrice. In the curious and half-forgotten image of Beatrice on the platform before the Palladian bridge I saw nothing now but the power of the mind's self-deception. Certainly there was no light in her face. There were blemishes under the skin if one looked for them, and beneath the corner of each eye a little triangle of darkness that told of long nights. Her only power now was that of the accuser, the skeleton in the cupboard; and in this bounded universe we can easily put paid to that.

So Taffy and I went our way regardless. She was a lady by my low standards. She was fastidious except when she remembered that we were the spearhead of the proletariat. She also had a little money—not enough to support a husband or a lover but enough to help. So I left my room and address—gave no notice and paid no rent; and where in the bomb-broken basement, the square of blasted concrete, the crazy leaning brickwork that flowers are bursting should I post the money—but sneaked back to take the letter out of the box after a day or two; the letter that Beatrice wrote to me when she could not find out where I was. It was full of upbraiding, weak, gentle, frightened upbraiding. I saw Taffy and we were estranged for a while. She knew something and she sulked. We had one of those interminable, reasonable conversations about the relationship between men and women. One would not be jealous, one would understand enjoyment taken with a third person. Nothing was permanent, nothing was more than relative. Sex was a private business. Sex was a clinical matter and contraception had removed the need for orthodox family life. And then suddenly we were clinging to each other as though we were the only stable thing in an earthquake. I was muttering into the back of her neck.

"Marry me, Taffy, for Pete's sake marry me."

And Taffy was sniffing under my chin, cursing hoarsely, grabbing and rubbing her face against my jersey.

"You cock an eye at another woman and I'll have your guts for a girdle."

I left my temporary bed at the Y.M.C.A. and we shifted into a studio on Taffy's money. We got married at a registry office as an afterthought and the ceremony meant nothing to us except that we were free now to go back to the studio. I got a letter from Beatrice by way of Nick Shales who was still teaching at school then; and I did not know whether to open it or not. Nick wrote too, a wounded letter. Beatrice had been to every common acquaintance, looking for me. I saw her in my mind's eye standing on doorsteps, crimsoning with the shame of it all yet forced to go on.

"Do you know where Sammy Mountjoy is? I seem to have mislaid his address——"

I opened the letter and the first lines were a plea for forgiveness; but I read no further because the sight of the first page stabbed me with a knife. In the top left-hand corner she had drawn a little cross. We were out of danger.

I have one more memory of her, memory of a dream so vivid that it has taken a place in my history. I am receding along a suburban road that is infinitely long and the houses on either side are mean, unpainted, but drearily respectable. Beatrice is running after me, crying out with a shrill bird cry. It is evening in that horrible country and the shadows are closing round her. And the water is rising from the basements and gutters so that her feet trip and splash: but I have avoided the water somehow. It rises round her, always rises.

But as for Taffy and I, we made ourselves a place between four walls and we faded out of the party as the bombs began to fall and the time of my soldiering drew nearer. We explored our histories, mine edited a bit, and perhaps hers, too. We achieved that extraordinary level of security when we did not expect entire truth from each other, knowing it to be impossible and extending a *carte blanche* of forgiveness beforehand. Beatrice faded from me, like the party. I told Taffy about her and the small cross did it. Taffy had a baby.

What else could I have done but run away from Beatrice? I do not mean what ought I to have done or what someone else could have done. I simply mean that as I have described myself, as I see myself in my backward eye, I could do nothing but run away. I could not kill the cat to stop it suffering. I had lost my power to choose. I had given away my freedom. I cannot be blamed for the mechanical and helpless reaction of my nature. What I was, I had become. The young man who put her on the rack is different in every particular from the child who was towed along the street past the duke in the antique shop. Where was the division? What choice had he?

I saw Johnny about then—saw him for one perfect and definable instant that remains a measure in my mind of the difference between us. I was walking away from myself one afternoon in the country—coming to the top of Counter's Hill where the road seems to leap over. Johnny leapt over towards me on his motor-bike and I had to jump out of the way. He must have come up the other side at about a hundred miles an hour so that when he reached the top and appeared to me he seemed to go straight on in the air and fly past. I remember him against the sky, six inches clear of the road. His left hand is on the handle-bars. He leans back and turns his helmeted head round and back as far as he can to the right. The girl has her head over his shoulder, her right arm reaching round him and her mop flies in the wind. Johnny's right arm is round her head with his hand prone on top and they are kissing there at that speed on a blind hill-top, careless of what has been and what is to come; because what is to come might be nothing.

I welcomed the destruction that war entails, the deaths and terror. Let the world fall. There was anarchy in the mind where I lived and anarchy in the world at large, two states so similar that the one might have produced the other. The shattered houses, the refugees, the deaths and torture—accept them as a pattern of the world and one's own behaviour is little enough disease. Why bother to murder in a private capacity when you can shoot men publicly and be congratulated publicly for it? Why bother about one savaged girl when girls are blown to pieces by the thousand? There is no peace for the wicked but war with its waste and lust and irresponsibility is a very good substitute. I made poor use of destruction because I was already well enough known to be a war artist.

No gun for Sammy. He became a recording angel instead.

"Here, then?"

"No. Not here."

7

Then where? I am wise in some ways, can see unusually far through a brick wall and therefore I ought to be able to answer my own question. At least I can tell when I acquired or was given the capacity to see. Dr. Halde attended to that. In freedom I should never have acquired any capacity. Then was loss of freedom the price exacted, a necessary preliminary to a new mode of knowing? But the result of my helplessness out of which came the new mode was also the desperate misery of Beatrice and the good joys of Taffy. I cannot convince myself that my mental capacities are important enough to justify either the good or the harm they started. Yet the capacity to see through the brick wall rose directly and inevitably at Halde's hands out of my sow's ear. I have an over-clear picture of the room in which he started the process. The Gestapo whipped the coverings off yesterday and unveiled the grey faces.

The room was real and matter of fact and sordid.

The main bit of furniture was an enormous table that occupied one-third of the floor area. The table was old, polished and had legs like the bulbous legs of a grand piano. There were papers piled at each end, leaving the centre for the commandant's blotting-pad. We faced him across the pad, man to man, except that he sat and we stood. There were filing cabinets behind him and the card slips on each drawer were lettered in careful gothic script. Behind and above the commandant's chair was a large photograph of the Fuehrer. It was a harmless room, dull and comfortless. Some of the piles of paper had been on the table for a long time because you could see what the dust was doing to them.

March in, right turn, salute.

"Captain Mountjoy, sir."

But the commandant was not sitting in his chair neither was his fat little deputy. This man was a civilian. He wore a dark lounge suit and he sat back in the swivel chair, elbow on each arm, finger-tips together. Left and behind him was the commandant's deputy and three soldiers. There were also two anonymous figures in the uniform of the Gestapo. We were a full house; but I could look nowhere but straight at the man in front of me. Is it hindsight to say that already I liked him, was drawn to him, could have spent as much time with him as with Ralph and Nobby? I was fearful, too, my heart was beginning to run away with me. We did not know for certain in those days how bad the Gestapo were, but we heard rumours and made guesses. And he was a civilian—too high up to wear uniform unless he felt like it.

"Good morning, Captain Mountjoy. Shall we say mister or even Samuel or Sammy? Would you like a chair?"

He turned and spoke rapidly in German to a soldier on my left who placed a metal chair with a fabric seat for me. The man leaned forward.

"My name is Halde. Dr. Halde. Let us get to know each other."

He could smile, too, not a wintry smile but a genuine one of joy and friendliness, so that the blue eyes danced and the flesh lifted to his cheek-bones. And now I heard how perfect his English was. The commandant spoke to us mostly through an interpreter or briefly in throaty German-English. But Dr. Halde spoke better English than I did. Mine was the raw, inaccurate stuff of common use, but his had the same ascetic perfection as his face. His enunciation had the purity that goes with a clear and logical mind. My enunciation was slurred and hurried, voice of a man who had never stilled his brain, never thought, never been certain of anything. Yet still his was the foreign voice, nationless, voice of the divorced idea, a voice that might be conveyed better by the symbols of mathematics than printed words. And though his P's and B's were clearly differentiated they were a little too sharp, just a fraction too sharp as though his nose were pinched inside.

"Better?"

Doctor of what? The whole shape of his head was exquisitely delicate. At first it looked roundish, because your eye was caught by the polished bald top where the black hair streaked across; but then as you came down from there you saw that round was the wrong word because the whole face and head were included in an oval, wide at the top, pointed at the chin. He had a great deal of forehead, the widest part of the oval and his hair had receded. His nose was long and the hollows of his eye shallow. The eyes themselves were an astonishing cornflower blue.

Philosophy?

But what was most striking about his face was not the fineness of the bone structure but the firmness of the flesh over it. There are many things that can be learned from the general condition of such tissue. If it is wasted away solely by disease the general effects of suffering cannot be concealed. The eyes are dull and the flesh bags under them. But this flesh was healthy, was pale and the least amount compatible with decent human covering of the front of the head. Any less and the skull would start through. The lines were not necessarily the lines of suffering but of thought and good-humour. Taken with the fine hands, the almost translucent fingers and the answer was asceticism. The man had the body of a saint.

Psychology?

Psychology!

Suddenly I remembered that I should have refused the chair. Thank you, I prefer to stand. That was what a Buchan hero would do. But I had this engrossing face before me, this assured and superior English. I had sat down already in a chair that rocked slightly on an uneven floor. All at once I was vulnerable, a man trapped in a mountain of flesh, a man wielding a club against a foil fencer. The chair tipped again and I heard my voice, high and absurdly social.

"Thanks."

"Cigarette?"

This ought to be refused, should be waved away—but then I caught sight of my fingers, stained to the second knuckle.

"Thanks."

Dr. Halde reached behind the right-hand pile of papers, produced a silver cigarette-box and flicked it open. I leaned forward, groping in the box and saw what was behind the pile of papers. Nobby and Ralph had been at great pains to find out how to avoid the archaic smile of the seventh century; but those papier mâché heads of hair with the clownish ill-made faces would not have deceived a child. They would have done better after all to let me help, or relied on hair and the blankets pulled right up.

Dr. Halde was holding out a silver cigarette lighter with a quiet flame. I put half an inch of cigarette in the flame and drew back, puffing out smoke.

Nonchalant.

Dr. Halde began to laugh so that the flesh of his cheeks rolled up into a neat sausage under either eye. He remained pale mostly; but there was the faintest suggestion of rose under each sausage. His eyes danced, his teeth shone. A little V of wrinkles creased the skin outside each eye. He turned and included the deputy in his delighted laughter. He came back to me, put his fingers together and composed himself. He was an inch or two higher than I. He looked down at me therefore, friendly and amused.

"We are neither of us ordinary men, Mr. Mountjoy. There is already a certain indefinable sympathy between us."

He spread his hands out.

"I should be in my university. You should be in that studio to which it is my sincere wish you may return."

The nationless words had in them an awful quality of maturity as though the next sentence might well be all the answers. He was looking me in the eye, inviting me to lift this affair above the vulgar brawl into an atmosphere where civilized men might come to some arrangement. All at once I dreaded that he should find me uncivilized, dreaded so many indefinable things.

Suddenly I was fumbling with my cigarette.

"Did you burn yourself, Mr. Mountjoy? No? Good."

He was holding out a china ashtray with a Rhineland

river scene on it. I took the ashtray carefully and set it near me on the table.

"You're wasting your time. I don't know how they got away or where they were going."

He watched me for a moment in silence. He nodded gravely.

"That may well be."

I scraped back my chair and put a hand on either side of the seat to get up. I began to play unbelievingly with the fiction that the interview was over.

"Well, then——"

I was rising; but a heavy hand fell on my left shoulder and clamped me down. I recognized the colour of the fabric at the wrist, and the physical touch of what ought to be feared made me angry instead so that I could feel the blood in my neck. But Dr. Halde was frowning past my shoulder and making quietening gestures with both hands, palms down. The heaviness left my shoulder. Dr. Halde took out a white cloud of lawn and blew his nose precisely. So he was suffering from catarrh then, his nose really was pinched and his English really perfect.

He folded away the lawn and smiled at me.

"That may well be. But we must make certain."

My hands were too big and clumsy. I shoved them into the pockets of my tunic where they felt unnatural. I took them out and worked them into my trouser pockets instead. I said the phrases in one mechanical movement as I had learnt them. Even as I spoke I knew they were nothing but a nervous reflex.

"I am a commissioned officer and a prisoner-of-war. I demand to be treated in accordance with the Geneva Convention."

Dr. Halde made a sound that was half a laugh and half a sigh. His smile was sad and expostulatory as if I were a child again, making a mistake in my classwork.

"Of course you are. Yes indeed."

The deputy commandant spoke to him and there was a sudden quick exchange. The deputy was looking at me and back at Halde and arguing fiercely. But Halde had the best of it. The deputy clicked his heels, shouted an order and left the room with the soldiers. I was alone with Halde and the Gestapo.

Dr. Halde turned back to me.

"We know all about you."

I answered him instantly.

"That's a lie."

He laughed genuinely and ruefully.

"I see that our conversation will always jump from level to level. Of course we can't know all about you, can't know all about anybody. We can't know all about ourselves. Wasn't that what you meant?"

I said nothing.

"But then you see, Mr. Mountjoy, what I meant was something on a much lower level a level at which certain powers are operative, at which certain deductions may be made. We know, for example, that you would find asceticism, particularly when it was forced on you, very difficult. I, on the other hand—you see? And so on."

"Well?"

"You were a communist. So was I, once. It is a generous fault in the young."

"I don't understand what you're saying."

"I shall be honest with you though I cannot say whether

you will be honest with me. War is fundamentally immoral. Do you agree?"

"Perhaps it is."

"One must be for or against. I made my choice with much difficulty but I have made it. Perhaps it was the last choice I shall ever make. Accept such international immorality, Mr. Mountjoy, and all unpleasantnesses are possible to man. You and I, we know what wartime morality amounts to. We have been communists after all. The end justifies the means."

I ground the cigarette out in the ashtray.

"What's all that got to do with me?"

He made a circling gesture with the cigarette-box before holding it out again.

"For you and me, reality is this room. We have given ourselves over to a kind of social machine. I am in the power of my machine; and you are in my power absolutely. We are both degraded by this, Mr. Mountjoy, but there it is."

"Why pick on me? I tell you I know nothing!"

I had the cigarette in my fingers and was fumbling for a match. He exclaimed and reached out the lighter.

"Oh, please!"

I got the cigarette into the flame with both hands and sucked at the white teat. There were the shapes of two men standing at ease, but I had not seen their faces, could not see any face but the worried, donnish face behind the lighter. He put the lighter down, set his hands on the blotter and leaned towards me.

"If only you could see the situation as I see it! You would be willing, so willing, I might say anxious"—the hands gripped—"Mr. Mountjoy, believe me, I—Mr.

Mountjoy. Four days ago over fifty officers escaped from another camp."

"And you want me to—you want me——"

"Wait. They are—well, they are still at liberty, at large, they are not back in the camp."

"Good for them, then!"

"At any moment a similar escape may be made from this camp. Two officers, your friends, Mr. Mountjoy, have done that already. Our information is that morale makes a large-scale escape from this camp unlikely, but not impossible. It must not happen—if you only knew how much it must not happen!"

"I can't help you. Escape is the prisoner's business."

"Sammy—I beg your pardon, Mr. Mountjoy—how well you have responded to your conditioning! Am I wrong after all? Are you really nothing but a loyal, chuckle-headed British soldier of the king?"

He sighed, leant back.

"Why did you call me Sammy?"

He smiled with me and at me and the winter of his face turned to spring.

"I've been studying you. Putting myself in your place. An unpardonable liberty of course, but war is war."

"I didn't know I was all that important."

He stopped smiling, reached down and fumbled papers out of a briefcase.

"This is how important you are, Mr. Mountjoy."

He threw two small folders across the blotter. They were drab and worn. I opened them and examined the paragraphs of incomprehensible gothic print, the scribbled initials and names, the circular stamps. Nobby looked up at me from the photograph in one and Ralph from the other—Ralph posing for the photograph, being deliberately half-witted and deadpan.

"You got them then."

Dr. Halde did not reply; and something about the silence, some tension perhaps, made me look up quickly and turn my statement into a question.

"You caught them?"

Dr. Halde still said nothing. Then he took out the cloud of white lawn and blew his nose on it again.

"I'm sorry to tell you that your friends are dead. They were shot while trying to escape."

For a long time I looked at the dim photographs; but they meant nothing. I tried to stir myself, said silently and experimentally in my mind: their chests have been beaten in by a handful of lead, they have come to the end both of them, those indefatigable cricketers, have seen and recognized the end of the game. They were my friends and their familiar bodies are rotting away.

Do you feel nothing then?

Maybe.

Halde was speaking softly.

"Now do you understand, Mr. Mountjoy? It is vitally necessary that not another man should get outside the wire—necessary for their sakes, for our sakes, for the sake of humanity, for the sake of the future——"

"Bloody swine."

"Oh, yes, of course. That goes without saying, et cetera."

"I tell you I know nothing."

"And then when I am given, or if it comes to that, take the task of preventing a recurrence of this—where else should I look? Of all the men in this camp, who has a record so accessible, who has talked about painting and pigments, about lithography? And besides"—he was peering at me closely with those enormous cornflower eyes —"who among all these men is so likely to be reasonable? Should I chose as my lever Major Witlow-Brownrigg, that stiff gentleman and bend him till he breaks, or shall I choose material more pliable?"

"I tell you——"

"It is essential that I should be able to raid the camp swiftly and suddenly and with absolute certainty of what I am going to find, and where. Please, please listen to me. I must break up the printing press, confiscate the tools, the uniform, the civilian clothes, I must smash the radio, I must go straight to the tunnel and fill it in——"

"But I——"

"Please listen. I choose you not only because you must be part of the organization but because you are an artist and therefore objective and set apart from your fellows; a man who would know when betrayal was not betrayal and when one must break a rule, an oath, to serve a higher truth——"

"For the last time, I know nothing!"

He spread his hands palm uppermost on the table.

"Does that seem reasonable, Mr. Mountjoy? Consider all the indications that could point to the opposite conclusion—your various skills, your friendship with the two officers—even your past membership of a party famous for underground activities—oh, believe me, I have a great respect for you and a great distaste for my own work. I also understand you as far as one man may understand another——"

"You can't. I don't understand myself."

"But I am objective because although I can get inside

your skin I can leave it at will, can get out before the pain starts——"

"Pain?"

"And so I know, objectively, surely, serenely, that at one level or other of our alas, unfortunate association you will, how shall I put it——?"

"I won't talk. I know nothing."

"Talk. Yes, that is the word. At some point, Mr. Mountjoy, you will talk."

"I know nothing. Nothing!"

"Wait. Let us begin by giving you something of great value. I shall explain you to yourself. No one, not a lover, a father, a schoolmaster, could do that for you. They are all inhibited by conventions and human kindness. It is only in such conditions as these, electric furnace conditions, in which the molten, blinding truth may be uttered from one human face to another."

"Well?"

"What embryo if it could choose, would go through the sufferings of birth to achieve your daily consciousness? There is no health in you, Mr. Mountjoy. You do not believe in anything enough to suffer for it or be glad. There is no point at which something has knocked on your door and taken possession of you. You possess yourself. Intellectual ideas, even the idea of loyalty to your country sits on you loosely. You wait in a dusty waiting-room on no particular line for no particular train. And between the poles of belief, I mean the belief in material things and the belief in a world made and supported by a supreme being, you oscillate jerkily from day to day, from hour to hour. Only the things you cannot avoid, the sear of sex or pain, avoidance of the one suffering repetition and prolongation of the other, this constitutes what your daily consciousness would not admit, but experiences as life. Oh, yes, you are capable of a certain degree of friendship and a certain degree of love, but nothing to mark you out from the ants or the sparrows."

"Then you'd better have nothing to do with me."

"Have you not yet appreciated the tragicomedy of our situation? If what I have described were all, Mr. Mountjoy, I should point a gun at your head and give you ten seconds to start talking. But there is a mystery in you which is opaque to both of us. Therefore, even when I am almost certain that you would speak if you had anything to tell I must go on to the next step, the infliction of more suffering because of the gap between 'almost' and 'certain'. Oh, yes! I shall loathe myself, but how will that help you?"

"Can't you see I couldn't stand a threat?"

"And therefore I must go through the motions as though I knew nothing about you at all. I will pretend you can neither be bribed nor swayed by fear. I offer you nothing, then, but a chance to save lives. Tell me everything you know about the escape organization and you shall be what you were before, neither more nor less. You shall be taken from this camp to another camp neither more nor less comfortable. The source of our information shall be concealed."

"Why don't you talk to the senior officer?"

Blue cornflowers.

"Who would confide in a senior officer?"

"Why won't you believe me?"

"Who would believe you, Mr. Mountjoy, if he had any sense?"

"What's the good of asking me for the truth then?"

A sad, wry, reasonable face. Hands spread.

"Even if that is true, Mr. Mountjoy, I must go on. Surely you realize that? Oh, I agree, we're in the sewer together—both of us up to the neck."

"Well, then!"

"What do you want most in the world? To go home? That could be arranged—a mental breakdown—just a month or two in a pleasant sanatorium, a few papers signed and there you are—home, Mr. Mountjoy. I implore you."

"I'm feeling a bit dizzy."

The inside of my hands slipped on my face. I could feel the oily stuff running.

"Or if home does not seem so immediately attractive—how about an interim period of entertainment? I try to phrase this as delicately as one not born to the use of your ample language can manage; but do you not sometimes feel the deprivation of the companionship of either sex? The resources of Europe are at your disposal, I am told they are, are——"

His voice went right away into the distance. I opened my eyes and saw that I was holding on to the edge of the table, saw that where my fingers had slipped they left wet marks. Just the tiniest little prick. A kind of sobbing rage swelled up in my throat.

"You bloody fool! Do you think I wouldn't tell you if I knew? I tell you I know nothing—nothing!"

His face was white, shining with perspiration and compassionate.

"Poor boy. How beastly the whole thing is, Sammy. I may call you Sammy? Of course, you care nothing for the resources of Europe. Forgive me. Money? No. I think not. Well there. I have taken you up to a pinnacle of the temple and shown you the whole earth. And you have refused it."

"I haven't refused it. Can't you see, you, you—I don't know anything——"

"You have bidden me get behind you. Or perhaps you are right and you really know nothing. Are you a hero or not, Sammy?"

"I'm no hero. Let me go."

"Believe me, I wish I could. But if anyone else escapes they will be shot. I can't take any risks at all. No stone unturned, Sammy, no avenue unexplored."

"I'm going to be sick."

He fell silent. I swayed back in the dentist's chair which unbalanced incongruously as though it were metal and fabric on an uneven floor. The Fuehrer in his awful power slid apart and then closed like the hands of a hypnotist.

"Let me go. Can't you see? They wouldn't trust me. Nobby and Ralph—they tossed up perhaps, but even if they had not, nothing would have induced them to put me in the picture—I know now what they wanted with me; but all the time they must have had a reservation. Can't trust him. He'd squeal. Curious contorted chap—something missing in the middle——"

"Sammy. Sammy! Can you hear me? Wake up, Sammy!'

I came back out of chaos, was collected together mercilessly from those unnameable places. For the first time I had a pause in which I could have willingly remained for ever. Not to look, not to know or anticipate, not to feel, but only to be conscious of identity is the next best thing to complete unconsciousness. Inside me I neither stood nor sat or lay down, I was suspended in the void.

"Well, Sammy?"

Memory of the cornflowers tugged at me. I opened my eyes and he was still there opposite. I spoke to his understanding out of our naked souls.

"Can't you be merciful?"

"It is the karma of our two nations that we should torture each other."

With my hands on the edge of the table I spoke to him carefully.

"Isn't it obvious to you? You know me. Be reasonable. Do you think I'm the kind of man who can keep anything back when I am threatened?"

He did not answer immediately and as the silence stretched out I began to know what was inevitable. I even looked away from him, unable now to influence the event. The Fuehrer was there, both transparent pictures now slid exactly into one. The plaster round the photograph was institutional buff and needed redecorating. One of the Gestapo was standing easy and as my eyes swung to his face I saw him put one hand to his mouth and hide a yawn. The interminable argument in a foreign language was keeping him from his grey coffee and sticky bun. Dr. Halde waited till my eye came back to his face.

"And you can see, Sammy, that I have to make certain."

"I told you I know nothing!"

"Think."

"I won't think. I can't think."

"Think."

"What's the good? Please!"

"Think."

And the generalized sense of position, of a war on, of prison, of men shut in——

"I can't——"

—men who lay in their bunks, rotting away, men with bright faces who went in and out of chapel, incomprehensible as bees weaving their passes before a grassy bank——

"I tell you I can't!"

—the men going round the bend, wire-happy, running wildly as the guns tucked them in——

"I tell you——"

The men.

For, of course, I knew something. I had known something for more than a year. It was the standard of knowledge required that I did not know. But I could have said at any time that out of the hundreds of us there were perhaps twenty-five who might actually try to escape. Only the information had not been required. What we know is not what we see or learn but what we realize. Day after day a complex of tiny indications had added up and now presented me with a picture. I was an expert. Who else had lived as visually and professionally with these faces and taken knowledge of them in through his pores? Who else had that puzzled curiosity about man, that photographic apprehension, that worried faith in the kings of Egypt?

"I tell you——"

I could say to him quite simply; I do not know when or where the escape organization operates or how—but take these twenty men into your trawl and there will be no escapes.

"Well, Sammy? You tell me what?"

And he was right of course. I was not an ordinary man. I was at once more than most and less. I could see this war as the ghastly and ferocious play of children who having made a wrong choice or a whole series of them were now helplessly tormenting each other because a wrong use of freedom had lost them their freedom. Everything was relative, nothing absolute. Then who was most likely to know best what is best to do? I, abashed before the kingship of the human face, or Halde behind the master's desk, in the judge's throne, Halde, at once human and superior?

He was still there; but I had to focus again to bring my eyes back from the map of Europe and the locked armies. His eyes were not dancing but intent. I saw he was holding his breath because he let it out with a little gasp before he spoke:

"Well?"

"I don't know."

"Tell me."

"I've just told you!"

"Sammy. Are you being an exceptional man or are you tying yourself to the little code? Are you not displaying nothing more creditable than a schoolboy's sense of honour when he refuses to tell on his naughty comrades? The organization will steal sweets, Sammy; but the sweets they steal are poisoned——"

"I've had enough of this. I demand that you send for the senior officer——"

As the hands fell on either shoulder Halde made his placatory gesture again.

"Now I shall be plain with you. I will even give you some trumps. I dislike hurting people, I loathe my job and everything that goes with it. But what rights have you?

Rights still apply to your prisoners *en masse*, but they bend and break before necessity. You are too intelligent not to know that. We can transfer you from this room to another camp. Why should you not be killed by your own R.A.F. on the way? But to kill you now would benefit nobody. We want information, Sammy, not corpses. You saw the door to your left because you came through it. There is another one to your right. Don't look round. Choose, Sammy. Which door is going to be your exit?"

And, of course, I might be deceiving myself, might be building up a whole façade of knowledge which would collapse when tested by fact—I could feel something stinging in my eyes.

"I don't know anything!"

"You know, Sammy, history will be quite unable to unravel the tangle of circumstances between you and me. Which of us is right? Either of us, neither? The problem is insoluble, even if they could understand our reservations, our snatched judgments, our sense of truth being nothing but an infinite regression, a shifting island in the middle of chaos——"

I must have cried out because I heard my voice rise against the palate.

"But look. You want the truth. All right I'll tell you the truth. I don't know whether I know anything or not!"

I could see the moulding of his face more clearly now for the top of every fold shone with perspiration.

"Are you telling the truth, Sammy, or must I admire you, foolishly and jealously? Yes, Sammy. I admire you because I dare not believe you. Your exit is a better one than mine."

"You can't do anything to me. I'm a prisoner of war!"

His face shone. His eyes were like bright blue stones. The general light on his forehead increased as it ran together. It became a star that moved down the long line of his nose and fell on the blotter with an audible tap.

"I loathe myself, Sammy, and I admire you. If necessary I will kill you."

There is a heard beating of the heart when each beat is like the blow of a stick on concrete. There is also the soggy beat, in the indulged life of the chain smoker, a confusion in the breathing that struggles with phlegm and that centre in there—in here—dumping sacks of wet vegetables on a wooden floor and shaking the building to pieces. There was heat, too, that rose to the ears so that the chin lifted and the mouth opened, swallowing on hard nothing.

Halde swam.

"Go!"

There was a strange obedience about my two hands that grasped the sides of the seat and helped to lift me. I did not like to see the new door for the first time so I turned back to Halde, but he would not meet my eye and he was swallowing on nothing as I had done. So at last in this awful trance of obedience I turned away towards the ordinary wooden door and beyond it there was a corridor of concrete with a strip of coconut matting down the centre. My mind was reeling along, trying to say inside; now this is happening, this is the moment! But my mind could not take it. Therefore the feet trod obediently one in front of the other, there was no rebellion from the body, only astonishment and doom in the mind. And the flesh that quivered and jumped had a sense of occasion. My eyes went on with their own life, presented to me as precious trophies, the stains on the floor—one in the likeness of a brain. And there was another one, a long mark on the scrubbed concrete that might have been the crack in the bedroom ceiling, the raw material out of which imagination had constructed so many faces.

Tie. Belt. Shoelaces.

I stood there with neither belt nor braces and my one conscious thought was that I needed both hands to hold my trousers up. Some soft, opaque material was folded over my eyes from behind and this seemed a matter for expostulation because without light how can a man see and be ready for the approaching feet of the last terror? He may be ambushed, cannot assess the future, cannot tell when to give up his precious scrap of information if he indeed has a scrap and it is indeed precious——

But I was walking, propelled not ungently from behind. Another door was opened, for I heard the handle scrape. Hands pushed me and pressed down. I fell on my knees, head down, hands out protectively. I was kneeling on cold concrete and a door was shut roughly behind me. The key turned and feet went away.

8

How did I come to be so frightened of the dark?

Once there was a way of seeing which was a part of innocence. Far back on the very edge of memory—or further perhaps, because the episode is outside time—I saw a creature four inches high, paper-white, changing shape and strutting along a top edge of the open window like a cock. Then later, when I saw her first there was perhaps still time; but no one told me, no one knew what we might see and how easily we might lose the faculty.

The verger stepped in, opened me up with one blow of his hand. Now for the first time I was awash in a sea where I might drown, was defenceless against attack from any quarter. I wore vest and pants, grey shirt and tie, socks up to the knee, gartered and turned down. I wore half-shoes and a jacket; and presently I wore a bright blue cap. Father Watts-Watt fitted me out and threw me into a new life. He directed his housekeeper to see to me; and I was seen to. I was taken from the ward to the vast rectory and Mrs. Pascoe made me bathe at once as though all those weeks in the ward had not cleansed me of Rotten Row. But though the ward had accustomed me to baths, this bathroom was very different. Mrs. Pascoe went with me along a corridor then up two steps to the door. Inside the bathroom she showed me the new things I had to do. There was a box of matches tied to—but what was it tied to? What did I think that structure was? A man in copper armour? That would have gone with the whole structure of the room; for it was taller than long, with one high, glazed window, that looked at nothing; and a single naked bulb. But the copper, brass-bound idol dominated everything, even dominated the huge bath on its four splayed tiger feet, dominated me, with a blank look over my head from two dark caverns and an intimidation of pipes. Mrs. Pascoe turned on the water, struck a match and the idol roared and flamed. Later, when I read about Talus, the man of brass, in my mind's eye he had just such a voice, such flames, just such a copper, brass-bound body. But that first time I was so plainly terrified that Mrs. Pascoe stayed with me while the bath filled and the electric light was haloed in steam that bulged down from the ceiling and the yellow walls looked as though they were sweating in the heat. Then, when there was water enough in the bath—less than I would have liked—for in the womb we are immersed completely—she turned off the gas and the water, showed me the bolt on the door and left me. I bolted the door, put my new clothes on the chair and hurried to the bath with one eye on Talus. I squatted over the water, running cold and inspecting the long yellow smear on the white enamel so far away from me.

The bathroom door rattled and shook. Father Watts-Watt spoke softly outside.

"Sam. Sam."

I said nothing at all, before the idol, in that defenceless place.

"Sam! Why have you bolted the door?"

Before I could answer I heard him walking away along the corridor.

"Mrs. Pascoe!"

She said something and for a moment or two they muttered.

"But the child might have a fit!"

I could not hear her answer but Father Watts-Watt cried out jerkily.

"He must never bolt the bathroom door—*never*!"

I squatted there in the hot water and shivered with cold while the argument, if such it was, faded away downstairs. A door shut somewhere. After that bath when I had dressed and crept downstairs, it was an astonishment to find Mrs. Pascoe sitting so quietly in the kitchen and mending his socks. I had my supper with her and she shooed me off to bed. I had two lights for myself. One hung from a bulb in the middle of the ceiling and one was hidden in a little pink shade on a table by the bed. But Mrs. Pascoe saw me into bed and then, just when she was leaving, she took the bulb out of the bedside lamp.

"You won't want that one, Sam. Little boys should go to bed to sleep."

She hovered for a moment and paused by the door.

"Good night, Sam."

She turned out the other light and shut the door.

This was my first meeting with the generalized and irrational fear which attacks some children. They cannot localize it at first; and when at last they succeed, it becomes more unbearable still. I went down in that bed, hunched up and shivering, taking up a foetal shape first that only unfolded a little because I had to breathe. In Rotten Row I had never seemed to be so alone—there was always the brass knob of the pub's back door; and, of course, in the ward we were legion we little devils—but here, in this wholly not-understood milieu, among these strange, powerful people—and at that the church clock struck with a sound that seemed to make the rectory shake—here I was utterly and helplessly alone for the first time in darkness and a whirl of ignorance. Fear was spasms, any of which might have made me faint clean away if I had known of that refuge; and when, gasping for air, the disarranged clothes allowed me a glimpse of the glimmering window, the church tower looked in like an awful head. But there must have been in me still some of the prince whom Philip used, for I determined then and there that I would have a light at any cost. So I got out of bed into a white flame of danger that burnt and gave no light. I put a chair under the single bulb in the middle of the room because I planned to transfer the bulb to the lamp by my bed and put it back in the morning. But if you are undefended in bed, you are helpless out of it and utterly the sport of whatever dark thing waits for you when you stand on a chair in the middle of the room. I stood on that chair in the middle of the room with my back twitching. I was reaching up, I was holding the bulb when both my hands burst into cherry red and the lightning flashed at me from between them. I dropped from the chair and bounded into bed with a dactylic rush dumtydy umtydy and huddled there sitting knees up and bedclothes drawn to my ears.

Father Watts-Watt stood in the open door, his hand on the switch. The light shone at me from his knees and his eyes and the swinging bulb moved all the shadows of the room in little circles. For a time we looked at each other through this movement. Then he seemed to pull his eyes away from me and look for something in the air over my bed.

"Did you call out, Sam?"

I shook my head without saying anything. He moved

away from the door, watching me now, trailing his right hand behind him on the switch and then letting it go consciously, like a swimmer who takes his feet off the sand and knows now he is out of depth. He struck out into the room where I was. He went first to the chair and examined my clothes, rubbing them between his fingers; and then he looked down past me.

"You must not play with the light, Sam. If you touch the bulb I shall have to take it away."

Still I said nothing. He came to the bed and very slowly sat himself down sideways near the foot. He could sit anywhere there without touching me. I did not stretch down so far. He began to tap with his fingers on the counterpane. He watched his fingers carefully as though what they did was very difficult and very important. He tapped slowly. He stopped tapping. His fingers had so occupied me that I was startled when I looked up to see that he was watching me sideways and that his mouth was open. When I looked up, he looked down and began to tap again, quickly.

He coughed and spoke.

"Did you say your prayers tonight?"

Before I could answer him he had hastened on. He talked fast about how necessary prayer was before sleeping as a protection from wicked thoughts which all people had no matter how good they were, no matter how hard they tried and so one must pray—pray in the morning and at midday and at night so that one could put away the thoughts and sleep quietly.

Did I know how to pray? No? Then he would teach me—but not tonight. Tonight he would pray for us both. There was no need for me to get out of bed. He prayed there, writhing his bony hands together, moving them and his head up and down so that the black patches of his eye-hollows changed shape. He prayed long, it seemed to me, sometimes in broken sentences of English and sometimes in another language. Then he stopped and put his hands down on either side of him so that they rested on the ribbed pattern of the counterpane. His two black patches, still moving a little as the hanging bulb settled deeper into the spiral, regarded me opaquely. Each was topped with a tangle of white and black hairs, as though youth and extreme age contended in that body without hope of compromise; and the lowish forehead shone and the bridge of the sharp nose. Then as I watched, the bedclothes still drawn up to my mouth, I saw the whole lower part of his face shorten and broaden, move upward. Lighted skin appeared under each patch. Father Watts-Watt was smiling at me, moving the set flesh of his face, rearranging the muscles of the cheek, showing folds and creases and bumps and teeth. I could hear him breathing, fast and shallow—and once he reared up with a curious jerk of the neck just as on that first evening, a shudder from feet to head, a goose walking over his grave. At last he moved six inches nearer on the counterpane. I could see his eyes now in the patches. They were peering at me closely.

"I suppose your mother used to kiss you good night, Sam?"

Dumbly I shook my head. Then for a long time there was silence again and no motion but the tiny dying circles of the shadows on the floor, no sound but breathing.

Suddenly he jerked off the bed. He strode to the window and then to the door. He turned with his hand on the switch and he seemed to me to be twice the height of a man.

"Don't let me catch you signalling again, Sam, or I shall take away this light, too."

He switched off the light and banged the door behind him. I dived into the bedclothes again, shielding myself from the church tower that looked in through the window with its black, concealing patches. Now there was not only the threat of the darkness but a complete mystery added to it.

Yet here, if I look for the moment of change I cannot find it; I was still the child from Rotten Row and if I had no freedom it was taken away physically not mentally. For Father Watts-Watt never repeated his advances, if that is what they were. Instead, he wrapped me in an occasional mystery of signals to the unnamed foes who surrounded him. He had a developing persecution mania; and presently the world saw him less and less. He watched me from far off to see if I would communicate with these enemies; or perhaps he wrapped me into his fantasies because that was a way of concealing his true motives from himself. On some involved level he pretended to be mad in order to evade the responsibility for his own frightening desires and compulsions and therefore in a sense he was not mad at all—yet is a man who pretends to be mad completely sane? This, for Father Watts-Watt and Samuel Mountjoy is another of those infinite regressions, an insoluble relativity. Thus when Father Watts-Watt stopped me on the gravel path outside the rectory side door, neither he nor I could have analysed his motives now or then.

"If anyone appears at your window, Sam, in the middle

of the night and tries to make you believe things about me, you are to come to my room at once."

"Sir."

And then it was such a long, writhing look across the garden, round and up the wall of the church, back above my head, his hands together—Father Watts-Watt moving with vast improbability like the caterpillar in Alice, then hands clasped up by his left cheek and looking past my own:

"I could tell you such things! They will go to any expense, Sam, any length——"

This was an example, I thought, of the elongating clergymen mentioned by the verger, here was one in fact before me on the daylight gravel now writhing sideways, winding up, flinging his arms wide with a gasp and smile:

"Back to work, eh, Sam? Back to my study——"

He moved away and then stopped, looking back in the door.

"You won't forget, Sam? Anything unusual—anything in the middle of the night——"

He went away and left me unfrightened. The curious intuition of childhood sensed his lies and did not mind them. He added nothing to the terror of the dark, the terror generalized and mindless that had to be endured nightlong and night after night. Once or twice more, I remember, he covered up that first passionate movement towards me by hinting at mysteries so that now I can piece them together.

His delusion or pretence, whichever it was, was basically that people were trying to take away his reputation. They were, I suppose, accusing him, trying to pin on him publicly all the acts of his fantasies. There was a complex system of lights employed as signals so that each of them should know where he was and what he was doing. The Russians—still in those days, *Punch* Bolshies—were at the back of it. Father Watts-Watt brought into his mania all the features of existence as it appeared to him, just as Evie had brought in hers. The only difference was that Evie told me everything whereas Father Watts-Watt only gave me hints. I did not believe Father Watts-Watt because I had known Evie. There had come a time and I cannot remember when or where, when I had realized that Evie's uncle did not live in the suit of armour because a duke would not do such a thing. I knew that Evie was telling stories—that childish, far more accurate description of half our talking—and now I knew that Father Watts-Watt was telling stories, too.

I knew that no lights would flash, no messages be passed; that no one would sidle up to me with a whispered condemnation of my guardian. There were laws which I knew as applying to this play. At the bottom of it all, of course, stood Ma's fantasy of my birth and her fictitious steady. As I progressed from person to person the fantasy changed in character but remained substantially the same in its relation to the teller. They were all trying to adjust the brute blow of the fist that daily existence dealt them till it became a caress. He and I at various crises in our lives, pretended to others that we were mad or going mad. He at least, ended by convincing himself.

I should be disingenuous if I pretended to be uncertain about what these frightening desires of my guardian's were. And yet I must be very careful in the impression I convey because although he teetered on the edge he never went further towards me than I have said, never went near anyone as far as I know. There was, to account for his shining knees and his complex lies of persecution, there was an awful battle that raged year in year out in his study where I could sometimes hear him groaning. There was nothing ludicrous in this, either then, or in memory. He was incapable of approaching a child straight because of the ingrown and festering desires that poisoned him. He must have had pictures of lucid and blameless academes where youth and experience could walk and make love. But the thing itself in this vineless and unolived landscape was nothing but furtive dirt. He might have kissed me and welcome if it would have done him any good. For what was the harm? Why should he not want to stroke and caress and kiss the enchanting, the more than vellum warmth and roundness of childhood? Why should he in his dry, wrinkled skin, his hair falling and his body becoming every day less comely and masterful, why should he not want to drink at that fountain renewed so miraculously generation after generation? And if he had more savage wishes why they have been common enough in the world and done less harm than a dogma or a political absolute. Then I could have comforted myself in these later days, saying: I was of some use and comfort to such a one.

The more I have thought over his action in adopting me, the more I have seen that there is what I might call one and a half explanations. First, of course, he would tell himself and perhaps believe that I must be suffered to come, that the shame of my reception at the altar must be atoned for, that it were better for a millstone and except ye do it to one of these little ones and so on. That is what I call the half explanation. The whole one is nastier if you have the conventional view of things, but if not, heroic. I was like the full bottle of gin that the repentant cobbler stood on his bench so as to have the devil always in full view. He must have thought that to know a child properly, to have as it were, a son, might exorcise the demon; but he had not the art of getting to know. We remained strangers. He became, if anything, more eccentric. He would be walking in the street shaking his head, striding along, knees bent, arms gesticulating—and then he would cry out from the heart of his awful battle.

"Why? Why on me?"

Sometimes half-way through his cry he would recognize a face and turn his voice down into the social gesture:

"Why—how do you do?"

Then he would writhe away, muttering. As he got older he got higher and higher in this attempt to get away from himself; and finally I think he came right out at the top to find himself a man who has missed all the sweetness of life and got nothing in exchange, a derelict, old, exhausted, indifferent. I cannot see then that we did each other much harm but little good either. He fed me, clothed me, sent me to a dame school and then the local grammar school. He was well able to afford this and I do not make the mistake of confusing his signatures on cheques with human charity. He effectually lifted me from the roaring squalor and happiness of Rotten Row to the luxury of more than one room to a person.

But where does the fear of darkness come in? The rectory itself was more daunting than he, full of unexpected levels and cupboards with one storey of vast rooms and two others of shadows and holes and corners. There were religious pictures everywhere and I liked the bad ones much better than the few that had any aesthetic merit. My favourite Madonna was terribly saccharine, coming right out of the picture at me with power and love, buckets of it. Her colours were lovely, like the piled merchandise in Woolworth's, so that she eclipsed that other lady floating impossibly with her child in Raphael's air. The house itself was cold with more than lovelessness. It was supposed to have central heating from some arrangement of gas tubes in a cellar like the engine-room of a ship. Mrs. Pascoe told me that if the arrangement was turned on it ate money; a vivid phrase which combined with the dark house and the rector's eccentricity to give me much thought. But whether the machinery ate money or not, what could a few puffs of lukewarm air do against those twisting stairs and corridors, those doors that never met the floor, those dormer windows, those attics where the warmth poured up and away through the warped boards? I have sat in the great drawing-room at the rectory, warming my hands at my Madonna before going up to bed and I have heard the slow tapping as a picture beat against the brown panelling though all the doors and windows were closed. I got little warmth in that house to take up to bed with me. And bed meant darkness and darkness the generalized and irrational terror. Now I have been back in these pages to find out why I am frightened of the dark and I cannot tell. Once upon a time I was not frightened of the dark and later on I was.

9

After the sound of the feet died away I did not know how to react or what to feel. My pictures of torment were unformed and generalized. Somewhere there was a bench in my mind, a wooden bench with clamps and a furrowed surface; but Nick Shales stood behind that bench and demonstrated the relativity of sense impressions. So I began to wonder on which side of my confusion the bench was and where my tormentors were. All that I felt or surmised was conditioned by the immediacy of extreme peril. I could not know how much warning I should have before they hurt me. I could not know whether they would speak or not or whether theirs was only the more bitter business of dealing with excruciated flesh. So I knelt in the thick darkness, holding my trousers up with both hands and flinched and listened for breathing. But an outside breathing to be heard must have been gusty indeed to penetrate that riotous duet of my lungs and heart. Also the composition of experience was disconcerting and unpredictable. Who could have told me, for example, that the darkness before my blindfolded eyes would take on the likeness of a wall so that I would keep lifting my chin in order to look over it? And I held up my trousers not for decency but protection. My flesh, though it crawled, cared nothing for the recent brain nor the important, social face. It cared only to protect my privates, our privates, the whole race. So at last in the riot of air and pulse, one hand still down at my trousers, I put up the other and tore the soft bandage away.

Nothing happened at all. The darkness stayed with me. It was not only trapped under the folds of cloth, it wrapped me round, lay close against the ball of the eye. I lifted my chin again to see over the wall which rose with me. A kind of soup or stew of all the dungeon stories flew through my head, oubliettes, walls that moved, the little ease. Suddenly, with pricking hairs, I remembered rats.

If necessary, I will kill you.

"Who's there?"

My voice was close to my mouth as the darkness was to the balls of my eyes. I made a sweeping movement out into the air with my right hand, then down, and felt smooth stone or concrete. I had a sudden panic fear for my back and scrabbled round in the darkness and then round again. Now I could no longer remember where the door was, and cursed suddenly as I felt the first thrust of Halde's ingenuity. He wanted me to move myself towards whatever there was here of torment and deception, would play with me, not to increase any suffering but solely to prove conclusively that he could call any reaction out of me he wanted—I let my trousers slide down and moved cautiously back on hands and knees. I found the back of my neck was hurting with the strain of my rigidity, I saw flashes of unreal light that obstructed my absence of view. I told myself fiercely that there was no view to be seen and I loosed the strain in my neck, bowing my head down towards my hand so that the pain and the lights passed away. My fingers found the bottom of a wall and instantly I doubted that it was a wall, was prepared to agree that it might be one but was too clever to be trapped by an assumption, and began to feel up, inch by inch. But Halde was cleverer than I after all, inevitably cleverer, for I crouched up, squatted, stood, then stretched on tiptoe with one hand up; and still the wallness of the wall went with me and derided my refusal to be caught, went beyond my reach, up to where there might be a ceiling or might not according to some insoluble equation of guess and probability and me and Halde. I squatted, then crouched and worked my way to the right, I found an angle and then wood. All the time I was trying to hold a new diagram in my head without displacing the old conjectural, instinctive one of a bench and a judge. Yet the new diagram was so rudimentary that it furnished at least a place for my back. Here was a corner which was a concrete wall coming to the wood of a door. I was so glad to be guarded at my back that I forgot my trousers and huddled down, huddled into the corner, tried to squeeze my backbone into the right-angle. I got my knees up against my chin and put my crossed arms before my face. I was defended. The attack from no matter where would find me with flimsy bulwarks of flesh to ward it off.

Eyes that see nothing soon tire of nothing. They invent their own shapes that swim about under the lids. Shut eyes are undefended. How then, what to do? They opened against my will and once more the darkness lay right on the jellies. My mouth was open and dry.

I began to touch my face with my hands for company. I felt bristles where I should have shaved. I felt two lines from nose down, cheekbones under the skin and flesh.

I began to mutter.

"Do something. Keep still or move. Be unpredictable. Move to the right. Follow the wall along or is that what you want? Do you want me to fall on thorns? Don't move then. I won't move; I shall stay defended."

I began to hutch myself to the right out of the angle. I pictured a corridor leading away and this picture had definition and was restful therefore; but then I guessed that at the far end would lie some warped thing that would seize on the shrieking flesh so though I was not more than a yard from my corner I yearned for its safety and flurried back like an insect.

"Don't move at all."

I began again, moving right, along the wall, a yard, five feet, hutch after hutch of the body; and then a wall struck my right shoulder and forehead, cold but a shock so white sparks spun. I came hutching back, knowing that I was returning to a right-angle next to a wooden door. I began to think of the diagram as a corridor leading sideways, a concrete corridor with a stain like a face.

"Yes."

Hutch and crawl. My trousers got under my knees and I allowed myself enough freedom from the wall to pull them up again. Then, on knees and not hutching, I crawled sideways along this wall and hutched along that one.

Another wall.

I had a whirling glimpse in my head of mazy walls in which without my thread and with my trousers always falling down I should crawl for ever. But trousers can only fall to the feet. I tried to work out in my head how many walls would be sufficient to strip me completely. I lay in my right angle, eyes shut, hearing the various sentences of my meeting with Halde and watching the amoeboid shapes that swam through my blood. I spoke aloud and my voice was hoarse.

"Took it out of me."

I? I? Too many I's, but what else was there in this

thick, impenetrable cosmos? What else? A wooden door and how many shapes of walls? One wall, two walls, three walls, how many more? I visualized a curious shape and an opening leading to a corridor—with many angles, a bench and an oubliette? Who was to say that the floor was level? Might this very concrete beneath me slope down, gently at first then turning more steeply till it became a footless skitter into the ant-lion's funnel, ant-lion not in the children's encyclopaedia, but here with harrow-high jaws of steel? I hutched and cowered my flesh over my slack pants into my angle. No one to see. A solo performance, look no eyes. No one to see a man turning into a jelly by the threat of the darkness.

Walls.

This wall and that wall and that wall and a wooden door——

But then I knew and had to confirm, even though until I could touch proof with my finger-tips I should not let the knowing loose in me. Busily I hutched along the walls, knees down, hands against concrete, fingers searching; and I came round four walls to the same wooden door, back to the same angle.

I scrambled up, trousers down, arms stretched against the wood.

"Let me out! Let me out!"

But then the thought of the Nazis outside the door hit me and a sense of the terrible ways in which steps might go down, many steps to the ultimate whatever that was, but at least worse off, worse even than uncompanioned darkness. So with instant appreciation I choked off that cry before it could bring them in. I whispered instead against wood.

"You Nazi bastards!"

Even this defiance was terrible. There were microphones which would pick up a whisper at half a mile. My bare knees ground down the floor to the concrete, I knelt among the concertina'd folds of my trousers, face crushed against wood. All at once defeat became physical and movement therefore too much effort. To flex a muscle was more than a man could do. The only life was to lie huddled, every fibre let lie as it would.

Not a corridor. A cell. This was a cell then, with concrete walls and floor and a wooden door. Perhaps the most terrible thing was the woodenness of the door, the sense that they did not need steel in their power but kept me there by sheer will of Halde. Perhaps even the lock was a fake, the door yielding to a touch—but what good was that? The old prisoner fooled by such a ruse, the man who had wasted twenty years, lived in a plain time when an open door was synonym for exit. Christian and Faithful pushing the door were escapers as soon as they found a way out. But the Nazis mirrored the dilemma of my spirit in which not the unlocking of the door was the problem but the will to step across the threshold since outside was only Halde, no noble drop from a battlement but immured in dust behind barbed wire, was prison inside prison. And this, I saw clearly as a demonstrated proposition when I lay huddled, this view of life blighted my will, blighted man's will and was self-perpetuating. So I lay on the concrete, having discovered that the place was a cell: examined dully the view of total defeat.

And then the arithmetic of Halde's intentions stood up before me. I was accepting something as final which was only the first step. There were many steps to follow so that the whole flight would be an accurate picture of his learning and genius. On which step would a man at last give up his scrap of information? If a man had a scrap of information to give up?

Because—and the strength of a nervous spasm came into my muscles—how could a man even be sure that he knew anything? If he had not been told where the radio was, but nevertheless could plot back through the months how the news had reached him, till all the plots pointed to one group of three men and still he had nothing but that plot to go on, did he know anything? How good is a guess? What use is an expert?

I began to mutter against the concrete, like Midas among the reeds.

"There are two men in that hut—I can't remember the number and I don't know the names. I might be able to point them out to you on parade—but what would be the good? They would deny everything and they might well be right. If they are like me then they know nothing; but if I am right and they know where the radio is hidden, do you think white hot hooks would tear the place out of them? For they would have something to protect, some simple knowledge, some certainty to die for. They could say no because they could say yes. But what can I say who have no knowledge, no certainty, no will? I could point out to you the men like myself rather who are to be ignored, the grey and hapless helpless over whom time rolls bringing them nothing but devaluation and dust——"

But there was no answer. Nothing communicated with nothing.

How large a cell? I began to move and break up the granite of my immobility, stretched myself carefully along my own wall; but before my knees were straight my feet came against the concrete of the other wall; and hutching round through what might be ninety degrees until my body lay along by the door I found the same. The cell was too small for me to stretch myself out.

"What did you expect? A bed-sitting room?"

Of course I could lie slantwise across the cell and then my feet would be in the unvisited far corner and my head in my own angle. But who could sleep with only the level floor as a contact? What dreams and phantoms might visit one unprotected at his back and not rolled up in cloth? And for that matter who could push his feet forward across the open space in the middle of this cell and not care what they might meet? Halde was clever, knew what he was at; they were all clever, far cleverer than one rotting prisoner whose hours were beginning to drip on him one by one. The centre was the secret—might be the secret. Of course they were psychologists of suffering, apportioning to each man what was most helpful and necessary to his case.

Unless, of course, they are cleverer even than you think. Why should they not sit back and wait for you to take the next step for yourself? Why should they rely on chance, and let you discover it in the middle there by accident? He was a student of Samuel Mountjoy, knew that Mountjoy would stay by the wall, would deduce the thing there in the middle, would endure all torment guessing and wondering and inventing—and would be forced in the end by the same insane twitch that avoids all the cracks between paving stones or touches and touches wood, would be forced, screaming but forced, forced by himself, himself forcing himself, compelled helplessly deprived of will, sterile, wounded, diseased, sick of his nature, pierced, would have to stretch out his hand——

They knew you would explore. He knew you would not be British you would be downhearted. They knew you would find this not-impossible confinement and go further, you might have sat slumped against the door, but *they* knew you would add a torment to the discovery of the confinement, would add the torture of the centre—and therefore would do. Would do what? Would put nothing there? Would let the whole thing be a joke? Would put there.

Would put there what is most helpful in your case, sum of all terror.

Accept what you have found and no more. Huddle into your corner, knees up to the chin, hand over the eyes to ward off the visible thing that never appears. The centre of the cell is a secret only a few inches away. The impalpable dark conceals it palpably. Be intelligent. Leave the centre alone.

The darkness was full of shapes. They moved and were self-supplying. They came, came and swam before the face of primordial chaos. The concrete ceased to be a material visualized because felt and became nothing but a cold feeling. The wood of the door was warm and soft by comparison; but not a female warmth and softness—only an absence of cold and immediate wounding. The darkness was full of shapes.

Was not the size of the cell adjusted to the exact dimension so that the impossibility of stretching out would become little by little more than the feeble will could bear?

I wiped my face with my hands, I gaped with blindness. The first step was an absence of light, light taken from the visual artist. He is an artist, they must have said and smiled at each other. If he had been a musician we would have plugged his ears with wool. We will plug his eyes with cotton-wool. That is the first step. Then he will find that the cell is small and that will be the second step. When the discomfort of not being able to stretch out at full length becomes more than he can bear, they said, he will stretch out diagonally and find what we have put there for him; find what he expects to find. He is a timid, a morbid and sensitive creature and he will crush himself against the wall until discomfort drives him into telling us what he knows, or drives him to stretch out on the diagonal——

"I don't know whether I know anything or not!"

Now more than the generalized dark, the centre of the cell boiled with shapes of conjecture. A well. Do you not feel that the floor of the cell slopes downward? You will begin to roll inward if you move, down to the well and the ant-lion at the bottom. If you are worn out with the fears of conjecture you will fall asleep and roll——

We want information, not corpses.

We want you to feel forward, inch by inch, line by line over the concrete, with one ungloved hand. We want you to find a curious half-moon of hardness, polished, at the edge polished, but in the centre rough. We want you to feel forward over the slope and spread your fingers till you have found the sole of a shoe. Will you go on then, pull gently and find that the sole resists? Will you, under the erected hair in the blindness, deduce without more effort the rigor, the body curled there like a frozen foetus? How long will you wait? Or will you stretch out your fingers and find our surprise curled there not eighteen inches from your own? It has a moustache of white swan's feathers. You never touched his sharp nose then. Touch his nose now. All those dark roads of grue were unnecessary. The test is here.

We want you to take the third step. We know you will because we are never wrong. We have beaten the world. We have hung in a row the violated bodies of Abyssinia, Spain, Norway, Poland, Czecho-Slovakia, France, Holland, Belgium. Who do you think we are? Our Fuehrer's photograph hangs on the wall behind us. We are the experts. We do not torture you. We let you torture yourself. You need not take the third step towards the centre; but your nature compels you. We know you will.

The darkness was tumbling and roaring. I lost the door.

Don't let them know you've lost it. Find it again. Ignore those green, roaring seas, ignore the mouth agape, the hair erected, the eyes now streaming with wetness down both cheeks. And then I was back in my corner again after that frantic scramble round the wall, was back in a recognized corner with the wood of the door pressing against me. The patch in the middle was perhaps three feet across or even less. Then the body could not be lying there, must be standing up, balanced on the frozen feet like a statue. They had stood him up to wait for me. If I touched him he would sway forward.

I came out of the storm. I was saying nonsense, nonsense, nonsense to myself without remembering clearly what the nonsense was. I began to talk aloud in a croaking and jerky voice.

"If they stood a body there it could not be our lodger because he died and was buried in England thirty years ago. Thirty years ago. Thirty years ago. He was buried in

England. The huge car came for him with frosted and chased glass. He was buried there. This could not be his body——"

Then I lifted my face away from the wall and spoke in great anger.

"What is all this about bodies?"

Up there is up and down there is down. There where the concrete is getting harder every moment is down. Don't forget which is which or you will be seasick.

Whatever else you do don't take the third step.

They know what they are about. They have you on the fork. One way you take the next step and suffer for it. The other way, you do not take it but suffer on your own rack trying not to think what the next step is. They are past-masters.

A square not three feet each way. No, not so much. Not much room. And, of course, nothing could be standing there. Whatever held the centre must be small. Curled up.

Snake.

I was standing up, pressed back against the wall, trying not to breathe. I got there in the one movement my body made. My body had many hairs on legs and belly and chest and head, and each had its own life; each inherited a hundred thousand years of loathing and fear for things that scuttle or slide or crawl. I gasped a breath and then listened through all the working machinery of my body for the hiss or rattle, for the slow, scaly sound of a slither, except that in the zoo they made no sound but oozed like oil. In the desert they would vanish with hardly a furrow and a trickle of sand. They could move towards me, finding me by the warmth of my body, the sound of the blood in my neck. Theirs was the wisdom and if one of them had been left at the centre there was no telling where it would be next.

My knees had their automatic fear, too, but my body was weakened by it, lost all sense of gravity, fell clumsily into my corner. I lay there huddled, pulling my hands back to my face. I stared blindly at the place where the thing might be. Of course he would not have a snake or a tarantula on tap and if he had he would not leave it about in a cell as cold as the inside of a coffin. Nothing lived in the cell but me. Whatever lay out there at the third step could not be living and could not be a body because a body could not stand up.

I began to creep round the wall again. I forced myself challengingly into each corner and I kept my eyes shut because that way they did not water so and I could imagine daylight outside them.

Four corners, all empty.

I knelt in my own corner, muttering to myself.

"Well? Well then?"

Let me find out before my mind invents anything worse, anything still unimaginable.

I crept along the wall again, making my eighteen inches into twenty-four. There was a space in the centre no bigger than a big book. Perhaps that was what was there, a book waiting for me to read all the answers.

I let my fingers creep out of my corner. They ate away part of the unknown patch, they went line by line and as they went they chilled and prickled. The space that might be a large book, minutely decreased.

Fingers ate away another line of concrete.

The feeling changed at the tips. They were in some

other mode, now. Or no. The concrete was changing, was not the same, was smoother.

Smooth. Wet. Liquid.

My hand snatched itself back as though the snake had been coiled there, whipped back without my volition, a hand highly trained by the tragedies of a million years.

My eye stung where a flung-back nail had grazed the ball, one deep physical automatism outsmarted by another.

Be reasonable. Did you weep there in the centre, or did you wipe the tears of strain from your cheeks?

Another hand crept forward, found the liquid, even rubbed a tiny distance backwards and forwards, found the liquid smooth like oil.

Acid?

"Nothing has happened to you yet. Be reasonable. All the torments he implied have not yet begun. Though the steps of approach are as real as the steps of a town hall, yet still you need not climb them. Even if they had spilt poison there in the centre I need not lick it up. They want information not corpses. Cannot be acid because fingertips are still smooth and cold, not burning and blistered. Cannot be lye because as with acid, no pain. Only cold, cold as the air, as the concrete where I can hear the stridulation of fabric under my hip. Nothing has happened to you yet. Don't be tricked into selling cheap."

Selling what? What was the information that I was so uncertain I really had? What could I have said? What was it, my last bargaining token, last scrap of value, only chock between me and a sliding descent of infinite length and cleverness, torment after torment? He said it was for my own good, for all our goods—so the last of human faces had said, that delicately adjusted face, so delicate over the delicate, fragile bones.

But now there began to build up in me the conviction that even if I wanted to I could not remember, would never remember. I could see a layer of concrete build up in my mind over the forgotten thing, the thing down there that I had meant to say. But when that concrete forms in the mind, no internal road drill can break it up.

"Wait a minute. Let me remember——"

For, of course, you can only remember such a thing by forgetting to remember and then glancing back at it quickly before the concrete has a chance to form; but Halde would use a road drill, he would know of one. Yet no pain will break that concrete; hammer and you leave no mark——

"I tell you I've forgotten—I'd remember if I could! You must give me a moment——"

But there would be no moment of mercy. I knew now that I had forgotten and that I should never remember. The ladder of pain would stretch away from this stone pillow to an unknown height, I forced to climb. Let the road drill dance on the nerves savagely, on the flesh, spill the blood. What is your name? Muriel Millicent Mollie? Mary Mabel Margaret? Minnie Marcia Moron?

Oil, acid, lye. None of them.

No.

I could feel my cheekbone against wood; and a voice was talking loudly and hysterically through the cotton-wool.

"I tell you I can't remember! I would if I could—why don't you let me alone? If you only gave me a time not to think but a time to lie down under the sky without steps or pain then the concrete would slip away and the information come blurting out if there is any information and then we could start fair——"

There was that harvest picture yearned for, a harvest under one star and the moon. The light lay heavy on the heads of corn and he was going down through the light, leaning on his stick, a man soon to be harvested, too, creeping towards peace. There was the blue girl leaning back, a quiet river under her shoulder, the meal having crept on towards the shared siesta time.

But I was standing up again, shuffling through my trousers round the wall, facing it with hands feeling. But the wall was still there, right round. I reached up again as high as I could and still there was no ceiling—only darkness weighing heavy, smothering like a feather bed.

Oil. Acid. Lye.

No.

My body slid down and its right hand crept out, touched smoothness. Its fingers slipped on with tiny steps in smoothness that nibbled away the unknown space.

He knew they would nibble, he is the master.

Something, not touched yet or not with the sensitive tips, something touched, lying against the nail of the third finger, the weak one. Something touched my nail about a third of the way from the pared edge, cold as the smoothness. Mercilessly the fingers lifted in the darkness and explored, sending back their messages from the sensitive tips.

The thing was cold. The thing was soft. The thing was slimy. The thing was like an enormous dead slug—dead because where the softness gave way under the searching tips it did not come back again.

I could see everything now except the slug-thing because there was almost no darkness left. There was light falling away in a torrent, there were shouts and screams visible as shapes, long curves that shone and vibrated. But the shape of the thing on the floor was communicated to me through one enslaved finger that would not let go, that rendered the outline phosphorescent in my head, a strange, wandering haphazard shape with here a tail drawn out in slimy thinness and there the cold, wet bulk of a body. But this was no complete body of any animal or man. I knew now why this was the shape of no animal, knew what the wetness was. I knew too much. I should have touched his sharp nose and been armoured. Their cleverness was to shatter all the taboos of humanity, to crash through with an exhibition so brutal, a warning so unequivocal that the third step was like standing on a step of sheer horror above the others. They had laid there this fragment of human flesh, collapsed in its own cold blood. So the lights fell and spun and blood that was pumped out of the heart was visible too, like a sun's corona, was part noise, part feeling, part light.

A darkness ate everything away.

When I came together again, moaning, sick, huddled there was no intermission of knowledge. As soon as I remembered who I was I knew where I was and what thing lay there in the darkness, flung down from what misused body? And how long, my mind thought busily to itself, how long had that fragment been lying there? But they were not infallible then, for this morgue-like coldness gave me some protection. Yet even so, my nose now noticed in the air, noticed and tried to reject, certain elements other than the fetor of confinement. Or perhaps they were infallible indeed, when dealing *ex cathedra* with a matter of faith and morals such as this one and even the rate of decomposition was nicely calculated to increase. I recognized and miserably applauded the virtuosity of their torture for torture it was. This third step, they said, is unbearable, becomes unbearable, yet he must continue to bear it because the fourth step is worse. Do you think the cliff of loathing on which you are now huddled is our highest point? It is nothing but a preparatory ledge on our Everest. Base camp. Climb now. Try.

I felt upwards for the ceiling and in that moment the fourth step revealed itself. There was a whirlpool which had once been my mind but which now was slipping round, faster and faster; and a story leapt into the centre of it, a story completely remembered, vividly visualized—story of the small cell and the ceiling that came down slowly with all the weight of the world. I was scrabbling at the high wall, but the ceiling was still out of reach and I could not tell. But I knew that there were crushed things hanging from it that stank as the cold scrap in the centre was stinking; and presently I should hear the sound of its descent as it made unbearably small what was too small already, and came mercilessly down. So I was crouched in my fetid corner, gasping, sweating, talking.

"Why do you torment yourself? Why do you do their work for them? Nothing has touched you physically yet——"

For of course he knew. That fine, intellectual head was dedicated. What had I with my feelings, my gross sensuality, my skipping brain to put against a man who taught in a German university? Reason and common sense told me there was no body hanging crushed from which other pieces might fall and yet I believed in the body because Halde wanted me to.

I started to cry out.

"Help me! Help me!"

Let me be accurate now if ever. These pages I have written have taught me much; not least that no man can tell the whole truth, language is clumsier in my hands than paint. And yet my life has remained centred round the fact of the next few minutes I spent alone and panic-stricken in the dark. My cry for help was the cry of the rat when the terrier shakes it, a hopeless sound, the raw signature of one savage act. My cry meant no more, was instinctive, said here is flesh of which the nature is to suffer and do thus. I cried out not with hope of an ear but as accepting a shut door, darkness and a shut sky.

But the very act of crying out changed the thing that cried. Does the rat expect help? When a man cries out instinctively he begins to search for a place where help may be found; and so the thing that cried out, struggling in the fetor, the sea of nightmare, with burning breath and racing heart, that thing as it was drowning looked with starting and not physical eyes on every place, against every wall, in every corner of the interior world.

"Help me!"

But there was no help in the concrete of the cell or the slime, no help in the delicate, the refined and compassionate face of Halde, no help in those uniformed shapes. There was no file for prison bars, no rope ladder, no dummy to be left in the pallet bed. Here the thing that cried came up against an absolute of helplessness. It struck with the frantic writhing and viciousness of a captive snake against glass and bars. But in the physical world there was neither help nor hope of weakness that might be attacked and overcome. The bars were steel, were reinforcements of this surrounding concrete. There was no escape from the place, and the snake, the rat struck again from the place away from now into time. It struck with full force backwards into time past, saw with the urgency of present need that time past held only balm for a quieter moment; turned therefore and lunged, uncoiled, struck at the future. The future was the flight of steps from terror to terror, a mounting experiment that ignorance of what might be a bribe, made inevitable. The thing that cried fled forward over those steps because there was no other way to go, was shot forward screaming as into a furnace, as over unimaginable steps that were all that might be borne, were more, were too searing for the refuge of madness were destructive of the centre. The thing that screamed left all living behind and came to the entry where death is close as darkness against eyeballs.

And burst that door.

10

Therefore when the commandant let me out of the darkness he came late and as a second string, giving me the liberty of the camp when perhaps I no longer needed it. I walked between the huts, a man resurrected but not by him. I saw the huts as one who had little to do with them, was indifferent to them and the temporal succession of days that they implied. So they shone with the innocent light of their own created nature. I understood them perfectly, boxes of thin wood as they were, and now transparent, letting be seen inside their quotas of sceptred kings. I lifted my arms, saw them too, and was overwhelmed by their unendurable richness as possessions, either arm ten thousand fortunes poured out for me. Huge tears were dropping from my face into dust; and this dust was a universe of brilliant and fantastic crystals, that miracles instantly supported in their being. I looked up beyond the huts and the wire, I raised my dead eyes, desiring nothing, accepting all things and giving all created things away. The paper wrappings of use and language dropped from me. Those crowded shapes extending up into the air and down into the rich earth, those deeds of far space and deep earth were aflame at the surface and daunting by right of their own natures though a day before I should have disguised them as trees. Beyond them the mountains were not only clear all through like purple glass, but living. They sang and were conjubilant. They were not all that sang. Everything is related to everything else and all relationship is either discord or harmony. The power of gravity, dimension and space, the movement of the earth and sun and unseen stars, these made what might be called music and I heard it.

And now came what is harder to confess than cruelty. It happened as the first of my fellows left our hut and moved along the path towards me. He was a being of great glory on whom a whole body had been lavished, a lieutenant, his wonderful brain floating in its own sea, the fuel of the world working down transmuted through his belly. I saw him coming, and the marvel of him and these undisguised trees and mountains and this dust and music wrung a silent cry from me. This cry travelled away and along a fourth dimension at right-angles to the other three. The cry was directed to a place I did not know existed, but which I had forgotten merely; and once found, the place was always there, sometimes open and sometimes shut, the business of the universe proceeding there in its own mode, different, indescribable.

The awesome and advancing creature so arranged his flesh that sounds came visibly out of his mouth.

"Have you heard?"

But then he noticed the water on my face and was embarrassed by the sight of a crying Englishman.

"Sorry, Sammy. They're a lot of bloody murderers."

He looked away because he would have found it very easy to cry himself. But I was surrounded by a universe like a burst casket of jewels and I was dead anyway myself, knowing how little it mattered. So he wandered off, thinking I was round the bend, not comprehending my complete and luminous sanity. I returned to my fourth dimension and found that love flows along it until the heart, the physical heart, this pump or alleged pump makes love as easy as a bee makes honey. This seemed to me at that time the only worth-while occupation; and while I was so engaged the pace became so hot that a flake of fire, a brightness, flicked out of the hidden invisible and settled on the physical heart for all the world as though the heart is what poetry thinks it to be and not just a bit of clever machinery. Standing between the understood huts, among jewels and music, I was visited by a flake of fire, miraculous and pentecostal; and fire transmuted me, once and for ever.

How can a man listen and speak at the same time? There was so much to learn, so many adjustments to make that prison life became extremely busy and happy. For now the world was reorientated. What had been important dropped away. What had been ludicrous became common sense. What had had the ugliness of frustration and dirt, I now saw to have a curious reversed beauty—a beauty that could only be seen, out of the corner of the eye, a beauty which often only became apparent when it was remembered. All these things, of course, were explicable in two ways; the one explained them away, the other accepted them as data relevant to the nature of the cosmos. There was no argument possible between people holding either view. I knew that, because at different times of my life I had been either kind in turn. It seemed natural to me that this added perception in my dead eyes should flow over into work, into portraiture. That is why those secret, smuggled sketches of the haggard, unshaven kings of Egypt in their glory are the glory of my right hand and likely to remain so. My sketches of the transfigured camp, the prison which is no longer a prison are not so good, I think, but they have their merit. One or two of them see the place with the eye of innocence or death, see the dust and the wood and the concrete and the wire as though they had just been created. But the world of miracle I could not paint then or now.

For as time went on and I became accustomed to the rhythm of silence I began to learn about the new world. To be part of it was not just an ambition, but was a necessity. Therefore the thing in here, the dead thing that looked out must adapt its nature to conform. What was the nature of the new world outside and what was the nature of the dead thing inside?

Gradually I came to see that all this wonder formed an order of things and that the order depended on pillars. But the substance of these pillars when I understood what it was, confounded me utterly. We had thrown it away in the world, it was a joke. The brilliance of our political vision and the profundity of our scientific knowledge had enabled us to dispense with this substance. It had not been perceptible in the laboratory test-tube when we performed our simple qualitative analysis. It had caught no votes, it had not been suggested as a remedy for war, it was accounted for, if any account was needed as a byproduct of the class system, the same way as you get aniline dyes from the distillation of coal—an accident, almost. This substance was a kind of vital morality, not the relationship of a man to remote posterity nor even to a social system, but the relationship of individual man to individual man—once an irrelevance but now seen to be the forge in which all change, all value, all life is beaten out into a good or a bad shape. This live morality was, to change the metaphor, if not the gold, at least the silver of the new world.

Now at last, the eyes of Sammy turned and looked where Halde had directed them. To die is easy enough in the forcing chamber of a cell and to see the world with dead or innocent eyes is easy enough, too, if you can find the trick. But when the eyes of Sammy were turned in on myself with that same stripped and dead objectivity, what they saw was not beautiful but fearsome. Dying, after all, then was not one tenth complete—for must not complete death be to get out of the way of that shining, singing cosmos and let it shine and sing? And here was a point, a single point which was my own interior identity, without shape or size but only position. Yet this position was miraculous as everything else since it continually defied the law of conservation of energy, rule one as it were, and created shapes that fled away outwards along the radii of a globe. These shapes could be likened to nothing but the most loathsome substances that man knows of, or perhaps the most loathsome and abject creatures, continuously created, radiating swiftly out and disappearing from my sight; and this was the human nature I found inhabiting the centre of my own awareness. The light that showed up this point and these creatures came from the newly perceived world in all its glory. Otherwise I might have been a man who lived contentedly enough with his own nature.

But now to live with such a thing was unendurable. Nothing that Halde could do seemed half so terrible as what I knew myself. Was this thing common? Did I underestimate the privacies of the kings, would they too make such a showing? I did not think so then and I do not think so now. I knew one of them, Johnny Spragg, and I understood how there had been in him what had been missing in me; namely a natural goodness and generosity so that even his sins were peccadilloes because all the time the root of the matter was in him. But either I had been born without this natural generosity or I had lost it somewhere. The small boy trotting by Evie was nothing to do with me: but the young man waiting on the bike for the traffic lights to change from red—he and I dwelt in one skin. We were responsible the one for the other. So that when I thought back and came on the memory of Beatrice the beauty of her simplicity struck me a blow in the face. That negative personality, that clear absence of being, that vacuum which I had finally deduced from her silences, I now saw to have been full. Just as the substance of the living cell comes shining into focus as you turn the screw by the microscope, so I now saw that being of Beatrice which had once shone out of her face. She was simple and loving and generous and humble; qualities which have no political importance and do not commonly bring their owners much success. Like the ward for children, remembered, they shine. And yet as I remembered myself as well as Beatrice I could find no moment when I was free to do as I would. In all that lamentable story of seduction I could not remember one moment when being what I was I could do other than I did.

Oh, the continent of a man, the peninsulas, capes, deep bays, jungles and grasslands, the deserts, the lakes, the mountains and high hills! How shall I be rid of the kingdom, how shall I give it away?

If I could say with Nick Shales that the word freedom is a pious hope for an illusion I might accept the drag of all those half-dead days and not mind them. If I could say with Rowena Pringle only believe, might I not subside into some calming system of reward and punishment, profit and loss? But I know the taste of potatoes and I do not believe merely—I see. Or if I could only take the mud as mud, if I could only see people as ciphers and be bored by the average impact of a day! If I could only take this world for granted!

Somewhere, some time, I made a choice in freedom and lost my freedom. I lost nothing before the verger knocked me down; or perhaps that blow was like death and paid all debts. Between there, then and the boy on the bike, the young man—that was the whole time of the other school. There, somewhere there? Back among the flowers and smell of cloakrooms, among the exercise-books and savage emotions, back among the rewards and penalties, back with the sense of life going on like that for ever?

That school catered for both sexes. Mixed, officially, I can think of no other institution so rigidly divided. This division, however, was not forced on us. We created it ourselves from the very first day. In the first hours of awe, we sat by instinct, girls on the left-hand side of the classroom, boys on the right. A line was drawn then, and by our common consent was never broken. No boy, not even I, who still remembered the majesty of Evie's hair-ribbons, could have sat among the girls. Had I done so the sky would have broken apart and fallen on us. We did our best to pretend that we went to a boys' school; we understood that the pattern of education for us in our little country grammar school was dictated not by theoretic pedagogy but by economics. We were being done on the cheap and ought to be thankful for being done at all. So our gang warfare that rioted by the stream at the bottom of the playground was for boys only. Here, my anomalous position in the rectory gave me a rootless background so that I boasted in compensation—boasted with rudimentary feeling for the shape of our social pyramid that I was the rector's son, sort of—and became unpopular. It was in the shadows of this unpopularity that I moved slowly into adolescence, when the skin is flayed off and a feather weighs like lead and pricks like a pin. I was at home nowhere. There was bed, but bed with the irrational fear of ghosts and horrors; so that at this time I discovered how to huddle up and pull out of the body that comfort which the world could not give. Gradually I learned to short-circuit my own current and be sufficient, running myself down like a battery in one incandescent flash.

Under what sign in the sky did Sammy develop then? There were two of them. They loom now in my memory, the virgin and the water-carrier. They form an arch, not of triumph but of defeat, they are supporters to my shield, if anyone made me, they made me, spiritual parents, but not in the flesh.

She was the one who taught Scripture and various form subjects. She was the form mistress over us for a year, she was a middle-aged spinster with sandy hair and the beginnings of a sandy moustache and beard, she was Miss Rowena Pringle and she hated me partly because I was hateful and partly because she was hateful and partly because she had a crush on Father Watts-Watt—who had adopted me instead of marrying her—and who was slowly going mad. She had an exquisite niminy-piminy lady-like air. To see her find that she had a blot of ink on her finger—hand up, fingers tapping in a bunch at each other like a tiny, lily-white octopus—was to appreciate how hysterically clean a lady can be. She withdrew from anything that was soiled—not dirty, soiled—and her religious instruction was just like that. Her clothes were usually in tones of brown. In rainy weather she would come to school in a brown macintosh neatly belted, she would wear goloshes and gloves, and be protected over all by a brown umbrella with scallops and silk tassels. She would vanish into the women's staffroom and presently appear in class, picking her way to her high desk, as delicately neat and clean as a chestnut. She wore pince-nez, gold rimmed with a fairy gold chain of almost invisible gold links that descended to the frilly lace on her bosom and was pinned there with a teeny-weeny gold pin. Near the pin there was the watery-gold glimmer of a cut topaz. She had sandy hair, a freckled, slightly fattened face that usually wore a smile of professional benevolence, as arranged and external as her clothes.

Miss Pringle never touched anyone. A good, solid clout such as the verger gave me, was not in her repertoire. You knew that for Miss Pringle to touch human flesh would be a defilement. Those white fingers, with the gold ring on the right hand, were private and set apart. She ruled, not by love but by fear. Her weapons were no cane, they were different, subtle and cruel, unfair and vicious. They were teeny, arch sarcasms that made the other children giggle and tore the flesh. She was a past-master of crowd psychology and momentum. She could give our giggles a touch at the right moment, wait, touch again, like a man with a pendulum, wait, touch, wait, touch until her victim was savaged by the storm of derision, was gasping for breath in the wretched flayed flesh—was on the hooks. And all the time she would be smiling her professional smile while the gold chain of her pince-nez flicked and twinkled; for, after all, it is a joy to practise one's religion and be paid for it.

She need not have disliked me so much for I was with her. I was still innocent of the major good and evil; I thought no evil, I believed when she made me suffer that the fault was mine. I condemn her out of my adult stature. The flayed child that I was in her hands did not understand that truth is useless and pernicious when it proceeds from nothing but the mouth.

For I was with her. To me, these stories of good and

wicked men, these stories where the scale is good and evil seemed the hub of life, the essential business. Agincourt was a great victory; but Jacob laid his head on a stone—I saw how hard it was and uncomfortable—and dreamed of a ladder of gold that reached into heaven. Watt invented the steam-engine; but a voice spoke to Moses out of a bush that burned and was not consumed away. Yes. I was with her.

For in that way she was a good teacher. She told her stories with the vivid detail you sometimes get from people who are frustrated mentally and sexually. It was years before I saw the stories of the Old Testament in any way but through her eyes. It was years before I saw how she had achieved the apparently impossible by bowdlerizing the stories and yet keeping their moral implications clear to us. My hand was always the first up with an earnest question, my maps of the Holy Land were the most detailed, my illustrations of lightning flashing from Mount Sinai the most vividly realized. All would not do. My question was sure to turn into nothing but a dolly service to Miss Pringle who could ace me with a return as vivid as my own lightning; as for my maps, they were marked in such a way that her red ink contrived to ruin them.

I pry round my memories of this relationship. Did she perhaps know that I had spat, however dryly, on the altar? Did she resent my presence as a piece of slum-land that was in process of reclamation? Did she resent my living in the rectory? Did she perhaps divine intuitively what was unusual about Father Watts-Watt and credit me with his affection? Were we simply incompatible temperaments, the involved, frustrated spinster and the boy, tough—but now not so tough—simple and incredibly still innocent? What did I do that I should always be her target? Or can I place my hand on my heart and claim for once to be a blameless victim? Is there something that is not my fault? Certainly she was not always in such ordered control of herself. She was not invulnerable. She bore the curse of Eve like all women and with less stoicism than most. As time went on we found that she had occasional days when teaching was too much for her altogether. She would sit at her high desk, lolling back, eyes closed, rolling her head from side to side and sighing. Then, such was the force of her cruelty and discipline that we would not dare to sympathize or exploit—we were mouse-still all the period until the heavenly bell. It was almost a relief to return to her a day or so later and find her in control again, smiling and dangerous.

I see her with my fatal eye, I span the gulf. Her mouth is flapping open and shut. Is the electric light on? If only I could hear as well as see!

There is a chalk triangle on the board behind her, an irrelevant triangle. The lace is light brown, extends halfway up her neck. If I drove my elbow sideways I should hit Johnny Spragg in the ribs. Philip is in front of me and to the right. But this is not that sort of lesson, this is important, can be breath-taking. Moses.

I am deeply interested in Moses. He is more important than the composition of water. I am willing to be told about water when we get to Mr. Shales's lesson but Moses is far more important. I want to know all about Moses that can be known. I know the story from infant school days, have had it here and there, till the plagues and all that are etched in me. But they—Miss Massey, pugilistic

Miss Massey—they stop just where you want to know. His story turns into the story of the Israelites, that wearisome bunch who can be relied on to do the wrong thing. Perhaps Miss Pringle—I recognize her expertise—will not make this mistake, if it is a mistake. Perhaps she can fill in the gaps for me. I know that the Bible contains many laws that Moses is alleged to have ordained; but these, too, are irrelevant. What was that rock in which he was hidden, where the Lord passed by and covered Moses meanwhile with one hand? There should be as full an account of that end of his life as there is of the beginning. Perhaps—I think as the class settles itself—perhaps Miss Pringle who knows so much will let us into that secret. This, then, will be a real step up, a step forward; to be old enough for her to lift the curtains from that end of his life——

For she could lift curtains, could Miss Pringle. She told us why the veil of the temple was torn at the crucifixion, told us directly and explicitly why it was torn not transversely nor destroyed but torn from the top to the bottom. This was deeply satisfactory; and sometimes she did the same for Moses. We understood the relationship between the speaker Aaron and the seer Moses by the time she had finished with us. Yet she would mix this profound exegesis with matter that was useless and even distressing. I would sit in my desk, and wonder why when she could speak so deeply to us, she could also say such cheap and silly things, like the Red Sea sometimes being parted—the waters driven back—by the wind; or snakes being cataleptic like lobsters when you stroke them or chicken at a chalk line; and therefore the rods thrown down were not a plain and lovely miracle but explicable, if you leant over backwards.

And Moses came to the mountain, even to Horeb.

Flap, flap, twinkle from the spectacles, watery glimmer of topaz——

I cannot hear her.

You did these things to me. In some ways you were wise; but you were cruel. Why can I not hear you? You did these things, you said the words that have vanished. They did not go into the air and die; they sank into me deep, they have become me, they are so close to me I cannot hear them. You said them and passed on, you were preoccupied with your own affairs. Will you not stand to them? Is the world truly what the world looks like to the outward eye, a place where anything goes if you can get away with it?

Flap, flap, twinkle.

There were three ways she might have taken. She might have explained that there is a kind of bush in the desert which burns for a very long time and sometimes catches fire in the sun.

No.

Flap flap.

She might have told us that Moses saw this with the eyes of the spirit. There was no bush to the outward eye; and only to dwell on this bush—for bush will do as well as any other word—only to dwell, is to find it expanding, filling all space and being, taking fire with colours like the rainbow.

Flap——

"I am sure you have all heard this part of the Bible before. So I shall ask you some questions about it. After all you are supposed to be a little wiser now than you were a year ago. Mount Horeb. What did Moses see on Mount Horeb?"

"A bush, miss, a burning bush'n the Angel of the Lord spoke out of the bush 'n——"

"That will do. Yes. Was there anyone in the bush?"

"Miss! Miss! Miss!"

"Wilmot? Yes. Did Moses ever meet him again?"

"Miss! Miss!"

"Jennifer? Yes. On Mount Sinai. Did he see clearly?"

"Miss!"

"Of course not. Even Moses had to be content with 'I am that I am'."

"Miss! Miss!"

"What is it, Mountjoy?"

"Please, miss, 'e knew more'n that!"

"Ah——"

I knew then what a fool I was; I knew that if explaining myself to Father Watts-Watt was impossible it was dangerous with Miss Pringle. How could I say—of course you know, too, I am only reminding you or perhaps you were only pretending so that one of us would please you by giving more than a dull agreement—but I was too late.

Miss Pringle spread a delighted beam over the class and invited them to share with her the enjoyment of this captive.

"Mountjoy is going to tell us something we do not know, children."

There was, as she knew, a little ripple at that. She took the ripple just before it had died away.

"Mountjoy knows the Bible better than we do, of course. After all, he lives very near the church."

The pendulum began to swing.

"Silence for Mr. Mountjoy, children. He is going to explain the Bible to us."

I could see how red my nose was getting.

"Well, Mountjoy? Aren't you going to give us the—scholarly results of your researches?"

"It was later on, miss, after 'e'd——"

"He'd, Mountjoy, not 'e'd. I'm sure the rector wants you to improve your accent as quickly as possible. Well?"

" 'E—He wanted to see, miss, but it would 've been too much for—him."

"What are you talking about, Mountjoy?"

"Miss, Moses, miss."

Now the laughter flailed. There were cries of Miss Moses that Miss Pringle allowed to increase just this side of riot.

"It was after, miss."

"After?"

"It would 've been too much. So he was hid in a crack in the rock 'n 'e—he saw 'is backparts it says, miss, an' I was going to ask you——"

"What did you say?"

Now I was conscious of the silence, shocked off short.

"It says 'e saw——"

"When did you read that?"

"It was when you told us to learn the, learn the——"

"That was the New Testament lesson, Mountjoy. Why were you looking at the Old?"

"I'd finished, miss, 'n I thought——"

"So you'd finished? You didn't say so. You didn't think to tell me and ask my permission for this, this——"

The topaz shook and glittered.

"Very well, Mountjoy, so you'd finished your verses. Say them."

But next to my mind as I stood, blinded and dumb in

the desk was the picture of this event as a journey on the wrong track, a huge misunderstanding.

"It was jus' that I wanted to know, miss, the way you said about the veil and all that——"

"Say them!"

The blackness of torment turned red. There were no words on my tongue.

"Say them, Mountjoy. 'Blessed are the——' "

Don't you understand? I'm on your side, really. I know that the openings are more important to you than the silly plausibilities of explaining away. I know that the book is full of wonder and importance. I am not like Johnny on my left who will take it as read, or Philip in front who is looking at you and wondering how he can learn to use you. My delight is your delight.

Miss Pringle shifted her hand forward to another manual. Here was *vox humana*. We heard this voice sometimes, her wounded voice, voice of Rachel weeping for her children, always the prelude to savagery.

"—thought I could trust you. And so I can, most of you. But there is one boy who cannot be trusted. He uses a lesson—not even an ordinary lesson——"

"But, miss! Please, miss——"

Miss Pringle had me standing up where she wanted me. If I did not understand the enormity of my offence, if I was still acquainted with innocence and held the belief that there was room for me somewhere in the scheme of things, nevertheless Miss Pringle felt herself able to undermine me and dedicated herself to that end.

"Come out here in front of the class."

There was a strange obedience about my two hands that grasped the sides of the seat and helped to lift me. My feet trod obediently and deeper into the dark. She had implied so much in one sentence. By an inflection, a quiver of the topaz she had lifted this episode now above laughing so that the rest of the class had to readjust to seriousness. Miss Pringle had enough showmanship to know that she must not run away from her audience. She gave them time to settle into the new mood by looking so long and searchingly into my face that my blush burned and their silence began to fill with excitement.

"That's what you think the Bible is for then. Oh, no, Mountjoy, don't start to deny it. Do you suppose that I really don't know what you're like? We all know where you come from, Mountjoy, and we were willing to regard it as your misfortune."

I saw her brown leather shoes that were polished like chestnuts take a little step back.

"But you have brought the place with you. Money has been spent on you, Mountjoy. You have been given a great opportunity. But instead of profiting by it, instead of being grateful, you use your time here, searching through the Bible with a snigger, searching for—for——"

She paused and the silence was deeper still. They all knew what little boys searched the Bible for, because most of them did it. Perhaps that was why my crime—but what was it, I thought?—my crime seemed monstrous to them, too. I thought then, that the trouble was my lack of ability to explain myself. I had a hazy feeling that if only I could find the right words, Miss Pringle would understand and the whole business be disposed of. But I know now that she would not have accepted even the most elaborately accurate explanation. She would have dodged it with furious agility and put me back in the wrong.

She was clever and perceptive and compelled and cruel.

"Look at me. I said, 'Look at me!' "

"Miss."

"And then—then! To have the insolence—there is no other word for it—to have the insolence to throw your nastiness in my face!"

She had both white hands up and away. They were cleaning their own fingers as if they would never be clean. The cascade of lace was moving quickly in and out. Now the class understood that this was to be execution in form, public and long drawn out.

Miss Pringle proceeded to the next step. Justice must not only be done, must be seen to be done. She required evidence of misdoing more than my unfortunate slip in theology. Of course there was one sure way of getting that. Most of the masters and mistresses in that school did not care enough about us to be cruel. They even recognized our right to separate existence and this recognition took a pleasant shape. We were made to keep our exercise-books very clean and neat; but we had rough work books, too; and by custom, unspoken, undefined, these books were private. So long as you did not defile them too openly or be outrageously wasteful, they were as private to us as his study to the scholar.

Had she convinced herself? Did she believe by now that I regularly searched the Bible for smut? Did she not understand that we were two of a kind, the earnest metaphysical boy and the tormented spinster, or did she know that and get an added kick from hatred of her own image? Did she really think she would find smut in my rough book; or was she willing to take anything legally wrong if she could find it?

"Get your rough work book."

I went back to my desk underground. The silence vibrated and Johnny would not meet my eye. One of my stockings was down round my ankle. My right ankle. There was no cover on the rough work book. The first four pages were crumpled and then the pages got flatter and cleaner. Since the first page now did duty for the cover most of my drawing there had worn away.

"Ugh!"

Miss Pringle refused my offer.

"I am not going to touch it, Mountjoy. Put it on the desk. Now. Turn over the pages. Well? What do you say?"

"Miss."

I began to turn the pages and the class watched eagerly.

Arithmetic and a horse pulling the roller over the town cricket pitch. Some wrongly spelt French verbs, repeated. A cart on the weighing machine outside the town hall. Lines. I must not pass notes in class. I must not—the old DH coming round a tower of clouds. Answers to grammar questions. Arithmetic. Latin. Some profiles. A landscape, not drawn, so much as noted down and then elaborated in my own private notation. For how could a pencil convey the peculiar attraction of a white chalk road seen from miles away as it wound up the side of the downs? In the middle distance was a complication of trees and hillocks into which the eye was drawn and into which the troubled spectator could vanish. This was not sketched but put down meticulously. This was so much my own private property that I turned a page hurriedly.

"Wait! Turn back."

Miss Pringle looked from me to the landscape, then back again.

"Why do you hurry over that page, Mountjoy? Is there something there that you don't want me to see?"

Silence.

Miss Pringle examined my landscape inch by inch. I could feel the excitement of my fellows, now transformed to bloodhounds on the trail and hot on the back of my neck.

Miss Pringle extended a white finger and began to give the edge of the rough work book little taps so that it moved round and presented my hillocks, my scalloped downs and deep woodlands to her, upright. Her hand clenched and whipped away. She drew a shuddering breath. She spoke and her voice was deep with awe and passionate anger, with outrage and condemnation.

"Now, I see!"

She turned to the class.

"I had a little garden, children, full of lovely flowers. I was glad to work in my little garden because the flowers were so gay and lovely. But I did not know that there were weeds and slugs and snails and hideous slimy, crawling things——"

Then she turned on me and tore a vivid gash through my soul with the raw edge of a suddenly savage voice.

"I shall see that the rector knows about this, Mountjoy, and I'm going to take you to the headmaster now!"

I waited outside the door with my book while she went into the headmaster's study. I heard their voices and the interview was short. She came out and swept past me and then the headmaster told me sternly, to come in.

"Give me the book."

He was angry, there was no doubt about that. I suppose she had pointed out what was unnecessary—that we were a mixed school and this sort of thing must be stamped on immediately. I think perhaps he was resigned to having an expulsion on his hands.

He thumbed through the whole book, paused and then thumbed through it again. When he spoke next, the gruffness had gone from his voice—or rather was modified as though he knew that he must retain some outrage for the sake of appearances.

"Well, Mountjoy. Which page does Miss Pringle object to?"

She seemed to object to all of them. I was confused by events and unable to answer.

He thumbed through again. His voice became testy.

"Now listen, Mountjoy. Which page is it? Did you tear it out while you were waiting outside?"

I shook my head. He examined the sewn centre of the book, saw that there was no odd page. He looked back at me.

"Well?"

I found my voice.

"It was that one, sir, there."

The headmaster bent over the book. He examined my landscape. I saw that the complex centre trapped his sight, too. His eye went forward, plunged through the paper among hillocks and trees. He withdrew from it and his forehead was puzzled. He glanced down at me, then back at the paper. Suddenly he did what Miss Pringle had done—turned the book so that my lovely curved downs were upright, the patch of intricate woodland projecting from them.

We entered a place then which I should now call chaos. I did not know what was the matter, I felt nothing but pain and astonishment. But he, the adult, the headmaster, he did not know anything either. He had taken a pace forward and the ground had disappeared. He had realized something in a flash and the knowledge had presented him at once with a number of insoluble problems. But he was a wise man and he did what is always best in such circumstances; that is, nothing. He allowed me to watch his face on which so much became visible. I saw the results of his knowledge even though I could not share it. I saw an appalled realization, I saw impotence to cope, I saw even the beginning of wild laughter.

Then he went and looked out of the window for a little.

"You know, Mountjoy, we don't give you a rough work book to draw in, do we?"

"Sir."

"Miss Pringle objects to your wasting so much time with a pencil."

There was nothing to be said to this. I waited.

"These pages——"

He turned round then and opened the book to show me, but caught sight of something. It was a page where I had drawn as many of the form as I could. Some of them had defeated me; but for one or two I had drawn face after face, elaborating then simplifying so that the final result gave me a deep satisfaction as I sent the passionate message down the pencil. He pushed his spectacles up on his forehead and held the page close.

"That's young Spragg!"

At that the chaos came out of my eyes. It was wet and warm and I could not stop.

"Oh, now, look here!"

I felt round me for a handkerchief but, of course, I had

none. I took out my bright school cap and used it instead. When I could see again the headmaster was stroking his moustache and looking defeated. He gave himself another breather out of the window. Gradually I dried up.

"Well, there you are then. Keep your drawing within bounds. I think perhaps I'd better keep this rough work book. And try to——"

He paused for a long time.

"Try to understand that Miss Pringle cares deeply about you all. See if you can please her. Well?"

"Sir."

"And tell Miss Pringle that I—should be glad to have a word with her in break. Right?"

"Sir."

"You'd better go and—no. Go now. Straight back to the class as you are. I'll see that you get a new rough work book."

I went back to the class with my stained face and gave her the headmaster's message. She ignored me save for one imperious sweep of the hand and a pointing finger. I saw why. In my absence she had had my desk moved out of the body of the class. It rested now against the wall right out in front where I should not contaminate the others by my presence. I sank into the seat and was alone. Here I was, with the waves of public disapprobation beating on the back of my neck. I have never minded them since. There I remained for the rest of that term. Sitting alone, I was introduced to the Stuarts. Sitting alone I followed Miss Pringle forward from Gethsemane.

Nowadays I can understand a great deal about Miss Pringle. The male priest at the altar might have taken a comely and pious woman to his bosom; but he chose to withdraw into the fortress of his rectory and have to live with him a slum child, a child whose mother was hardly human. I understand how I must have taxed her, first with my presence, then with my innocence and finally with my talent. But how could she crucify a small boy, tell him that he sat out away from the others because he was not fit to be with them and then tell the story of that other crucifixion with every evidence in her voice of sorrow for human cruelty and wickedness? I can understand how she hated, but not how she kept on such apparent terms of intimacy with heaven.

But now, on that first ignorant and chaotic day we were still with Moses. The harrow had been over my soul and I cared a little less about him.

"And so as a sign to Moses that the Lord was present, the bush burned with fire but was not consumed away."

High in the belfry, relief sounded. We piled out of the room, I uncertain of my reception after my crucifixion and went straight into the lecture-room for general elementary science.

Mr. Shales, Nick Shales, Old Nick was there, waiting for us. He was impatient to begin. The light shone from his enormous bald head and his thick glasses. He had cleaned the board with the tail of his gown and a pillar of white dust hung in the air round him. There was bent glass on the demonstration bench and he stood, leaning his weight on his knuckles, and watching us as we clambered up the steps between the ranged forms.

Nick was the best teacher I ever knew. He had no particular method and he gave no particular picture of brilliance; it was just that he had a vision of nature and a passionate desire to communicate it. He respected children too. This was not a verbal respect for children's rights because it never occurred to Nick that they had any. They were just human beings and he treated each one with serious attention indistinguishable from courtesy. He kept discipline by ignoring the need to enforce it. See him now, waiting impatiently for us all, he included, to examine some fascination of fact, some absorbing reality which never could fail to astonish——

"Better take this down in your books because we are going to try and disprove it. Ready? Here you are then. 'Matter can neither be destroyed nor created'."

Obediently we wrote. Nick began to talk. He was imploring us to find a case where matter was either destroyed or created.

"In a shell."

"A candle burning——"

"Eating."

"When a chicken comes out——"

Eagerly we gave him examples. Sagely he nodded and disposed of each.

Yet not one of us thought of Miss Pringle next door and her lessons. We might have shouted together that a burning bush that burned and was not consumed away surely violated the scheme of Nick's rational universe as he unfolded it to us. But no one said a word about her. We crossed from one universe into another when we came out of her door and went into his. We held both universes in our heads effortlessly because by the nature of the human being, neither of them was real. Both systems were coherent—was it some deep instinct that told us the universe does not come so readily to heel and kept us from inhabiting either? For all Miss Pringle's vivid descriptions that world existed over there, not here.

Neither was this world of Nick's a real thing. It was not enveloping; each small experimental result was not multiplied out to fill the universe. If he did the multiplication we watched and marvelled. Nick would paint a picture of the stars in their courses as a consequence of his demonstrations of captive gravity. Then not science but poetry filled him and us. His deductions stood on tiptoe reaching out to the great arithmetical and stellar dance; but neither he nor we looked at the sky. A generation was to pass before I myself saw the difference between the imaginary concept and the spread picture overhead. Nick thought he spoke of real things.

A candle burnt under a bell-jar. Water rose and filled the space once occupied by oxygen. The candle went out but not before it had lighted up a universe of such orderliness and sanity that one must perforce cry; the solution to all problems is here! If there were problems, nevertheless they must contain their own solution. It would not be a rational universe in which problems were insoluble.

What men believe is a function of what they are; and what they are is in part what has happened to them. And yet here and there in all that riot of compulsion comes the clear taste of potatoes, element so rare the isotope of uranium is abundant by comparison. Surely Nick was familiar with that taste for he was a selfless man. He was born of poor parents and had nearly killed himself working his way up. Knowledge, therefore, was most precious to him. He had no money for apparatus and made things work from tin and bent glass and vulcanite. His mirror galvanometer was a wonder of delicacy; and once he produced the aurora borealis for us, captive like a rare butterfly, in a length of glass tubing. He did not care to make technicians of us, he wanted us to understand the world around us. There was no place for spirit in his cosmos and consequently the cosmos played a huge practical joke on him. It gave Nick a love of people, a selflessness, a kindness and justice that made him a homeland for all people; and at the same time it allowed him to preach the gospel of a most drearily rationalistic universe that the children hardly noticed at all. At the beginning of break he could not get away to the staffroom for the crowd of children round his dirty gown who were questioning, watching, or just illogically and irrationally wanting to be near. He would answer patiently, would say when he did not know the answer, would receive the creature before him openly as of equal stature and importance. Nick had come out of a slum as I had, but by his own brains and will. He was not lifted; he lifted himself and his short body was the legacy of semi-starvation and years of overwork. He was a socialist and had been one in the heat of the day; but his socialism was like his natural philosophy; logical and kind and of astonishing beauty. He saw a new earth, not one in which he himself would have more money and do less work for it, but one in which we country children would have schools as good as Eton. He wanted the whole bounty of the earth for us and for all people. Sometimes now that the British Empire has been dissolved and I meet natives of one hot land or another who are triumphant in their claims to have freed themselves, I think of Nick; Nick who would have freed them sixty years ago to his own cost. Yet he had no possessions himself; he neither drank nor smoked nor had a car. He had nothing that I saw except an old blue serge suit and a black gown gnawed into a net by acid. He denied the spirit behind creation; for what is nearest the eye is hardest to see.

These two people, Nick Shales and Rowena Pringle, loom larger behind me as I get older. Mine is the responsibility but they are part reasons for my shape, they had and have a finger in my pie. I cannot understand myself without understanding them. Because I have pondered them both so deeply I know now things about them which I did not know then. I always knew that Miss Pringle hated Nick Shales; and now, because I am so much like her, I know why. She hated him because he found it easy to be good. The so-respectable school marm with her clean fingers was eaten up with secret desires and passions. No matter how she built up the dam on this and that, the unruly and bilious flood of her nature burst forth. May she not have tortured herself in despair and self-loathing, every time she tortured me? And how she must have writhed, to see Nick, the rationalist, followed by children as if he were a saint! No one liked her, except a succession of dim and sycophantic girls, a line of acolytes not worth having. Perhaps she half understood how flimsy a virtue her accidental virginity was, perhaps sometimes in a grey light before the first bird she saw herself as in a mirror and knew she was powerless to alter. But to Nick the rationalist, the atheist, all things were possible.

I needed Nick that lesson, not to teach but be there. I think he noticed my stained face and this led him into his usual error of exercising charity for the wrong reason. He fancied, I believe, that the contrast between my position at the rectory and my known, my almost brandished bastardy had been flung at my head. So he took pains to keep me back after the class had gone, to help him put the apparatus away.

But I said nothing. I was incapable of explaining what had happened. So Nick talked instead. He cleaned the board again with his filthy gown and put his notes away in the desk.

"Have you got any more drawings to show me, young Mountjoy?"

"Sir."

"What I like about your drawings is that they look like the things they're meant to be."

"Yes, sir."

"Faces. Now how do you manage to draw faces? I can see that a landscape might need rearranging; but faces have to look like somebody. Wouldn't a photograph be better?"

"I s'pose it would, sir."

"Well then!"

"Haven't got a camera, sir."

"No. Of course not."

We had finished putting away the apparatus. Nick turned and sat perched on his high stool and I stood near him, one hand on the demonstration bench. He said nothing at all; but there was in his silence a placid acceptance of me and all my ways. He took off his spectacles, polished them, put them on and looked up out of the window. There were rich bulges of cloud unfolding above the horizon and he began to tell me about them. They were thunderheads, anvil-shaped spaces in which power was building up. This time he went from the particular to the general for my benefit. The weather from the Arctic down became a gorgeous dance in slow, tremendous time. When he finished, we were side by side, contemplating this together and as equals.

"You wouldn't think people could be cruel. You wouldn't think they would have the time, not in a world like this. Wars, persecutions, exploitations—I mean, Sammy, there's so much to look at, for me to examine and for you to paint—put it this way. If you took all this away from a, a millionaire, he'd give all his money for no more than a glimpse of the sky or the sea——"

I was laughing and nodding back at him; because it *was* so obvious to us both and so astonishingly not obvious to all the others.

"—I remember when I first learnt that a planet sweeps out equal areas in equal times—it seemed to me that armies would stop fighting—I mean—I must have been about your age—that they would see how ridiculous a waste of time——"

"Did they, sir? Did they really?"

"Did who?"

"The armies."

Slowly the difference between the adult and the child re-established itself.

"No. They didn't. I'm afraid not. If you do that sort of thing you become that sort of animal. The universe is wonderfully exact, Sammy. You can't have your penny and your bun. Conservation of energy holds good mentally as well as physically."

"But, sir——"

"What?"

Understanding came to me. His law spread. I saw it holding good at all times and in all places. That cool allaying rippled outward. The burning bush resisted and I understood instantly how we lived a contradiction. This was a moment of such importance to me that I must examine it completely. For an instant out of time, the two worlds existed side by side. The one I inhabited by nature, the world of miracle drew me strongly. To give up the burning bush, the water from the rock, the spittle on the eyes was to give up a portion of myself, a dark and inward and fruitful portion. Yet looking at me from the bush was the fat and freckled face of Miss Pringle. The other world, the cool and reasonable was home to the friendly face of Nick Shales. I do not believe that rational choice stood any chance of exercise. I believe that my child's mind was made up for me as a choice between good and wicked fairies. Miss Pringle vitiated her teaching. She failed to convince, not by what she said but by what she was. Nick persuaded me to his natural scientific universe by what he was not by what he said. I hung for an instant between two pictures of the universe; then the ripple passed over the burning bush and I ran towards my friend. In that moment a door closed behind me. I slammed it shut on Moses and Jehovah. I was not to knock on that door again, until in a Nazi prison camp I lay huddled against it half crazed with terror and despair.

Here?

Not here.

Yet the future was not wholly in her hands or his, for now there was wine spilt in our blood to emerge in pimples and fantasies of the wakeful bed and in sniggers, in sexual sniggers, the lore of the small town and the village. There were catchwords only mentioned to call forth the dirty laugh. There was a sense of inferiority because Self did not know why the guffaw, would like to be on the ball, know the inside story, the dirt, would like the social security of belonging to the tribe, to those who know. And, of course, here Nick's universe of cause and effect, his soulless universe fitted like a glove. I was more intelligent than Nick. I saw that if man is the highest, is his own creator, then good and evil is decided by majority vote. Conduct is not good or bad, but discovered or got away with. Self, then, emerging from his preoccupation with Moses and trying to find out why for two days cherries are so ludicrous and somehow to do with the silent country girl Selina. Self listening to Johnny and getting in on a bit of current dirt for the first time. Self hearing Mr. Carew use the crash word in history and laughing before anyone else and getting fifty lines but well, well worth it. Self right in, knowing all the dirt, inventing dirt, a leading muck raker in the warm sniggery world, home.

Self looking in the mirror.

I saw myself as a very ugly creature. The face that looked at mine was always solemn and shadowed. The black hair, the wiry black eyebrows were not luxuriant but coarse. The features set themselves sternly as I strove to draw them and find out what I really was. The ears stood out, the forehead and the jaw receded. I felt myself to be anthropoid and tough, in appearance, no lady's man but masculine.

But I would have liked to be a girl. This was in the fantasy world where their skirts and hair, their soft faces and the neatness of their bellies had always been. But now when the wine spilt, with added intensity came the scent of talcum, the difference of a breast, glitter of brooches in Woolworth's, round, silk knees, the black treacle of their celluloid mouths, their mouths like wounds. I wanted to be one of them and thought this unique as self-abuse and very shameful. But I was mistaken all round. Masturbation is universal. Our sex is always uncertain. I wanted not so much to become as to enjoy. Then when the mechanism of sex became clear to me I knew only too well what I wanted. In the pages of my rough book the girls' faces began to outnumber the others. The currents were running. Ambivalent and green we had sat for three years in the same room, neutral as anemones on the wet rock. The tide was stirring us. There was scent in the air and on the lips of the celluloid beauties. We looked across the room, searching among the live creatures for a trace of those lineaments that had launched a thousand films.

How if Miss Pringle had been as good and as attractive as Nick? Would prayer and meditation have cooled the fever? Would the beauty of holiness have triumphed over the cheap scent and the flickering, invented faces? Should I have drawn the nine orders of the angels?

Philip could not draw at all. He sat by me in Art and it was an understood thing that I would do his work quickly before I did my own. Miss Curtis, the spinster who taught us, was a sensible woman. She let sleeping dogs lie though she knew well enough what was going on. The morning I think of was no more outwardly noteworthy than she—yet she first encouraged me and I liked her well enough. We sat round in a hollow square; and sometimes the platform in the middle would have a cone or ball on it, sometimes a chair and a violin: sometimes a live model.

The girl who sat there that morning was known to me slightly. She sat usually across the room and to the back. She was a mouse. I proposed in my mind not to draw her, but to concentrate on little stick men besieging a castle instead. But Philip nudged me. I glanced at the girl and scrawled her in with about two lines and a couple of patches of offhand shading. Then I returned to my scaling ladders.

Miss Curtis moved round behind the desks. I began to make tokens of working at this model. Perhaps there was something unusual in my decision not to draw her. I may have—who knows? Seen with other eyes, or remembered the future. I may have been trying to avoid the life laid down for me.

"Philip Arnold! Why, Philip!"

Miss Curtis was behind and between us. We turned our shoulders together.

"That's very good indeed!"

She leaned forward, she seized the paper and walked quickly to the board with it. All the boys and girls leaned back and looked up. The model coughed and moved, Miss Curtis went over the drawing in detail. Philip sunned himself and I chewed up a pencil in my rage. She came back to the desk.

"Don't do any more work on it, Arnold. Just sign it."

Philip smirked and signed. Miss Curtis looked at me with creased cheeks and a glittering eye.

"If you could draw like that, Mountjoy, I would say that one day you might be an artist."

She went away, smiling a little and I examined my orphaned portrait. I was astonished. In carelessness and luck I had put the girl on paper in a way that my laborious portraitures could never come at. The line leapt, it was joyous, free, authoritative. It achieved little miracles of implication so that the viewer's eye created her small hands though my pencil had not touched them. That free line had raced past and created her face, had thinned and broken where no pencil could go, but only the imagination. Astonished and proud I looked back at the model.

There was a certain flamboyance in the pictures on the wall behind her, dancers by Degas, some rococo Italian architecture and a palladian bridge; and she took her place by appearance and cooled them. The egg and the sperm had decreed a girl and that difference was there in the bone. I could see that one of these fingers held against the light would be transparent; and possibly the palm also. I could assess the fragility of the skeleton, the hollows either side of the brow—like the reverse of a petal. I saw—let me be exact where exactitude is impossible—I saw in her face what I can neither describe or draw. Say she was beautiful to me. Say that her face summed up and expressed innocence without fatuity, bland femininity without the ache of sex. Say that as she sat there, hands in her lap, face lit from a high window she was contained and harmless, docile and sweet. Then know that nothing has been said to touch or describe the model set before us.

Only I now declare across a generation to the ghost of Nick Shales and to the senile shape of Rowena Pringle, I saw there in her face and around the openness of her brow, a metaphorical light that none the less seemed to me to be an objective phenomenon, a real thing. Instant by instant she became an astonishment, a question, a mountain standing in my path. I could tell myself before that first lesson ended that she was nothing but a girl with fair hair and a rather sweet expression; but even then I knew better.

How big is a feeling? Where does an ache start and end? We live from hand to mouth, presented with a situation before which and in which we execute our dance. I have said that our decisions are not logical but emotional. We have reason and are irrational. It is easy now to be wise about her. If I saw that light of heaven, why then it should have been a counterpoise to Nick's rationalism. But my model was flesh and blood. She was Beatrice Ifor; and besides that unearthly expression, that holy light, she had knees sometimes silk and young buds that lifted her blouse when she breathed. She was one of those rare girls who never have an awkward age, who are always neat, always a little smoother than their sisters. They become a blinding contradiction. Their untouched, bland faces are angels of the annunciation; and yet there is a tight-rope poise in their walk which is an invitation to what Father Watts-Watt would have called Bad Thoughts. She was demure but unconsciously so. She was like other girls in that she was a girl, but she was unique for me in being what I can only describe as a lot more so. She was untouched and unapproachable. She came from a home of respectable tradespeople and now that the barrier down the middle of the class was breaking, now that the currents were sorting us into types and groups and temporary pairs she remained remote and untroubled. No one could expect giggles or badinage from her. Her great eyes, light grey and lucent under the long lashes, looked at nothing, at a nothing hanging in the air. Now with passion I repeated her profile on the page but she eluded me. I never recaptured the inspired ease which came from luck and not caring. Yet my masterpiece lay there and Philip Arnold had written his name across the bottom right-hand corner. Miss Curtis extracted some amusement from the situation. When that stolen portrait, or if you like, when that freely given portrait was put up in pride of place at the prize-day exhibition she went out of her way to praise it. After I had resented Miss Curtis long enough she merely remarked to me that there was plenty more where that came from. But to my terror and continuing frustration I could not catch the being of Beatrice on paper no matter how I studied her. She was flattered by the portrait and gave Philip the beginnings of a smile that stabbed me to the heart. For now I was lost. She could not be avoided or walked round. The compulsion was on me. Somehow I must draw her again successfully; and this required careful study. But the careful study only blinded me. She was of fearful importance and yet when the door closed behind her I could not remember her face. I could not catch this particular signature of being which made her unique; I could not remember it. I could only suffer. Then when she appeared again my reeling heart recognized a beauty that is young as the beginning of the world. In my fantasy world the dreams were generous enough. I wanted to rescue her from something violent. She was lost in a forest and I found her. We slept in a hollow tree, she in my arms, close, her face on my shoulder. And there was the light round her brow of paradise.

Let us see if the outcome could have been different. To whom could I have gone and spoken of this? Nick would have dismissed that light. Miss Pringle would have had me expelled as a danger to her dim girls. As for Father Watts-Watt, by now everything about him was lack-lustre, including his knees. Because the whole situation had to remain inexplicable, suffering was at once inevitable and pointless. For Beatrice saw no light in my face. The tides of my passion and reverence beat on her averted cheek and she never looked round. I could not say I love you, or do you know there is a light in your face? In a desperate effort to make some contact I took to facetiousness. I heard myself being silly and rude and all the time I could have kissed her feet.

So she noticed me at last only to ignore me with point and I fell into the pit of hell. Calf-love is no worse or stronger than adult love; but no weaker. It is always hopeless since we come to it under the lee of economics. How old was Juliet?

Beatrice lived some miles out in the country and came to school by bus. That part of the landscape took on significance and any fact about it was relevant to me. With flayed off skin and a new knowledge of life I walked many miles spiralling in towards her village and flinching off again. What mysteries there were behind the white fence of her garden I could not tell but felt them. There was, in and around me, an emotional life strange as dinosaurs. I was jealous of her not only because someone else might take her. I was jealous of her because she was a girl. I was jealous of her very existence. Most terribly and exactly I felt that to kill her would only increase her power. She would go through a gate before me and know what I did not know. The tides of life became dark and stormy. The grey, failing man in the rectory thought of nothing but his book on Pelagianism. When I went near him now, no goose walked over his grave because he stood on the edge of it. What had we to do with each other? And those other adults that surrounded me, remote and august as images from Easter Island—how could I speak of my hell and let them in? Even today I can hardly speak of it to myself.

In this forcing bed I tried to come to decisions about the world. There was this terror that walked by day and night, referred to so casually by a four-letter Saxon word. There was the well in me from which occasionally came the need to express and the certainty of doing so. I could draw a face now in one swift line—any face but the one I could not remember—and the likeness leapt from the paper. I even tried indirect communication with Beatrice. I made a Christmas card for her. I painted it with desperate care, elaborating, tearing up and simplifying with such passionate intentness that I flashed through a whole history of art without knowing it. Those purples and reds became flying shapes in which the blue and white thing, once a star but now battered could scarcely survive. The black and jagged slash down the centre of my picture had been her profile, once drawn with literal, dead accuracy, but now acknowledged to be a symbol only. Behind that savage crack in daily life the torrential colours fought, an indescribable confusion. What did I think to achieve? Did I think that two continents could communicate on such a level? Did I not understand that none of my tide had come to trouble her quiet pool? Better if I had written two words on paper—help me! Then after all that I sent the card to her anonymously—strange, involved, proud contradiction! and of course nothing happened.

Sex, you say; and now we have said sex where are we? The beauty of Miss Pringle's cosmos was vitiated because she was a bitch. Nick's stunted universe was irradiated by his love of people. Sex thrust me strongly to choose and know. Yet I did not choose a materialistic belief, I chose Nick. For this reason truth seems unattainable. I know myself to be irrational because a rationalist belief dawned in me and I had no basis for it in logic or calm thought. People are the walls of our room, not philosophies.

My deductions from Nick's illogically adopted system were logical. There is no spirit, no absolute. Therefore right and wrong are a parliamentary decision like no betting slips or drinks after half-past ten. But why should Samuel Mountjoy, sitting by his well, go with a majority decision? Why should not Sammy's good be what Sammy decides? Nick had a saintly cobbler as his father and never knew that his own moral life was conditioned by it. There are no morals that can be deduced from natural science, there are only immorals. The supply of nineteenth-century optimism and goodness had run out before it reached me. I transformed Nick's innocent, paper world. Mine was an amoral, a savage place in which man was trapped without hope, to enjoy what he could while it was going. But since I record all this not so much to excuse myself as to understand myself I must add the complications which makes nonsense again. At the moment I was deciding that right and wrong were nominal and relative, I felt, I saw the beauty of holiness and tasted evil in my mouth like the taste of vomit.

In the year of manliness sex was demonstrated to us and because it involved those whom we admired in part, I at least thought that now I understood. Miss Manning taught us French. She was about twenty-five, a sleepy, creamy woman with gusty black hair and a splash of mouth. She taught; but all the time as if she were thinking of something else. Sometimes she would stretch, cat-like, and smile slowly as if she found us and the classroom and education amiable but ridiculous. She looked as if in some other place she could teach us something really worth knowing; and I have no doubt this was true. She excited us boys agreeably with the V of her bosom between blue lapels and with her round, silk knees, too; for this was the era of the knee if a woman sat down so that there was a little competition to get the strategic desks and our Miss Manning, I believe, was not unaware of it. She was never angry and never particularly helpful. She seemed to be thinking all the time: poor little green-stick girls and hopeful, pustular rowdies! Be patient—presently the gates will be unlocked and you will walk out of the nursery. Miss Manning, in fact, was altogether too attractive a woman to have her heart in her work.

Mr. Carew thought her attractive, too. We had believed him to exist for the twin purposes of rugby and Latin, but now we saw that he shared the common image with us. If he were coaching us on the field and Miss Manning appeared on the touchline not only we, but he, were driven to excesses of manly activity. How we hurled ourselves into a loose scrum! And taking up our positions for a kick-off, how loping, rangy and altogether unconscious of Miss Manning our strides became! But Mr. Carew would coach us twice as hard, would demonstrate that particular action with which he threw the ball like a torpedo far past the forwards in a line-out to where the threes might get it. Now all this activity was strange because Mr. Carew was married and had a small baby. He was a large, fair, red, sweaty man—or perhaps that was the rugby, but in my memory he always sweats. He had been to a minor public school and his rugby was much better than his Latin. He would not have found a job easy to get surely—but we had just changed over to rugby from soccer so we must have been his life's luck. But our Miss Manning took to appearing on the touchline very often, sensibly cautious of getting her feet muddy. With what laughter and care did Mr. Carew help her round a particularly dirty patch! Then the game would be delayed and he would hang round her, laughing very loud and sending up clouds of breath and steam into the November air. He displayed his club colours before her in male splendour and Miss Manning smiled her creamy smile.

Our school caretaker was a sodden old soldier who chased us off the grass when we were small and told us about life when our pimples were out. There was a pub handy to the school and when he returned after the dinner break, fumes went before him like a king's messenger. Then he would smooth out his grey, military moustache and tell us about being in action at two thousand yards against cavalry and show us the scar he got when he was serving on the north-west frontier. The more beer he had drunk the more military he became. This increase in martial ardour was paralleled by a rise in his moral temper. Normally he was opposed to puttees and lipstick; but when he had well drunken, short-skirted women in Parliament were unnatural. Bobbing, bingling, Eton crops—

but not apparently shaving—were flying in the face of providence and one of the reasons for the decadence of the modern army. He advocated the bayonet, Mr. Baldwin, and generally no nonsense.

At that time, a Novemberish time of short days and cold and mud, he was worried. He had something on his mind. Slurred by beer, fuming in our eager faces from veined nose, moustached mouth and eyes of yellow, he could only indicate that were he to tell us all, our mothers would remove us to a purer place. There were some things that young chaps had no business to know about, that's what. So don't you ask me no more, young Mountjoy. See?

He got so near letting on that we were wrought to a fever of conjecture and suspicion. We would not let him be. Our wings touched this honey and stuck there. Mr. Carew and Miss Manning were our Adam and Eve, were sex itself. This excitement was male, was kept from the green-stick girls, was knowledge, was glamour, was life. During the dinner-hour there was a master on duty for the boys and a mistress on duty for the girls; but who looks after the guardians? What more natural than that they should meet and that Benjie, going the round of the boiler-rooms or whatever he did, should see them, himself unseen? What was more, he now had a moral issue on his hands. What should he do? Should he tell the headmaster? This was what kept him awake and was turning him to drink. Where was his duty? Should he not, or should he tell?

There seemed to be only one way of pushing this crisis uphill. Yes, we cried, with a virtue even stronger than his, yes, of course he should. Roll on the crisis! After all, it was a bit thick if—so we delighted in our virtue and excitement. Miss Manning! Creamy, luscious Miss Manning! Mr. Carew, steaming and red!

Five of us sneaked after Benjie when he made up his mind. We hung about in a deserted corridor, watched as he tapped the study door and went in. After that we waited for nearly ten minutes with just too little courage to go and listen outside the door. Presently it opened and Benjie appeared backwards, cap in hand and talking. The headmaster came after trying to silence him. But Benjie was fuming and loud.

"I said it once, sir, and I'll say it again. It couldn't 'ave been worse if they was married!"

Then the headmaster saw us. I imagine it was perfectly obvious to him why we were there and why we were so interested. I, at least, expected a blast from him, but he said nothing to us. He only looked sad as if he had lost something. He was no fool, that headmaster. He knew when a story could be forgotten and when it had reached too many ears.

For the time of their stay Mr. Carew and Miss Manning were now most popular and admirable. They were not just teachers, they had reached the adult stature of those who sin. They were our film stars. We would have sat at Miss Manning's feet and listened to her with devoted attention if she had cared enough about us to tell us all the secrets of life. Whatever she said we should have believed her; and this is another contradiction. At her last lesson we examined our Miss Manning with bated breath for some sign of the experience that had been hers. But the gusty black hair, the V, the slow, creamy smile and the wide red mouth were the same. Her silk knees were the same. Once she caressed her leg, starting at the knee, running her hand down, stretching and drawing up the shin at the same time, running the silken snake through the palm of one hand, bending the instep back till you might have thought she could smooth the whole limb small and squeeze it through a ring. Then the end of the lesson came and as we stood in our desks she dismissed us with a strange phrase for someone who was about to disappear for ever.

"*Eh bien, mes amis. Au revoir!*"

Then they were gone, the two of them and the staff was grey and dingy again. Miss Pringle had a series of days when the world was too much for her—head lolling back, desperate sighing; but once when I presumed on her inattention she gave me a raving blast like a blowlamp. Nick reacted differently. He let me down for the first and last time in his life. I screwed up my courage and asked him a hesitant question about sex and all that, asked out of the fantasy life and our Miss Manning and Beatrice and having wanted to be a girl and wondering whether I was killing myself.

Nick shut me up violently. Then he spoke, flushing, his eyes watching water boiling in a flask.

"I don't believe in anything but what I can touch and see and weigh and measure. But if the Devil had invented man he couldn't have played him a dirtier, wickeder, a more shameful trick than when he gave him sex!"

So that was that. "It couldn't have been worse if they was married!" And though I scored a hit with my suggestion among the lads that what Benjie should have said was "It couldn't have been better——" nevertheless, I recognized the fallen angel. In my too susceptible mind sex dressed itself in gorgeous colours, brilliant and evil. I was in that glittering net, then, just as the silk moths were when they swerved and lashed their slim bodies and spurted the pink musk of their mating. Musk, shameful and heady, be thou my good. Musk on Beatrice who knows nothing of it, thinks nothing of it, is contained and cool, is years from mating if ever, and with another man. Musk if man is only an animal, must be my good because that is the standard of all animals. He is the great male who keeps the largest herd for himself. Do not tell us that we are highest animals and then expect from us only the fierce animal devotion to the young, the herd instinct and not the high, warring hooves of the stallion. As for that light round the brow, the radiance of the unending morning of paradise—that is an illusion, a side effect. Pay no attention to it. Forget it, if you can.

Therefore I moved forward to the world of the lads, where Mercutio was, where Valentine and Claudio and for this guilt found occasion to invent a crime that fitted the punishment. Guilty am I; therefore wicked I will be. If I cannot find the brilliant crimes to commit then at least I will claim to have committed them. Guilt comes before the crime and can cause it. My claims to evil were Byronic; and Beatrice looked the other way.

The time came for me to leave. Beatrice was going to a training college in South London where they would make a teacher of her. I was going to the Art School. I had no clear desire for success. I repeated the catch-phrases of the party because in that society one had the illusion of perpetual freedom, the monk's freedom in reverse. We had our blessings and farewells. Nick told me, in strangely religious phraseology, "Whatsoever thy hand findeth to do, do it with all thy might."

The headmaster took longer but said much the same.

"Going, Sam?"

"Yes, sir."

"Come to me for words of wisdom?"

"I've seen the others, sir."

"Trouble with advice is you might remember it."

"Sir?"

"Sit down, boy, for a minute and don't fidget. There. Cigarette?"

"I——"

"Look at your fingers and come off it. Throw the ash in that basket."

Sudden, inexplicable emotion.

"Want to thank you for all you've done, sir."

He waved his cigarette.

"What am I going to say to you? You'll go a long way from Rotten Row."

"That was Father Watts-Watt, sir."

"Partly."

Suddenly he swung round in the seat and faced me.

"Sam. I want your help. I want—to understand what you're after. Oh, yes, I know all about the party, it'll last you a year or two. But for yourself—you're an artist, a born artist, the Lord knows why or how. I've never seen anyone so clearly gifted. Yet these portraits—aren't they important to you?"

"I suppose so, sir."

"But surely—isn't anything important to you? No, wait! Never mind the party. I'll take that as read, Sammy, I'm a moderate man. But for yourself. Isn't anything important?"

"I don't know."

"You've got this gift and you haven't thought if it's important? Look, Sammy. We don't have to pretend any more, do we? You have an exceptional talent that makes you as distinct as if you had a sixth finger on each hand. You know that and I know it. I'm not flattering you. You're dishonest and selfish as well as being a—whatever you are. Right?"

"Sir."

"Your talent isn't important to you?"

"No, sir."

"You aren't happy."

"No, sir."

"Haven't been for some years now, have you?"

"No, sir."

"Happiness isn't your business. I tell you that. Leave happiness to the others, Sammy. It's a five-finger exercise."

He held up his right hand and twisted the fingers about.

"So your portraits aren't important in themselves. Are they a means to an end? No. Forget the dictatorship of the proletariat. What end?"

I don't know, sir."

"Aren't you looking forward to being famous and rich?"

Now it was my turn to think.

"Yes, sir. That would be very nice."

He gave a sudden jerk of laughter.

"Which is as much as to say you don't care a damn. And I'm supposed to advise you. Well, I won't. Good-bye."

He took my stub from me and shook me by the hand. But before I could close the door, the incorrigible schoolmaster in him had called me back.

"I'll tell you something which may be of value. I believe it to be true and powerful—therefore dangerous. If you want something enough, you can always get it provided you are willing to make the appropriate sacrifice. Something, anything. But what you get is never quite what you thought; and sooner or later the sacrifice is always regretted."

I went out of there and out of the school into high summer. It seemed to me, though in fact I was only exchanging one tutelage for another, that the world had opened to me. I would not go back to the rectory but walked out of the town instead and along beside the downs. There was the forest here, clinging to the downs between the escarpment and the river. I took my sudden excitement into them, I began to wade into the tall bracken as though somewhere in here was the secret.

Even the wood-pigeons co-operated for they sang the refrain of a dance tune over and over. "If you knew Susie" they sang from their green penthouses and all the forest, the bracken, the flies and uncatalogued small moths, the thumping rabbits, the butterflies, brown, blue and white, they murmured sexily for musk was the greatest good of the greatest number. As for the heavy sky, the blue to purple, it filled every shape between the trees with inch-thick fragments of stained glass, only at arm's length out of reach. The high fronds touched my throat or caught me round the thighs. There was a powder spilled out of all living things, a spice which now made the air where I waded thick. In basements of the forest among drifts of dried leaves and crackling boughs, by boles cathedral thick, I said in the hot air what was important to me; namely the white, unseen body of Beatrice Ifor, her obedience, and for all time my protection of her; and for the pain she had caused me, her utter abjection this side death.

There must have been a very considerable battle round me that evening. Every dog has his day and at last I see that this was mine. For the spices of the forest were taken away from me, I found myself hot and sticky, coming out below the weir where the pebbles shake under water year out and the moored lilies tug and duck and sidle. So that there should be no doubt, I now see, the angel of the gate of paradise held his sword between me and the spices. He breathed like his maker on the water below the weir and it seemed to me that the water was waiting for me. I stripped off and plunged in and I experienced my skin, from head to foot firm, smooth confinement of all my treasures. Now I knew the weight and the shape of a man, his temperature, his darknesses. I knew myself to shoot the glances of my eye, to stand firm, to sow my seed from the base of the strong spine. Dressed and cooled, contained as an untouched girl I moved away from the providential waters and up the hill-side. Already there were stars, large glossy stars that had been put in one at a time with the thumb. I sat there between the earth and the sky, between cloister and street. The waters had healed me and there was the taste of potatoes in my mouth.

What is important to you?

"Beatrice Ifor."

She thinks you depraved already. She dislikes you.

"If I want something enough I can always get it provided I am willing to make the appropriate sacrifice."

What will you sacrifice?

"Everything."

Here?

"Mr. Mountjoy? An appointment? I'll just ring through."

A lion gnashed from my left hand, high up, bloodshot about the eyes, blood and rage. To my left a python writhed over a lopped and polished branch—but where was the goat for the body? I searched for him while the receptionist spoke into her telephone and he was there, African with horns of fantastication and the yellow eyes of lust. I thought to myself that I seemed not to be on the pavement but standing a little above it. This was the house of the pay-off. Here the past was not a series of icebergs aground on some personal shore. This was the grey house of factual succession. Come here to the gate-house of the stuffed lion and stuffed python and stuffed goat. Examine your own experiment.

"Mr. Mountjoy, Dr. Enticott is not quite ready but asks if you would go down to his office. Do you know the way?"

"I'm afraid I've never—that is; no."

The receptionist traced out a route on a plan. Not at all, it was a pleasure to her, professionally smooth, helpful and untouched. Accustomed to deal with too much joy, too much sorrow.

The grounds were just recognizably the same. The cedar had survived and the branches each reached up to a level of water and defined it with floating leaves. The bulk of the house was the same as before, only a little smaller. There, stretching away from my feet along the back of the house was the terrace where the man had walked ritually. Johnny and I must have hidden behind the scruffy remains of that hedge. But there were other buildings that had sprung up within the grounds, low and functional, sprung up like fungus. The wide lawn was slashed by concrete paths and these were worn and cracked, though they had appeared since we had trespassed. I had been a prisoner so long that now, only a hundred yards from my own house and in the grounds of an English hospital I did not dare to step off the path and I zigzagged across the lawn where the concrete allowed me to walk. The gardens were as well kept as public gardens and the air was the air of the top of the hill. Yet the sense of institution lay over the whole house and gardens like the greyness of a prison camp. Two women walked arm in arm under the trees. They sauntered, but the greyness included them. There was a single figure standing in the middle of the lawn like an ungainly statue; a stolid woman who stood with arms akimbo as if time had found her like that and then stopped.

Kenneth's office was empty. There were green filing cabinets, papers, pen, blotter, ink and a couch for confidences. It was a good, airy office, workman-like and pleasant if it had been anywhere else.

He came in behind me.

"Hullo."

"Here you are."

But this was not the loud Kenneth of parties with his wonderful stories, his admiration of Taffy and his liking for me. This was no more Kenneth than I was Sam, sprawling in slacks and sweater. Here we met officially in suits and constraint.

"Won't you sit down?"

We looked at each other across the desk and I spoke first.

"I suppose this is very—irregular?"

"Why should you think that?"

"I'm not a relative."

"We are not in purdah. No."

"I can see her?"

"Of course. If she wants to see you, that is."

"Well then."

"Is Taffy coming on later?"

"She's not coming."

"But she said——"

"Why should Taffy come?"

"But she said—I mean—she wanted to meet Miss——"

"She couldn't have!"

"She said Miss what's her name was a friend of you both——"

"She said that?"

"Of course!"

"She's busy on this wine thing of hers for tonight. You'll be there, won't you?"

I saw the disappointment come into his face. He swung his pencil and bounced it on his blotter.

"Oh well."

So Taffy had been diplomatic. It looked better if we had both known Beatrice. The helping hand.

"Perhaps she can come and see Miss Ifor later on."

Kenneth adjusted his face.

"Of course, of course."

It is true then that these places are not necessarily forcing beds for humanity and understanding. You can walk a hospital and learn nothing.

Kenneth jumped up, opened a filing cabinet and took out a sheaf of papers. He thumbed through them, returning his face to what he thought was the proper face for a medical man, withdrawn and responsible. But youth will out and his mask was unmarked. He might have been my son.

"When can I see her, then, Kenneth?"

He started.

"Now, if you like."

Crestfallen a little. Yes, he has really come to see her, not me: and no, Taffy is not with him, she does not think of me.

"Well——"

He got up, abruptly.

"Come on then."

I stood up to follow. My feet were obedient but my mind was thinking strange things and behaving mutinously. There should be a pause of recollection, it thought. I will wash my hands before I. There should be deliberate thinking back, a straightening out of the time stream back to when you last saw her. Yet the spots are opening and closing in front of my eyes and Kenneth is in love with Taffy and that complex sticks a peninsula into this ocean of cause and effect that is Beatrice and me.

"This way."

She was in the main building, then, in the general's own house, the house for lucky people.

"Through here."

I remember now. It was that morning when I turned up outside the training college after walking all night, the morning when I first pretended to be half-way round the bend. I remember what she said. *You mustn't ever say such a thing, Sammy.*

But most of all I remember her terror.

"Just a moment."

Kenneth had stopped and was talking to a nurse. He did this to impress me with yes, Dr. Enticott, no, Dr. Enticott. I am not famous, Sammy, but this is my pitch.

Can't you see I am up to the neck in the ice on paradise hill?

"Here we are, Mr. Mountjoy. I'd better go first."

Formal, because on the job.

The room was huge, an old drawing-room perhaps, in which the moulded ceiling was heavily dependent, marked with dust in dull lines like the rubbing of brass or bark. The three tall windows on our left were too big for frequent cleaning so that although they let the light in they qualified it. There were no pictures or hangings, though the light-green room cried out for both. There was little enough fabric anywhere. There was only a scatter of heavy round tables, chairs, and one or two sofas arranged by the farther wall.

There was a scatter of women too, but left random as the furniture. One held a ball of string. Another stood looking out of the middle window, unnaturally still like the ungainly statue on the lawn. Nurse knew her way about this aquarium. She swam forward between the tables to the darkest corner, the right-hand one across areas of floor.

"Miss Ifor."

No.

"Miss Ifor! Your visitor's come to see you!"

There was someone sitting on a chair in front of one of the sofas. She faced the right-hand wall, hands in her lap. She was posed. Her weak, yellowish hair was cut short like a boy's so that the shape of the head was clear to see, a vertical back. I remembered then how my hand had sometimes supported her head deep in the hair at the back; and now the truth was out, in daylight, shorn. The high forehead was parallel to this vertical back, so that really there was not much room in the head, very little, I now saw when the crowning glory was away from it.

Somewhere one of the women began to make a noise. It was the same sound, over and over again, like a marsh-bird.

"Hi-yip! Hi-yip! Hi-yip!"

No one moved. Beatrice sat, looking at the wall, looking at nothing. Her face was in the shadow of her body; but a little light was reflected from the institutional wall and showed some of the moulding. Certainly the bones of the face were well hidden now. The flesh had hidden them in lumps—or was it the very bone that had coarsened? The knuckles of her hands seemed more prominent and under the green dress the body had thickened, was the same size from shoulder to hip.

There was a curious feeling in my hands. They seemed to be growing larger. The room was shuddering slightly as if a tunnel of the underground lay below.

I pulled my lips apart.

"Beatrice!"

She did nothing. The nurse moved briskly past my right shoulder and bent down.

"Miss Ifor dear! Your visitor's come to see you!"

"Beatrice!"

"Miss Ifor dear!"

"Hi-yip! Hi-yip! Hi-yip!"

There was a movement of sorts a kind of small lurch

of the whole body. Beatrice was turning. She was jerking round like the figure in a cathedral clock. An express was passing through the tunnel. Beatrice moved jerk by jerk through ninety degrees. Her back was to me.

Kenneth touched my arm.

"I think perhaps——"

But nurse knew this aquarium.

"Miss Ifor? Aren't you going to talk to your visitor? Come along now!"

She had the body by the shoulder and arm.

"Come along, dearie!"

Jerk jerk jerk.

"Hi-yip! Hi-yip! Hi-yip!"

The body was facing me. The entombed eyes were nittering like the hand of an old man.

"Aren't you going to say hullo, dear? Miss Ifor!"

"Beatrice!"

Beatrice was beginning to stand up. Her hands were clasped into each other. Her mouth was open and her eyes were nittering at me through my tears and sweat.

"That's a good girl!"

Beatrice pissed over her skirt and her legs and her shoes and my shoes. The pool splashed and spread.

"Miss Ifor dear, naughty—ah, naughty!"

Someone had me by the arm and shoulder and was turning me.

"I think——"

Someone was leading and helping me over acres of bare floor. Marsh-birds were sweeping and crying.

"Keep your head right down."

I could smell her still on my shoes and trousers. I struggled against a clamping hand at the back of my neck. Down, down, forced down in the fetor.

"Better?"

The words would not form. I could see them as shapes, hear them silently, could not twist them into my tongue.

"You'll feel better in a moment."

Cause and effect. The law of succession. Statistical probability. The moral order. Sin and remorse. They are all true. Both worlds exist side by side. They meet in me. We have to satisfy the examiners in both worlds at once. Down in the fetor.

"There."

The hand removed itself. Two, one on each shoulder pulled me back. I fitted a chair.

"Just sit still for a bit."

My mind wandered off into long corridors, came back, pictured Kenneth at his desk and opened my eyes. He was there. He gave me a smile of professional cheer.

"These things are a shock until you get used to them."

I made my mouth do its proper work.

"I suppose so."

I was coming back now into my body and I could hear Kenneth quacking on. But there was something I wanted from him. I felt round and found a cigarette.

"Do you mind?"

"No. Of course not. As I was saying——"

"Is there any hope?"

He was silent at last.

"What I mean is: can you cure her?"

More stuff. More quacking.

"Look, Kenneth. Can she be cured?"

"In the present state of our knowledge——"

"Can she be cured?"

"No."

The smell of the foul nursery rose from my shoes. Maisie, Millicent, Mary?

"Kenneth. I want to know."

"Know what?"

"What sent her——"

"Ah!"

He put his fingers together and leaned back.

"In the first place you have to remember that normality is a condition only arbitrarily definable——"

"Her life, man! What drove her mad?"

Kenneth gave a vexed laugh.

"Can't you understand? Perhaps nothing happened."

"You mean—she would have gone—like this—anyway?"

He looked at me, frowning.

"Why do you say, 'Anyway'?"

"For the love of—look. Did anything send her, send her——"

Puzzled, he looked at me, reached out for the file, opened the spring cover, looked down, flicked paper, muttered.

"Heredity. Yes. I see. Illnesses. School. Training College. Engaged to be——"

His voice faded away. I hit the desk with my fist and cried out.

"Go on, can't you?"

He was consuming himself in blood. He shut the file, looking anywhere but at me. He muttered in the corner of his office.

"Of course. It would be."

"Go on! Read it out to me."

But he was muttering still.

"Oh, my God. What a fool. I should have—now what shall I do?"

"Look——"

He swung round and down at me.

"You shouldn't have done it. How the hell was I to know? And I thought I was doing you both a favour——'

"No one can do her a favour——"

"I didn't mean—I may have done—I could be——"

"I had to see her."

He was whispering frantically now.

"No one must ever know. Do you hear? I could be struck off——"

"Paradise."

All at once his voice spat at me.

"I've always detested you—and this—that a man like you should have a woman like Taffy——"

He stopped speaking and sat down the other side of the desk. His voice was intentional.

"You and your bloody pictures. You use everyone. You used that woman. You used Taffy. And now you've used me."

"Yes. It's all my fault."

His voice ran up high.

"I'll say it's your fault!"

"Do you want it in writing?"

"That's right. Take all the blame, you think, and nothing happened. Kiss and be friends. Do anything you like and then say you're sorry."

"No. I don't believe like that. I wish I did."

Silence.

Kenneth pushed the back of his hand across his forehead. He looked at the file.

"Who can tell you anything certain? Perhaps you did. Yes. Perhaps you hurt her so badly it tipped her over. I should think so. She's been here ever since, you see."

"Seven years!"

"Your Beatrice is a foundation member."

"Seven years."

"Ever since you saw her last. In a condition which we think is rather like experiencing continual and exaggerated worry."

"Ever since."

"I hope it makes you happy."

"Do you think hurting me will help you with Taffy?"

"I'm glad we've got that straight at last. Yes. I'm in love with her."

"I know. She told me. We're both sorry."

"To hell with your sorrow. And her sorrow."

"Well there."

"And to hell with this place and life generally."

"I asked her, you see. She would have kept your secret."

Kenneth gave a high-pitched laugh.

"Oh, yes, you've got a good wife, she'll never let you down. She'll stand at your back and prop you up so that you can come across a few more suckers."

"It isn't like that, you know. Not from inside."

"Got what you came for."

"I did it then. I had a dream. Not your line of country—or is it? You could put this one in the file with the rest of the evidence. Mr. X after deserting Miss Y had a dream. She was following him, stumbling, and the waters were rising round her. Exaggerated worry, you said. Cause and effect holds good. Nick was right and Miss Pringle was right——"

"I don't know what you're talking about."

"Just that I tipped her over. Nothing can be repaired or changed. The innocent cannot forgive."

I smiled wrily at Kenneth; and as I smiled I felt a sudden gust of affection for him.

"All right, Kenneth. Yes. I got what I came for. And thank you."

"For what?"

"For being so—Hippocratic."

"I?"

Suddenly the image of thick Beatrice started up behind my eyes, green, tense and nittering. I covered them with one hand.

"For telling me the truth."

Kenneth moved about uneasily between his desk and the cupboard and then settled into his chair.

"Look, Sammy. I shan't be seeing much of you both from now on."

"I'm sorry."

"For God's sake!"

"I mean it. People don't seem to be able to move without killing each other."

"So I'm telling you what the chances were as far as I can see them. Then you'll know. You probably tipped her over. But perhaps she would have tipped over anyway. Perhaps she would have tipped over a year earlier if you hadn't been there to give her something to think about. You may have given her an extra year of sanity and—

whatever you did give her. You may have taken a lifetime of happiness away from her. Now you know the chances as accurately as a specialist."

"Thank you."

"God. I could cut your throat."

"I suppose so."

"No, I couldn't. Don't go. Wait. I want to talk to you. Listen, Sam. I love Taffy. You know that."

"I can't take it in."

"And I said I hated you. But I don't. In a sort of twisted way—it's that life you both lead together, that place you've got. I want to share that. In a sense I'm in love with both of you."

"I can't take it in."

I pulled myself up and made a sort of smiling grimace, mouth dragged down, in his direction.

"Well——"

"Sammy."

I turned at the door.

"Sammy. What am I going to do?"

I adjusted myself to his face. Useless to say that a man is a whole continent, pointless to say that each consciousness is a whole world because each consciousness is a dozen worlds.

"There's too much interpenetration. Everything is mixed up. Look. You haven't hurt us. It will pass. Nothing of what you go through now will peer over your shoulder or kick you in the face."

He laughed savagely.

"Thank you for nothing!"

I went out of the door then, and as I went, I nodded him my agreement.

14

I had my two speeches ready, one for each of my parents not in the flesh. Now I would go to Nick Shales and do him good. I would explain gently.

"You did not choose your rationalism rationally. You chose because they showed you the wrong maker. Oh, yes, I know all about the lip-service they paid. She—Rowena Pringle—paid lip-service and I know how much lip-service is worth. The maker they mimed for you in your Victorian slum was the old male maker, totem of the conquering Hebrews, totem of our forefathers, the subjectors and quiet enslavers of half the world. I saw that totem in a German picture. He stands to attention beside the cannon. There is a Hindu tied across the muzzle and presently the male totem of the Hebrews will blow him to pieces, the mutinous dog, for his daring. The male totem is jack-booted and topee'd and ignorant and hypocritical and splendid and cruel. You rejected him as my generation rejects him. But you were innocent, you were good and innocent like Johnny Spragg, blown to pieces five miles above his own county of Kent. You and he could live in one world at a time. You were not caught in the terrible net where we guilty ones are forced to torture each other..."

But Nick was in hospital dying of a tired heart. Even then it seemed to me he had less than his share, a bed in a ward in a town he always wanted to avoid. I saw him that evening from far off down the ward. He was propped up on pillows and leaned his immense head on his hand. The light from a bulb behind him lay smoothly over his curved cranium, snowed on him like the years, hung whitely in the eaves over his eyes. Beneath their pent his face was worn away. He seemed to me then to have become the image of labouring mind: and I was awed. Whatever was happening to him in death was on a scale and level before which I felt my own nothingness. I came away, my single verse unspoken.

To her my speech was to be simple.

"We were two of a kind, that is all. You were forced to torture me. You lost your freedom somewhere and after that you had to do to me what you did. You see? The consequence was perhaps Beatrice in the looney bin, our joint work, my work, the world's work. Do you not see how our imperfections force us to torture each other? Of course you do! The innocent and the wicked live in one world—Philip Arnold is a minister of the crown and handles life as easy as breathing. But we are neither the innocent nor the wicked. We are the guilty. We fall down. We crawl on hands and knees. We weep and tear each other.

Therefore I have come back—since we are both adults and live in two worlds at once—to offer forgiveness with both hands. Somewhere the awful line of descent must be broken. You did that and I forgive it wholly, take the spears into me. As far as I can I will make your part in our story as if it had never been."

But forgiveness must not only be given but received also.

She lived in a village some miles from the school now, a bitsy village with reed thatch and wrought-iron work. She cried out delightedly when she saw me at the end of the garden path.

"Mountjoy!"

And then she took off her gardener's glove and offered me her white hand while the speech and everything I knew flew out of my head. For there are some people who paralyse us as if we were chicken, our beaks at the chalk line. I knew at once I should say nothing; but even so I was not prepared for the position and opinion of Miss Pringle; nor did our pictures of the past agree. My fame and Philip's fame, were the consolations of teaching. She liked to think that her care of me—Sammy; may I say Sammy? And I muttered of course, of course, because my beak was on the chalk line—she liked to think that her care of me had been a little bit, a teeny bit (there was a plaster rabbit sitting by the plaster bird-bath) a teeny-weeny bit responsible for the things of beauty I was able to give the world.

And so, in ten seconds, I wanted nothing but to get away. My flesh crept. She was still this being of awful power and now her approval of me was as terrible as her hatred and I knew we had nothing to say to each other. For that woman had achieved an unexpected kind of victory; she had deceived herself completely and now she was living in only one world.

All day long the trains run on rails. Eclipses are predictable. Penicillin cures pneumonia and the atom splits to order. All day long, year in, year out, the daylight explanation drives back the mystery and reveals a reality usable, understandable and detached. The scalpel and the microscope fail, the oscilloscope moves closer to behaviour. The gorgeous dance is self-contained, then; does not need the music which in my mad moments I have heard. Nick's universe is real.

All day long action is weighed in the balance and found

not opportune nor fortunate or ill-advised, but good or evil. For this mode which we must call the spirit breathes through the universe and does not touch it; touches only the dark things, held prisoner, incommunicado, touches, judges, sentences and passes on.

Her world was real, both worlds are real. There is no bridge.

The bright line became a triangle sweeping in over a suddenly visible concrete floor.

"Heraus!"

Rising from my knees, holding my trousers huddled I walked uncertainly out towards the judge. But the judge had gone.

The commandant was back.

"Captain Mountjoy. This should not be happening. I am sorry."

The noise turned me round. I could see down the passage now over the stain shaped like a brain, could see into the cell where I had received what I had received. They were putting the buckets back, piles of them, were throwing back the damp floorcloths. I could see that they had forgotten one, or perhaps left it deliberately, when they emptied the cupboard for me. It still lay damply in the centre of the floor. Then a soldier shut the buckets and the floorcloths away with an ordinary cupboard door.

"Captain Mountjoy. You have heard?"

"I heard."

The commandant indicated the door back to the camp dismissively. He spoke the inscrutable words that I should puzzle over as though they were the Sphinx's riddle.

"The Herr Doctor does not know about peoples."

Books by William Golding
available in paperbound editions
from Harcourt Brace Jovanovich, Inc.

Free Fall (H 010)
The Hot Gates (HB 117)
The Inheritors (HB 64)
Pincher Martin (HPL 32)
The Pyramid (HB 145)
The Spire (HB 94)